Daughter of the Mountain

Daughter

of the

Mountain

Sherry Parnell

Library of Congress Control Number: 2023910498

Paperback: 978-1-7333077-3-4

Ebook: 978-1-7333077-4-1

Hardback: 978-1-7333077-5-8

Prologue

It wasn't because she was from the mountains, born and bred. It wasn't because she lived in a town so small and so destitute that the gas station fulfilled every need from groceries to entertainment. It wasn't because she had no more than an eighth-grade education and little need for more. It was because she was of the mountains, mind and soul. It was because the hill's dust had settled so deeply into her skin that it appeared a tawny hue. It was because the night winds had wrapped their coldness around her so tightly that her auburn hair twisted and curled. It didn't matter that Sarah was from the mountains; that's just geography. What mattered was that she was of the mountains; that's destiny.

PART ONE

May 17, 1983

Today is the day. I can't wait any longer. I don't want to leave my baby girl, but I have to trust that Mama will raise her up right, at least better than she done me. I ain't sure where I'll go. I just know that it's got to be better than here.

I pray my baby girl can forgive me. I pray that Mama can forgive me. I pray that God can forgive me.

Chapter One

Effie Bilfrey opened the screen door and stared at the tattered suitcase at her daughter's feet. "Sarah Bilfrey, what are you doing?"

Sarah stood firm with her hands clamped tightly around her daughter's tiny shoulders. "Mama, I have to leave, and I need you to look after the baby for me."

Effie eyed her daughter suspiciously before grunting, "You're leavin'? For how long?"

Nervously twisting a strand of her daughter's soft hair around her finger, Sarah mumbled, "Mama, please."

Effie said nothing. Not able to meet her mother's piercing stare, Sarah tried again.

"Mama, I know we ain't always got along, but you got to help me."

With her jaw set and jutted forward, Effie angrily stepped closer. "I ain't got to nothing, girl, and I sure as hell ain't going to help you leave," Effie snapped as fear wrapped itself in the only emotion Effie was willing to show.

At a familiar impasse, the two women stood for a moment in silence while the baby's wide eyes caught sight of the white mountain laurel blooming beside the porch. When Lottie toddled close to grab spring's first pink-tipped bloom, Sarah swiftly scooped her up and handed her to her mother. Shifting the child in her arms, Effie grabbed Sarah's wrist. She dug her fingers into Sarah's pale skin until it was scarlet ringed. "No, Sarah. No! You ain't going!"

Sarah's eyes, pooling with tears and pleading, met her mother's as she begged, "Please, Mama. Please."

Allowing her daughter's desperation to leave prevail over her own desperation to make her stay, Effie relented. Leaning close, Sarah buried her nose into the downy mass of the small child's hair, taking in her sweet baby smell. She whispered, "If you don't remember nothing, baby girl, remember that I love you."

Sarah turned quickly to leave, but before her foot touched the first step, Effie called out in a voice hoarse with emotion, "You remember the same, Sarah Bilfrey."

Suppressing a sob, Sarah nodded before running down the rutted dirt road away from all those she'd loved, all that she'd known, and all that she'd feared.

Drained of her anger, yet not filled with the grief to come, Effie stood stunned. Then, shaking her head ruefully, she took the barefoot, dirty-faced child inside. Effie sat the babbling baby down in the middle of the floor, which was nothing more than rough-hewed planks covered in rag rugs.

The child howled and searched the room frantically with wide eyes. "Hush now, it's a gonna be all right," Effie said, assuring both the baby and herself, before opening the door and calling out urgently, "Baby Curtis! Baby Curtis, you come on in now and give me a hand." Curtis was ten years from being a baby, but since he was Effie's youngest, his name was rarely uttered without the preface "Baby."

Curtis scrambled up the splintered wooden steps, carefully stepping over the second one with the rotted board, and then hesitated at the door. Irritated, Effie leaned out. Bumping her nose into Curtis's head, she said, "Damn it, Baby Curtis!" Pressing her hand into the small of his back, Effie shoved Curtis toward the door and said, "You get on in here. I need some help." Uneasy, Curtis went over and stood next to his now-wailing niece. "Well, you hear as good as I do. Make her stop her boo-hooing so I can get the breakfast made in some peace," Effie demanded before she stormed into the kitchen, keeping half an eye on Baby Curtis as he tried to coax a smile from the shrieking child.

Effie pulled her favorite cast-iron skillet from its resting place among the stack of chipped plates and plastic glasses. She then slammed it a bit harder than intended against the rusted cookstove, causing Curtis to jump and the baby to wail louder. Effie huffed in frustration, "I can't cook while she's making that racket." Turning on her heel, she snapped, "Baby Curtis, take Lottie on out of here."

Without looking up, Curtis reminded his mother, "Sarah don't like her called 'Lottie.'"

Effie snorted and spit back, "Well, I don't see her here to disagree, do you?"

Not wanting to further anger his mother, Curtis scooped up the baby. Nuzzling the girl's warm cheek, he whispered, "Let's go, Lottie," before they both escaped to the backyard, overgrown with thick grass and dotted with wildflower blooms.

Effie watched the screen door slam shut before turning back to her skillet and her thoughts. Effie was going to make biscuits—her specialty. Everyone raved about Effie's biscuits. What no one knew, however, was that before anyone swallowed the moist buttered bread or before anyone's lips touched the flaky, barely browned crust, something far more extraordinary took place. It was during the cooking—the mundane process of sifting flour, cracking eggs, and frying biscuits—that Effie dreamed, planned, and schemed. This time was no different, except that as Effie started her well-worn process, there were no plans, only memories.

Effie began as she always did, sifting the flour. As the powdery substance floated through her fingers, she was reminded of the delicate feel of her daughter's hair as she would brush it smooth. Sarah was only a girl then, small and trusting. Too trusting, perhaps, Effie thought.

Effie's composure in front of her son began to crack, just like the egg she grasped too tightly in her hand. Pieces of shell dropped to the floor, and as Effie moved her foot, she could hear the crunch beneath her shoe. Refusing even a tear, Effie shoved the broken pieces to the side, a process she had practiced for too many years.

The butter, unmeasured and thick, hit the hot skillet and began to sizzle before she delicately placed the doughy biscuits into the pan. A gesture so gentle, so rare, and reserved only for her cooking. As Effie waited for the biscuits to brown, she began to rub her calloused fingers. Hands well-worn from work and worry. Hands that have held together her loosely fit family of restless boys and an ever-aching girl, and a lifetime of scrapping, struggling, and finding a way to make it work.

She flipped the partially cooked biscuits with her favorite spatula—the one with the handle bent and scorched by Sarah's failed attempt to re-create her mother's perfect biscuits. She then slid the biscuits onto a chipped blue plate and threw the warm spatula into the sink.

"Baby Curtis!" Effie shouted, and after years of keeping his ear tuned for his mother's voice, he was at the door before Effie reached it. Years of taking whacks across the bottom had taught him that quick response and utmost respect were the surest ways to avoid his mother's wrath, which didn't come often, but when it did it was fierce.

"I see you got her to quiet down," Effie said as she nodded toward the baby approvingly. "Well, you sit her down, and I will give her some biscuits. She's got to be hungry." Effie tore the layers of the soft bread apart and blew on a piece to cool it before placing it in her granddaughter's mouth. The baby chewed it quickly, saliva dripping down her chin, before greedily reaching for more.

"Well, she's a Bilfrey all right, ain't she? She eats like you do." Effie grinned as Baby Curtis and the chubby pink-cheeked toddler sat on the kitchen floor, eating biscuits in silence.

Their quiet moment was soon disrupted by the crack of the screen door hitting the splintered wooden frame. "Who's here? Is that you, Frank or Gene?"

Only sixteen, Frank and his brother Gene, younger by only a year, were still more boys than men, which Effie often was forced to remind them even if their attitude and freewheeling boasted otherwise.

Effie craned her neck around the corner to have a look. "It's me, Ma." Frank, heavy footed, clomped toward the kitchen, looked down at the peaceful three, and gave a snort. "What's this about?"

Effie swept her arm over the plate and then toward her son and grandchild before saying, "This here is a picnic. We are celebrating our newest tenant."

Frank grinned. "You finally rented number three? Thank God, now I don't need to help Ernest shovel shit no more."

Effie shook her head. "Nope, I didn't rent three, and thanks to Sarah I am now looking after your niece. And you best remember, boy, that in this life, there will always be shit to shovel."

Scowling, Frank snapped, "You're doing what?"

Even-toned, Effie answered, "You heard me."

Stomping his foot to punctuate each word, Frank spat back, "I can't fucking believe this!"

Effie, covering Lottie's ears too late, snarled, "You mind your mouth, boy, and your manners."

Disgusted, Frank snatched a biscuit and headed back outside.

"Mom-mom, mom-mom," the tiny girl gurgled.

"Well, I don't think you will be needing that word now. Best you learn how to say Granmom." Effie took the toddler's hand and gave a small tug. "Come on, let's see what your mom thought was important enough to stick in that tiny little suitcase." Effie strode toward the case with determination as her granddaughter's wobbly legs stumbled to keep pace.

Effie squatted down and flipped the rusted latches on the shabby pink case. She pulled out the carefully packed contents and inspected each item. Effie turned every piece from front to back and over once more as if the answers to her daughter's sudden departure could be found in a rumpled sweater or in the folds of a tiny pair of jeans.

Chapter Two

With a determination only a mother on a mission has, Effie strode sure-footed and quickly across the yard. Curtis had to speed into a jog to keep up, and by the time he reached her, Effie was already halfway down the hill. "Wait up," he said, puffing as he tried to catch his breath.

"You got to keep up or catch up," Effie said over her shoulder, never slowing her pace a bit.

"But it's harder to go fast carrying Lottie."

Effie paused for a moment, considering his point. She decided to wait, even though the whole time she impatiently slapped her hand against her thigh and called out for him to hurry.

"I don't see what the hurry is now," Curtis reasoned. "She's already gone."

Effie, walking quickly again, called back, "Time always matters, boy, you just don't know that when you're ten."

Curtis muttered under his breath, but Effie, having already turned her head, didn't hear. It wouldn't have mattered anyway, nothing mattered to Effie right now but getting there.

Both breathless now, Effie and Curtis stood before Cabin 4. Even though there were only two steps to the porch, Effie eyed them with uncertainty and contempt. Her prolonged gaze made it difficult for Curtis to decide whether his mother was afraid of what she would find behind the door or if she was simply too tired to find out. Before Curtis could settle on which one, Effie inhaled deeply and started up the steps. Curtis stayed close behind, pulling Lottie's little body closer to his own before stepping inside.

The inside of Cabin 4, where Sarah and Lottie lived, was dimly lit with tattered homemade yellow curtains hanging loosely at dirty windows. The floors were made from rough pine boards, uneven with knotholes so wide and deep one could see the dirt beneath. Although colorful rag rugs were carefully laid to cover some of the most damaged boards, areas of dark rot peeked out in several places. The furniture was simple and sparse but clean. A few homemade quilts were placed over the couch and chair in an effort to make the room cozier.

Although the room was large, it was the only one. And as Effie slowly looked around, taking in each piece and part, it was as though she'd never seen the room before. A large five-drawer dresser sat catty-corner, a choice Effie wouldn't have made with the limited space. Above the dresser hung a poster purchased at the dime store. On it, Fonzi stared back at Effie from his glossy mount. Effie smiled, remembering the day Sarah dug into her pocket for the exact change to buy it. Sarah had never seen *Happy Days*, but the man in the picture seemed otherworldly enough to earn a place on the wall.

Effie turned slightly, her gaze falling upon the small crib resting empty in the opposite corner. Gone were the baby blanket and rag doll, but the faded pink sheet still showed the faint imprint of Lottie's tiny body. As Effie stepped closer, she saw another doll lying abandoned beneath the crib. It was a Cabbage Patch doll. Not real, of course. Homemade—with crooked stitches and cheap yarn—it was the second purchase Sarah made that day in the dime store. Effie held the doll to her nose and inhaled deeply before tenderly laying it in the crib.

The cabin didn't have indoor plumbing. Instead, there was an even smaller outbuilding behind it. Having to go outside to use the bathroom was more than an inconvenience to Sarah, it was an embarrassment. She felt it made her family nothing better than hillbillies. Sarah often argued that their backward ways weren't acceptable anymore, especially since it was now the eighties. Effie resented Sarah's opinion on the subject, since she felt she was more than generous giving her daughter a rent-free place to live regardless of the bathroom's location.

In truth, it wasn't much trouble for Effie to give Sarah, scared and pregnant at sixteen, a place to live since Effie owned the eight cabins on her property in Talon Ridge, but Effie expected some gratitude. Although Sarah's situation wasn't uncommon in these parts, it also wasn't that welcome, but Effie accepted it best she could by allowing Sarah to choose a cabin and helping her settle in. These small, poorly built buildings were shacks more than cabins. Each crudely built with rough-hewn wood and placed at varying distances from each other in a misshapen semicircle.

Cabins 1 and 2 were so dilapidated that they were all but boarded up waiting for repair or the truly desperate. Cabin 3 sat empty and was an option, but Sarah chose the fourth cabin because it was next to Mr. Goodwin; it was a choice with which Effie couldn't argue. These buildings were nothing more than run-down shacks, but Effie insisted that if someone could say they were living in a cabin, then no matter how ramshackle it was they could always feel better about their lot. Sarah disagreed with Effie's reasoning, but she wanted desperately to believe that the right name had the power to change even the meaning of one's life, or at least that was what she hoped when she named her daughter.

"What are you looking to find?" Curtis asked as he gently lowered Lottie to the floor. Even at such a young age, the baby recognized the room and began to toddle around, feeling freer in the familiarity.

"I guess I'll know when I find it," Effie said as she headed toward the dresser. Lottie was now running from one side of the room to the other, Sarah's obvious absence initially confusing the child and then frightening her. With Lottie's squeals now threatening to turn to shrieks, Effie ordered Curtis to take her outside.

"I don't know what to do with her," Curtis groaned.

"Play with her," Effie said through gritted teeth.

Curtis whined, "I don't know how to play with her."

Her patience now worn, Effie snapped, "I swear, Baby Curtis, some days you're about as useful as tits on a bull." Effie opened the door of the only closet, pulled out two cardboard boxes and ripped them both open. Taking a quick look, she thrust her hands inside the second one and pulled out a stack of torn and tattered children's books. "Here!" she snapped as she shoved them toward Curtis.

"I have to *read* to her?" Curtis moaned.

Effie, now standing at her full five-three height, clenched her hands onto her hips and leveled Curtis's will with her glare. Without another word, Curtis took Lottie's hand and coaxed the toddler outside.

Effie began her search. First, she carefully pulled each dresser drawer open, but seeing every one empty, she moved onto the bed. Effie pulled back the patch quilt, which she'd made years ago for Sarah, but nothing more than a faded sheet was underneath. She looked under the dresser and the bed—nothing. She explored the underside of the couch and chair cushions—nothing. Empty-handed and a bit more frantic, Effie started flipping pillows and tearing up rugs. As Effie turned to ransack the kitchen, she saw the two forgotten boxes that she'd taken from the closet.

Effie recklessly pulled out the contents of each box until papers, books, and a few photos lay scattered on the floor. Effie sat, exhausted and somewhat overwhelmed by the mess that now surrounded her. Sarah was always a neat child who was rarely chided for her messes, but she was also a girl who kept every item and object as though everything was a treasured keepsake. Effie, on the other hand, placed value only on what could protect her, keep her, or save her.

Effie set aside the few remaining children's storybooks then she sifted through the papers. The first was a stack of letters, some from a grade school playmate mixed in with a few from a first love. The others, clipped and kept, were school papers with high marks. Though never boastful, Effie felt proud as she leafed through them before placing the stack neatly next to her.

Taking in a deep breath, Effie picked up the letters. Twenty of them were from Sarah's childhood friend, Beatrice, otherwise affectionately known as Beatty. Effie leaned back against the wall, allowing the letter she was reading to rest in her lap. She closed her eyes to see if she could recollect the child's face, and sure enough, Beatty Bain appeared in her mind's eye, the fair-haired and pale-skinned little girl who'd occupied so many of her daughter's hours as a child. Beatrice was just a wisp of a girl and always looked, to Effie, to be more ghost than girl, even more so when she was at Sarah's side, which was often.

Sarah was leader of the twosome, which Effie attributed to Sarah's physical characteristics being in direct opposition to that of her friend. Sarah was tall for her age, and although thin, she possessed broad shoulders and a strong frame. Her thick auburn hair naturally curled into tight coils that reached halfway down her back. An often-unruly mane with red and chestnut strands intertwined wove around her head and hung softly beside high cheekbones and subtly defiant dark eyes. Her hair was let loose and always tangled, and Effie often threatened to cut the beloved locks, but Sarah would plead until Effie relented. Effie, of course, really never had any intentions, just the notion.

A day after Sarah turned one, the local witch woman came up to Effie on the street and asked to hold the baby. Hesitant, Effie handed Sarah to her. After staring at the child for several moments, the woman said brightly, "She has beautiful eyes." Turning the baby toward Effie, she said, "See how the gold flecks dance right around the edges? It's rare and special." Effie smiled, unable to contain her pride, until the woman said more ominously, "Some things are rare for a reason. You going to want to watch this one."

Frightened, Effie grabbed Sarah from the crazy old woman and hurried down the street. By the time she was home, Effie convinced herself that a woman who spent her days mixing mushrooms and snakeskin in a pot didn't know anything, especially about her baby. However, the raspy-voiced words of this haggard old witch never left Effie's mind.

She looked down at the now-crumpled letter in her tightened fist and wondered where her daughter had gone. Effie always knew that Sarah had a spirit that seemed ill at ease in its place in the world, but Effie had put her fears in the hope that Lottie would be the rope to tether Sarah to Talon Ridge—until today.

She read each letter until only one was left. Then, holding the last letter in her hand, she sighed, realizing that without Sarah's letters to Beatrice these were nothing more than the silly thoughts of a girl who had so little sense as to want eight bedrooms and no babies—a constant theme in Beatrice's letters.

It wasn't uncommon for most families in Talon Ridge to have a lot of children, but the Bains had, for generations, produced faster and more offspring than rabbits in heat. It was Effie's strongly held opinion that at least one of those Bain women could have kept her legs closed. It was an opinion that she knew she had no right to since she personally understood the demands of men, especially men who treated women more like property than people. Men whose demands led to too many mouths and whose laziness led to too little food. The Bain men were no better. And although there wasn't a family around who didn't know the pang of hunger occasionally or the discomfort of close spaces, the Bains lived in squalor, and for that Effie could find no excuse.

Effie tossed the last of Beatrice's letters onto the pile. Not one brought her closer to understanding why Sarah left. Effie did, however, have more sympathy for Beatrice.

As Effie gathered the letters together, the soft rustling sounded much like Margery Keefer's hushed whisper when she'd told Effie that Beatty had become a prostitute. In these hills, it was a fate all too common.

Margery Keefer was the young woman who rented Cabin 6, barely past twenty-two but the deep-set lines around her mouth clearly showed a life already hard-lived. Margery knew of Beatrice Bain's means of employment first-hand.

After all, in the mountains it was hard to make a living; at least Margery Keefer found a way to pay her rent each month.

Effie moved onto the love letters, three in all. They were from a young boy down the road. The proximity made calling on Sarah more practical than some of the other girls whose homes could be a half day's walk. Of course, that didn't mean he didn't love Sarah or at least as well as one can love at twelve. His name was Dallas Cutler. The rumor was that his mother couldn't think of a name, so she closed her eyes and placed her finger on a map, which confirmed Effie's opinion that the Cutlers were not the brightest bunch.

Dallas may not have been the smartest, but he was sweet, especially to Sarah, and that was all that Effie needed to see. Effie remembered the boy in faded jeans and a white tee standing on the porch, waiting for her daughter. Dallas was scrawny, but strong with coal-black hair that curled and refused taming in the same way as Sarah's. Effie thought Sarah too young for a boy to call on her, waiting on the porch like some feral cat wanting to be fed. But Effie relented when she realized that since Dallas, Sarah's eyes no longer seemed to hold the restlessness that often made Effie stiffen with fear. So, she allowed the long walks and late talks and relaxed in the new calm of Sarah's spirit.

The first letter was short, only two paragraphs. Effie noted that the handwriting was chicken scratch at best, and she struggled to make out the first few sentences. Although not dated, it seemed to be from early in their short-lived relationship as he wrote about the fun he had and his desire to see her again soon. Effie laid the letter next to Beatrice's and picked up the next; it was longer and more personal. Dallas talked of Sarah's beauty and his want to be with her, to kiss her, to touch her. Effie's fingers and thumb involuntarily clamped together, folding the paper in half as she looked upward. She then used the letter to fan the heat of the blush from her face. She didn't know if she felt embarrassment or shame. After all, even though Sarah was gone, these letters were personal and private; these letters were hers. But like any mother who has searched for answers in vain, Effie picked up the last letter, whispered, "I'm sorry," and began to read.

> Sarah,
> I know you told me not to write no more, but I got to know what's wrong. Did I do something? If I did, I'm sorry.
> Whatever it is, we can make it better but you got to talk to me. I still love you. I hope you still love me. If you do, meet me at Culver's Creek after school.
>
> Still yours (I hope),
> Dallas

"He no longer loves me," Sarah had told her mother at the time. Effie, ready to dry tears and watch a young girl's broken heart take months to mend, was surprised when Sarah, dry-eyed and unmoved, shrugged and said little more. At the time, Effie believed her daughter's indifference was due to a young girl's fickle nature and the passing affections of puppy love. Now though, as she read over each new line, Dallas's words were changing all that she thought she knew.

Effie gathered all the letters, clipped them once more, and placed them back into the box. She then pulled down the lid and folded the corners tightly. As she closed her eyes, she tried to keep her dark memories back, but like floodwaters, they swirled and seeped into all parts of her brain—drowning the few good memories.

Chapter Three

Curtis stomped down the porch steps, and Lottie toddled behind. She waddled off the bottom step, landing on her thickly diapered bottom with a soft thud, causing a puff of powdery dust to plume around her. She dug her little hands into the soft dirt and slid her fingers back and forth, making tiny tracks around her legs. Curtis was caught by the curiosity of her antics for only a few seconds before he stormed across the yard, muttering.

An empty soda can was the first thing to feel Curtis's ten-year-old wrath. He pulled back his foot and kicked hard enough to send the aluminum scrap soaring past the cabin. Not feeling any better, Curtis looked for something else to kick. Finding nothing, he picked up a handful of stones and pelted them across the yard. With every rock chucked against an unsuspecting tree or the corner of the house, Curtis listed another wrong he'd suffered. He began, of course, with his mother.

"How dare she?" he grumbled. "Stickin' me with the baby. She's Sarah's kid, not mine. It ain't fair!" With that, Curtis drove a rock into the side of the cabin. The loud crack startled Lottie, who began to cry; Curtis ignored her. It wasn't until those cries became ear-piercing howls that Curtis stormed back across the yard. He kicked the dirt and muttered a list of insults leveled at everyone until he reached Lottie, who was now in a complete lather.

Standing over the wailing child, Curtis halfheartedly attempted to sooth her. "It's okay, Lottie. Don't cry." But Lottie did cry, and now she cried louder. Frustrated, Curtis grabbed Lottie's rag doll and threw it at her, but the soft cloth toy only lightly landed by her leg.

Distracted from her tears for a moment, Lottie picked up the doll and, out of habit, chewed on the diminutive foot. Contented again, Lottie sunk her hands back into the dirt. Exhausted from his own fit, Curtis slumped down on the bottom step.

He stared at Lottie for a bit as she happily gnawed on her doll. Looking up at Curtis, Lottie, with her crookedly spaced teeth, grinned. No longer angry, Curtis felt his heart soften a bit. "I ain't really mad at you, ya know?" Curtis lightly tousled the top of Lottie's head. "I know it ain't your fault your mom run off, but I had plans. And ain't none of them was watching a baby all summer." Lottie kicked her chubby legs back and forth as she indulged in the attention.

"I was gonna prove this summer that I ain't a baby no more." Curtis crossed his arms and sunk his elbows into his knees. "I'm sick of being treated like one."

Curtis's anger at Lottie for having to be her keeper soon faded as he wondered where his sister had gone. Quiet, thoughtful, and smart, Sarah had a spark that Curtis, even as a little boy, could plainly see and admire. She was the lightness to his brothers' darkness, the sweetness to their bitter, and the kindness to their cruelty. Curtis couldn't remember a time when he didn't love Sarah or want to be near her.

Curtis, like his mother, could always see the wildness in Sarah that others couldn't. He, too, knew that she was always searching, wanting more, and waiting. Because he was a child, he believed that he was reason enough for her to stay. Curtis now grimly realized that he wasn't, nor was Lottie. Watching the baby chew on her doll, Curtis felt suddenly ashamed that he hadn't considered the pain of *her* loss.

Guilty, Curtis took the top book from the stack and flipped to the first page. He moved to the bottom step and sidled closer to Lottie. "Look, Lottie. Do you want me to read this to you?" The picture caught her attention, and Lottie dropped her doll.

Curtis began, and as he read page after page of *Goodnight Moon*, Lottie cooed and pointed and patiently waited for the next to be turned until he'd reached the end. Lottie then watched as Curtis traced his finger across the picture on the last page. The kittens curled on a rocking chair as darkness cast across the emerald walls of the room suddenly made Curtis homesick, not for a place, but for a time he knew was now gone.

Closing the book, Curtis whispered, "Good night, Sarah." He then quickly wiped his freshly wet cheeks and slid the book onto the bottom of the stack.

No longer wanting to feel sad, Curtis distracted himself by flipping through the pile of books as he looked for his favorite, *Tales of a Fourth Grade Nothing*. As he fanned out the books, a quick scan revealed that they were all for toddlers except one—one that caught his eye and kept his attention as he gently lifted it up from the others. He ran his fingers over the purple and yellow flowers randomly scattered across the shiny pink cover then he traced the curly, swirling letters written in script, spelling out the word "Diary."

"Diary?" Curtis whispered the word as a question. With no one to answer, he opened the book. Immediately recognizing his sister's small, staccato print upon the page, he knew. "Sarah's diary," Curtis murmured. Without hesitation, Curtis turned to the first page and began to read.

October 15, 1976

First of all, I ain't writing "Dear diary." It don't make no sense to write a letter to a book. It's not like I'm writing to a person. A book don't listen, it don't talk, and it don't care. Of course, I guess most people don't neither.

I'm only writing in this book because my teacher, Ms. Prindle, said if I wrote in it, I wouldn't have to read my essays in front of the class anymore. She knows I hate it. I just can't stand all those eyes watching me but not really seeing me. And I never know what to do with my hands. I just sway from one foot to the other. No matter how I try, I can't get my body to still itself. Mama says I have a restless soul—maybe so.

Ms. Prindle says it won't be graded. She says she ain't even going to read it. What sense does that make? Maybe she's not so smart or maybe she's lazy. I don't know. No one knows much about her other than she ain't never lived in the mountains. What I do know is that makes her lucky, damn lucky.

So, why write in a book that no one's never going to read? I guess because I gave my word. Mama always says that a person's word is their worth. And I don't know much, but what I do know is that I want to be worth something.

Tempted to turn to the next page, Curtis stopped. Feeling eyes on him, he craned his head to the right to see Lottie had scooted closer and was watching him. Suddenly guilty, he closed the book. Of course, he knew the child had no understanding of what he had found or what he was doing, but he still felt oddly ashamed. After all, these words were his sister's private thoughts, and although her abandonment made him angry enough to disregard the betrayal, his love for her wouldn't allow it. Even though Curtis decided not to read further, he also decided that he had to keep it. Looking around, he carefully tucked the small book into the back of his pants and pulled his shirt down over the part that still peeked out.

Curtis then stood and stretched, shaking the pins and needles loose from his legs. At ten years old, he was already almost as tall as his brothers, but he didn't seem to realize it. He often cowered under their height even though he nearly matched it. Staring across the yard, Curtis ran his fingers through his hair, which could have been described as the color of dirty dishwater if not for a few golden streaks. He pushed back loose curls—an uneasy habit—that stubbornly tousled back onto his forehead nearly covering his deep-set green eyes. His soft pale skin and light hair were in direct opposition of his brothers' darker complexion—an outward reflection, perhaps, of the differences in their natures.

When he saw Lottie happily kicking her baby feet and babbling, Curtis's heart filled with an ache for Sarah. He picked up his tiny niece, and cradling her in his arms, he sat back down on the bottom step. Although the feel of her tiny warm body and the softness of her downy hair against his cheek should have provided comfort, it only made Curtis sadder. He buried his face near her neck and began to bawl. No longer the quieted cries of a prideful boy, his tears flowed freely as his loud sobs carried across the small yard right to the ears of his older brother Frank.

Lost in self-pity and sadness, Curtis didn't hear his brother's heavy footfalls as he closed in on the boy who sat vulnerable in his grief. Frank shoved Curtis's shoulder with his boot before beginning his assault. "When you gonna stop being such a little shit? You got nothing better to do than cry, *Baby* Curtis." Hissing the word "Baby," Frank again shoved Curtis with his boot. Curtis, already defeated from the day, surrendered with a demand more plaintive than threatening. "Go away Frank. Please."

Frank, like a cat that releases a mouse too weak to provide amusement, leaned in and snarled, "You ain't nothing more than a fuckin' mama's boy sitting here rockin' your baby that also ain't nothing but a piece of shit." Finally satisfied at seeing the wounded look in Curtis's eyes, Frank turned and headed into the house, but not before flicking the hot ash of his cigarette onto Curtis's bare arm.

Chapter Four

With a wide gait, Frank smugly strode toward the house. His features were sharp like his words, and he had a shock of black hair, dark to match many of his moods. He wasn't very tall, but he was broad-shouldered and barrel-chested, appearing bigger than he was, which Frank exaggerated even more by walking with his shoulders back and chest out.

His forced bravado actually succeeded in intimidating many of the boys his age, and those who weren't still knew better than to tangle with him. Frank had earned, at an even younger age, the hard-won reputation of a fighter. He was quick to attack and slow to relent, which meant that many sidestepped his path rather than crossed it. Although he may have been feared, Frank wasn't respected, except by his younger brother Eugene, who followed him with the loyalty of a dog.

Being only ten months apart, the brothers were often mistaken for twins. Both had hair the color of soot and a grin that looked more snarl than smile. But the similarities stopped with appearance. Frank's abrupt mannerisms and clipped words were in contrast to Eugene's gentleness and softer ways.

Named after Effie's father, Eugene inherited only his grandfather's weakness, which to Frank was proof that a name can determine one's character and purpose. Although he insisted on being called Gene, Frank often ridiculed his brother's given name, trying to incite anger and fight in him. A failed effort, which only caused Gene hurt. Each strike and slight was never enough, however, to keep Gene from Frank's side.

Secrets, scrapes, and the solidarity of being bastard boys kept the brothers together, tight and united. Talon Ridge wasn't a place where fathers taught sons how to ride bikes and throw a ball. But at least the other boys knew their fathers. The same could not be said for Sarah, Frank, Gene, and Baby Curtis—mongrel pups dumped from mismatched litters. It made holding your head high difficult, but Frank found a way.

Stamping out the half-smoked cigarette with the toe of his boot, Frank tried to exhale the frustration he would feel the moment he opened the door. He stepped inside Sarah's house to find Effie sitting surrounded by boxes and loose papers, which, upon seeing him, she scrambled to gather.

"That's okay, Ma, I won't tell Sarah that you're snooping through her stuff," Frank sneered, trying to provoke an argument.

Refusing to take Frank's bait, Effie said calmly, "I'm not snooping. I'm searching. And I don't think Sarah is gonna mind much now." Then she methodically began stacking the boxes back into the closet, hoping that Frank would become disinterested and leave. Instead her strained attempt at indifference only piqued his interest and his desire to goad her a bit more.

"You find something interesting in those boxes? You discover Sarah's secret?" The word "secret" pierced Effie's ears then her heart, but appearing unruffled, she casually replied, "Nope. No secrets." Then she inhaled deeply, burying her own secret, and closed the closet door.

"She really not coming back? And you're just going to raise her kid, huh?"

Effie turned slowly to face her child, her eldest son, and her fiercest adversary. "What do you expect me to do, Frank? You want me to throw a two-year-old baby out on the road?"

Frank took his time answering as a sly smile slid across his face. "No. Why give her away when we could try selling her first?"

Effie, tired of Frank's sick humor, snapped back, "What I should've done was sold you. Of course, I didn't bother tryin' 'cause I knew there wouldn't be any takers."

Every word was punctuated with Effie's gall, and Frank felt each one. "Hell, I wish you would have given me away, then at least I wouldn't be stuck here in this hole."

Frank's words dared his mother's next move, which she made swiftly and without reserve. "You ain't stuck nowhere, boy! And from where I'm standing, your feet move just fine." Effie matched Frank's glare, never once taking her eyes from his.

Not admitting being defeated but knowing he was, Frank pushed past his mother and out the door onto the porch.

Not five feet from the steps, Curtis sat playing with Lottie. Frank watched, and as he did, bile rose in his throat. Enraged, he stomped toward them, jaw clenched, and hands curled into fists. Unaware of the moving force closing in on him, Curtis continued to pull Lottie's small feet, tickling them to hear her laugh.

"You're such a worthless little shit, you know that? And so is she. Both of you are worthless shits!" Frank leaned in, spitting each word into Curtis's face. Curtis stood stock-still and silent.

Suddenly, and without warning, Frank snatched Lottie from Curtis and held the howling baby just out of Curtis's reach. Curtis's fear faded as his anger flamed. "Put her down, Frank. Put her down. Now!"

Curtis latched on to Frank's arm, which only caused Frank to callously snigger as he easily pulled from his grasp. Then, like a ball kept high in a game of keep-away, he lifted Lottie into the air as Curtis tried unsuccessfully to reach for her.

"Is this what you want? Come on, little girl, get your baby," Frank taunted. Curtis's face, red with rage, burned hot as he again tried to grab Lottie, but Frank's large frame and swift side-to-side steps made it impossible. Each try only amused Frank and exhausted Curtis.

Missed swings and punches falling flat caused Curtis to resort to his only known successful defense. Grabbing Frank's left forearm, Curtis opened his mouth wide and clamped down hard. Howling, Frank pulled up, causing Lottie to tumble to the ground unhurt but screaming.

Both boys, unmatched in more ways than size, fell to the ground. Frank wrapped his now-bleeding arm around Curtis's neck as he tried to hold his brother's kicking legs. Curtis thrashed more than punched, but he did manage a few good hits before Effie, who'd heard the baby screaming, rushed to the porch and hollered for them to stop.

Timing his mother's steps, Frank got in one more good punch before Effie was at Lottie's side. Scooping up the baby first, Effie then snapped around and screeched, "Get out of here! Do you hear me, Frank Cashel Bilfrey?"

Frank shoved Curtis off then swiftly stood. Refusing to be humiliated again, Frank turned to stomp across the yard. He hadn't even taken one step before Effie shifted Lottie in her arms then slapped her hand hard across Frank's face.

Frank gingerly touched his stinging cheek before muttering, "That's right, pick him. You always pick him." Sulking, Frank stumbled toward home. Curtis, looking down, rubbed the rawness around his neck. Effie held Lottie close, snuggling the baby with soft kisses. They stood there in silence. No more words were needed.

Chapter Five

A fragrant wisp of honeysuckle floated on the warm May breeze blowing across Sarah's yard where Effie, Curtis, and Lottie still stood. The sweet smell wafted to Effie's nose where it nuzzled underneath, waking her from her trance. Effie breathed in the sugary scent before slowly exhaling. She then set Lottie down in the grass, allowing the soft blades to intertwine between the toddler's bare toes.

Lottie's sudden squeal of laughter, like sun breaking through clouds, broke Effie's outward gaze. "Dog," Lottie chirped as a longhaired black dog brushed against her little leg.

Leaning over, Effie placed one hand gently on Lottie's tiny shoulder, and with the other she tenderly scratched the back of Dog's neck. The animal laid his muzzle on her leg as he rolled his eyes up, looking at her with only love and loyalty. "Do you like that, boy? You're such a good dog. You're such a good boy," Effie cooed to Dog in a soft voice that her own children rarely heard.

Animals were easier for Effie to love because, for her, that kind of love didn't come at a price. And in her lifetime,

Effie felt she'd already paid dearly. "Here, Lottie, pet the doggy. He likes it." Effie pressed Lottie's hand against Dog's warm fur. The child lightly touched Dog's head, squealed again, and pulled her hand away.

Dog seemed to appear from nowhere yet also seemed to always have belonged. Although the animal loved everyone, he gave his allegiance to only one—Mr. Goodwin. Mr. Goodwin, seventy-three and alone, lived in Cabin 5. He was the only person who Effie ever felt deserved the respect of being called by his surname. A retired miner, he had a back curved and twisted like a meandering river, and his lungs, heavy with coal dust, caused him to wheeze when he talked. But Mr. Goodwin's stooped posture and raspy voice went unnoticed once one came to know his strong character and listened to the wisdom of his words.

Effie had known Mr. Goodwin a long time, the one remaining piece from her past that she actually chose to keep. He had worked with her father for twenty years; side by side they shoveled coal and drank half their earnings. Motherless and mostly alone, Effie clung to her father. Although he was often undeserving and rarely returned her love, Effie never stopped trying until the day she lay him in the ground next to her mother. The mother she never knew, whose last breath was taken when Effie took her first. The mother who left her with a lifetime of guilt and little else.

A young girl without a mother is like an untethered balloon, bobbing and floating to places unknown and to frightening heights that hold one for too long. Effie, left to her own devices for so many years, never understood the feeling of being held in place, secured to a spot of safety and comfort except for some brief moments spent with Mr. Goodwin. He reminded Effie of porch swings and summer songs sang out of tune but happily. He reminded Effie of sweet tea and evening talks. He reminded her that there were some memories that didn't need burying; there were some worth keeping.

Mr. Goodwin was Effie's first renter, and, in Effie's estimation, he would be the last to live in Cabin 5, for she couldn't imagine another soul filling the space or her life the way he so easily did. Thoughts of this gangly man with sunken cheeks and a wide grin caused something akin to a smile to surface on Effie's face.

"What are you thinking about, Ma?" Curtis cocked his head, trying much like Dog to understand.

"Days past, Baby Curtis, days long past."

Effie stood, stretched her back, and gently shooed Dog with her foot before saying, "Get on home now, Dog. Mr. Goodwin will feed you good." Turning to Curtis, Effie said, "You take Lottie and go on home now too, Baby Curtis."

Worried, Curtis whined, "You're not coming?"

Effie was not one to tolerate a child's whimpering, but considering Frank's dark mood and unpredictability, she understood. So, softly, she said, "You'll be just fine, Baby Curtis." Pointing to his mouth, she added, "With those teeth, you'll make out all right."

Grinning in spite of himself, Curtis grabbed Lottie's hand and headed home.

Effie watched the pair make their way across the yard and down over the hill, Curtis with his lanky strides and Lottie with short, hurried steps trying to keep pace. Four children and a grandchild, in what time did this happen? Effie wondered. Suddenly tired, she moved toward the porch and sat on the steps, resting bones too achy for her age. She looked up at the sky. Seeing the sun sitting only slightly above the treetops, she marveled how a day could feel so long before it was even dinnertime.

Seeing Frank's stamped cigarette butt nestled next to her foot, Effie quickly looked around, reached down, and snatched it. She didn't know why she hid her habit. After all, everyone knew she smoked, but she still felt the need to be secretive like a child fearing being caught. New to the vice, Frank left half the cigarette, so Effie grabbed a lighter from her shirt pocket, lit the end, and took a long drag, remembering her first cigarette. Twelve, curious, and bored, she stole one from her father's pack and snuck behind the house. In retrospect, Effie wasn't very cunning in her effort to escape her father's attention and subsequent wrath, but maybe that was the point; he noticed.

Effie's muscles involuntarily tightened, and her jaw clenched in a visceral response to the memory of her father lashing her with a hickory switch. It was only three times and not hard enough to break the skin, but it left welts and was a punishment not equal to the crime. Effie cowered, not from the thin, reedlike branch that struck her back, but rather from his words, which came faster and harder than the hits. Her father withheld nothing, spitting out each venomous word until Effie, teary-eyed, begged him to stop.

Seeing her small face creased and scrunched in pain, he broke from his trance of momentary madness and dropped the branch. The physical and emotional pain overwhelmed Effie, and her tiny body crumpled under the weight of it. Although her father stood over her, Effie thought he now seemed smaller. Unexpectedly less afraid, Effie sat up and waited for what was next.

When Effie's father finally spoke, it wasn't soothing words of comfort. Instead, he preached about the sins of stealing. But Effie, grateful for any attention her father cared to give, obediently nodded, and murmured an apology. Effie then promised to never again steal, even though she knew just as she knew when she was five and she now knew as a grown woman that her father's punishment was never for a lost shoe or a stolen cigarette. Effie's greatest sin was being given life at the cost of her mother's.

The red ember singed Effie's fingers, causing her to abruptly drop the cigarette and return to the present moment, rattled but safe—safe as a mother without her child can feel.

Effie slowly turned her body to face Sarah's cabin, but feeling too close, Effie stood and walked a few feet from Sarah's home. Effie studied the chipped paint, the broken windowpane with taped cardboard to catch the wind, and the rotted porch step. She saw the splintered wood and the warped boards. She saw the sagging roof and the broken rail. She saw that Sarah was right—it was a shack, worn and broken.

Effie hadn't reached the end of the yard to walk home before she looked back, knowing it wouldn't be long before she returned to this house and to her search for a daughter lost long before she ever left.

Chapter Six

Gene had spent the day shoveling manure for Ernest Weddell alongside his brother Frank. It was because of Gene that Frank got the job since most folks in Talon Ridge only trusted Frank Bilfrey under his brother's influence. Many simply assumed that Gene could keep Frank in line. Many didn't understand that Frank perceived Gene's integrity as weakness upon which he capitalized, and in doing so he eventually destroyed.

Coming home, Gene saw Baby Curtis playing in the yard with Lottie as he walked through the gate, but, unlike Frank, he felt no inclination to insult, tease, or torment them. Instead, Gene walked past with barely a nod of acknowledgment. It could have been that Gene was too tired to waste his breath on words with Curtis, or it could have been that Gene had more decency than Frank. Either way, Gene's decision to make the right choices did little to affect Frank's decision to make the wrong ones.

Ernest Weddell, however, was no fool. He recognized a cheat and crook when he came across one, mostly because he saw himself in the likes of Frank Bilfrey. The brothers hadn't even worked the job for two months before Frank conned the younger boys into doing his job in exchange for his protection. The scam was the only protection the boys needed was from Frank, but they quickly discovered that shoveling manure was easier than being shoved face-first into it. Gene tried to talk Frank out of his twisted scheme, but always the follower, Gene soon joined.

Gene opened the door to find Frank sitting at the table flipping a butterfly knife. The knife was Frank's prized possession, and most likely stolen. Frank believed the knife and the cuts on his body made him look tough, despite what Effie said to the contrary. The thud of heavy metal against the wooden table from another missed toss caused Gene to flinch.

"God, Gene, why the fuck are you so jumpy?" Frank snapped.

"I'm not. I'm just tired," Gene said.

Smirking and slowly nodding his head, Frank said, "Yeah, Genie. You're just tired." Sniggering, Frank added, "Or you're just a big pussy."

Ignoring his brother's snide remarks, Gene pulled off his boots and put them on the porch before sinking into the couch.

Not done, Frank taunted, "That's real good, Eugene. Ma is gonna be real proud that you put your shit boots outside like a good boy."

Gene snapped, "Come on, Frank. For once why don't you try not being a pain in the ass about everything?"

Frank snickered and said in a long drawl, "Eugene..." Before Frank could finish his sentence, Gene jumped to his feet, snatched the knife, and held it to Frank's throat.

Enraged, Gene leaned close to Frank, and with a lunacy-laced whisper said, "You call me Eugene one more time and you're going to be saying it through a mile-wide slit in your throat." Pressing the knife a little closer, Gene said louder, "You got that, Frank?"

Frank carefully nodded. Gene slowly released his grip of the knife, unwittingly giving Frank the opening to grab it. Overpowering Gene with his right hand, Frank twisted his brother's arm until he was bent on his knees in surrender. Frank didn't demand an apology or continue his torment, he simply let go, and with what could only be perceived as pride said, "Now that's the Gene I can respect." Giving his brother a friendly push on the shoulder, he added, "But you ever do that to me again, brother, it ain't me that's gonna be whistlin' through a slit in my throat." Bested again, Gene stood and shook his head, baffled and yet also awed at his brother's strength and darkness.

Stumbling back to the couch, Gene sat down and took a deep breath, trying to calm himself as he realized that the Bilfrey rage wasn't passed on to only Frank. Taking a few minutes' consideration, Gene tried to decide if his rare show of daring was due to genetics or courage. He knew, however, that regardless the reason, he was most comfortable at Frank's back, and that was where he'd stay, because he also knew that trying to change their roles would be as useless as trying to make the sun revolve around the earth.

Trying to break the tension that still hung heavy between them, Gene casually asked,

"Where's Ma? I'm gettin' hungry."

Because anger and grudges weren't held long between them, Frank answered offhandedly, "Last I saw she was at Sarah's digging through her closet like a thief."

Gene turned to face Frank. Now more interested in this latest piece of news, he asked, "Sarah's?"

Through pursed lips, Frank answered, "Mm-hmm."

Gene shook his head. "Sarah's gonna to be pissed when she finds out."

Frank snorted, "Sarah ain't gonna say shit because Sarah is gone."

Shocked, Gene abruptly stood and asked, "She's gone? Where'd she go?"

Frank grunted, "Hell if I know or give a shit."

Gene nervously rubbed his index finger across his chin. "No, Frank. You're wrong. I just saw Lottie in the yard."

Annoyed, Frank snapped, "Well, if you got all the god-damn answers then why the hell are you asking me?"

Not wanting to test Frank's patience twice, Gene said cautiously, "I'm just confused, Frank. I mean, if Sarah left, then why didn't she take Lottie?"

Frank said, "Look, all I know is she left. I don't know where she went. I don't know if she's coming back. And I sure as hell don't know why she didn't take her snot-nosed kid with her. What I do know is that I don't give a shit about the lot of it so stop asking questions. Got it?" Clearly done talking, Frank stomped over to the cupboard, took out a box of crackers, and began stuffing them into his mouth.

Gene went to the kitchen table and sat down followed by Frank, who tipped the box toward him. Gene shoved a fistful of crackers into his mouth. The brothers ate in silence; Frank sulked, and Gene brooded. Thirty more minutes passed before Effie opened the door and walked in followed by Curtis and Lottie. Disgusted, Frank, without a word, stomped outside.

Gene awkwardly stood by the door, waiting a moment before carefully saying, "So Ma, Frank says Sarah's gone."

Effie pulled a loaf pan from the bottom shelf and said, "So it seems."

Nervously rocking back and forth, Gene asked, "Where'd she go?"

Effie shrugged.

Gene asked, "Is she coming back? Who's going to take care of Lottie?"

Effie said nothing.

Gene pressed, "Ma, shouldn't we call someone? Maybe the sheriff could look into it?"

Effie wheeled around. "We ain't calling no one. This here is our problem, and it stays our problem."

More gently, Gene said, "Look, Ma, we can figure this out."

Looking more closely at her son, Effie wondered why he was suddenly so concerned about a sister who'd never been a cause for worry. Defensively, Effie snapped, "*We* ain't doing nothing. You just worry about Gene and let me worry about the rest." Without another word, Effie turned and pulled the rest of the ingredients from the cupboards.

Tired of his mother's mistrust of Frank resting on him, Gene sighed as he put his hand on the doorknob before quietly saying over his shoulder, "I ain't Frank." Looking at Baby Curtis standing comfortably at his mother's side, he added, "I ain't Baby Curtis, but I ain't Frank neither." Gene turned and went outside.

As the brothers sat side by side on the porch, Gene realized that his first impulse to be loyal to Frank was the right one. It was then that it happened. Without words, without actions, without anyone's real perception, Gene made the decision to always give his allegiance to Frank above all others. And although unspoken, this choice would reverberate loudly, causing chaos and sadness for the rest of both of their lives.

Chapter Seven

Frank, who rarely saw morning before the sun shone, stumbled into the living room and gruffly demanded, "What the hell is going on?"

Effie, still entranced by the happiness Lottie found in the simple pleasure of poking her cheeks, hardly noticed her son or his anger. But Frank always found a way to be noticed.

"Ma!" Frank shouted with a tone both indignant and needy.

The sharp sound of his call was earsplitting, silencing the laughter and causing Effie to turn to see her oldest son standing above her.

Frank took a wide stance, bent his head to the side, and cocked his eyebrow. Years of posturing to appear tough proved ineffective with his mother, who saw more boy than man as Frank, hair ruffled from the pillow and face creased with sheet marks, rubbed the remaining sleep from his eyes. Her perspective changed quickly when Frank snapped, "This shit woke me up." Frank saw the light in his mother's eyes momentarily dim without realizing that it was because she'd just watched the boy she loved surrender to the man she so disliked.

Frank waited for his mother's rage, but she said nothing. He found her wordless stare to be more unsettling than any curses, scolding, or swearing that had ever passed her lips. Frank ended the torture of Effie's silence by taunting, "That's all you got, Ma? You just gonna stare at me? You got plenty to say to Sarah's little bastard, but nothing to your own, huh?" Frank watched as his mother's eyes shone with a new light, lit from rage.

Effie wielded her words like the sharp, quick pull of a pointed blade. "Maybe we don't know what man this baby belongs to, but we know she belongs. But you, Frank, you don't belong nowhere. No one will have you 'cause no one wants you."

Feeling as though he had been knifed, Frank pitched forward, dropping his chin onto his chest and closing his eyes in pain. It wasn't the cruelty of his mother's words, but rather the truth of them that broke Frank's heart, or at least the pieces that were left.

Frank's pride never allowed him to walk away injured without seeking retribution from those who caused the wound. Pushing past the pain, Frank stood straight, squared his shoulders, and settled back into a fighter's stance. "That's all you got? Telling me I don't belong? You think that means shit to me? I'm happy I don't belong here with a crazy mother, a runaway sister, her snot-nosed bastard, and two worthless brothers."

In that moment, Frank felt no love and no allegiance to any of them. In that moment, Frank felt only hate; it warmed and fueled him and was the reason Frank believed he survived.

Taking a few steps backward, he slumped into the sunken folds of the couch. Frank sat and watched his new source of anger and resentment curled on his mother's lap. He didn't see the soft curls that fell around her cherubic face. He didn't hear the sweet words that slipped through her small pink lips. Frank didn't see the baby; he saw the burden.

A burden not just left for his mother but for them all. Another mouth to feed, another person to bear, another reminder of Sarah. A barely audible groan of pain escaped Frank's lips as he thought of his sister. Only two years older, Sarah seemed in many ways decades older. Early in their lives, she held Frank's hand, watched his step, and kept him safe.

Effie had always been a strong woman and a protective mother, but she was also weak and distant too often to be dependable. However, Sarah, even as a small child, showed no frailty. Frank loved her giddy dancing around the room, he loved her when she loved Dallas Cutler, and he loved her even when she no longer seemed to love him.

Sarah's "dark days," as Effie called them, came suddenly, casting a shadow across her and all those in her path, including Frank. His existence in Sarah's world receded until she no longer saw him—no one did. Frank struggled to hold on to the only good he was given, but the more he thrashed the more he suffocated under the weight of what he couldn't change until it changed him.

Frank was not a naturally born fighter, so he was forced to learn. He fought the boys at school until they feared him. He fought his mother until her indifference didn't matter. He fought until any weakness he felt was gone, replaced by a strength formed not from character and courage but rather from resentment and anger. Fatherless, many days motherless and without Sarah, Frank shored himself against the constant storms by refusing to feel anything but anger.

Frank felt that anger now, calming only in its familiarity. Effie had taken Lottie outside, leaving Frank alone inside the house. He sat upright on the couch before standing and stretching. Stumbling into the kitchen, he greedily stuffed a few cold biscuits into his mouth before peering out the tiny window.

Watching in silence, Frank examined the four figures standing in the yard as though they were another family. One that was normal and happy. He watched their lips wordlessly move, allowing him to imagine hearing kindness and sweet tones where there was usually none. He watched their quiet actions, allowing him to imagine ordinary lives—pleasant and uncomplicated. Frank rarely ever thought or longed for the unreachable commonness of a devoted family, but today, in this moment, he did.

Chapter Eight

The sun streamed through the budding trees. Pines and oaks were mirrored in shaded paintings upon the ground. Gene stepped to the side so as to stand in these shadows. He rarely sought the light, much of which was always blocked anyway, living in the thickly wooded Talon Ridge. Gene carried a heavy wooden bucket filled to the top with water, which sloshed and spilled onto his pant legs. Groaning, he heaved the bucket over his shoulder and tipped it, soaking the dry dirt until it was a wet mud.

Curtis trailed behind with Lottie close by. Hours of shoveling manure and hauling water to Effie's vegetable garden made Gene's muscles burn and his patience short. "Watch her, Curtis! She's stepping on Ma's plants." Curtis pulled Lottie to his side. Grumpy, Gene again snapped, "She just kicked up the seeds, Curtis! Pick her up! I ain't taking shit for you messing up Ma's garden." Curtis quickly lifted Lottie into his arms and stayed at a safe distance behind his brother.

Curtis stepped clear of the garden before setting down Lottie, who quickly toddled toward Effie. Curtis ambled behind her until they both settled near his mother's clothesline but not so close as to irritate Effie while she hung clothes. Gene, thankful for the peace, sat down and rested his throbbing legs. He surveyed the yard and noticed that in some quiet moment when he wasn't paying attention, when he was too busy working, the land had changed. The trees were dressed in green again, flowers poked colorful heads up between clumps of dirt and grass grown too long, and a subtle heat settled in the early morning air.

Gene's eyes continued to follow the trail that the spring season had put down until his gaze fell upon the kitchen window of their house where Frank still stood inside watching. Seeing Gene, Frank quickly ducked behind the curtain. Gene stared at the empty space Frank left, wondering what he'd been watching and why. After a few minutes, Gene saw an almost imperceptible movement of the thin, light, lacy curtain, and he knew Frank was still watching.

Slowly it dawned on Gene that Frank—strong, tough Frank—was hiding. Gene craned his neck and squinted his eyes as he tried to once again catch Frank looking, but his efforts were cut short by a hard slap across the back of his neck. Flinching from the sharp sting on his sunburned skin, Gene pulled back and looked up to see Piney standing there, his thin lips pulled tight in a sinister smile.

"What you starin' at, boy?" Piney Boyer sneered.

"I ain't lookin' at nothin.'" Gene's tone was level, nothing like he felt. Inside, his stomach churned, and the bile slowly rose to his throat. Gene coughed, trying to choke it back down, then said, "What are you doing here, Piney?"

Gene's effort to sound tough was quickly clipped when Piney cuffed the side of his head and spat back, "Ain't really none of your business, peckerwood, is it? 'Stead of worryin' about what I'm doin', you should be worrin' about how I'm gonna kick your ass if you talk to me like that again." Piney stressed his point by wedging the tip of his boot under Gene's backside and pushing hard, causing Gene to topple forward.

Landing on his side, Gene glared up at Piney and muttered, "Shit, Piney, why..." Seeing the look on Piney's face, Gene thought better of finishing his sentence. Another battle surrendered to someone stronger, meaner, and morally inferior left Gene defeated. He shifted his weight and stood as Piney slithered his wiry frame over toward Effie.

There wasn't a time in Gene's life when he didn't remember Piney Boyer lording over them, making demands and life, in general, miserable. Piney lived in Cabin 8 for as long as any of the Bilfrey children could remember, and Gene couldn't recall a time when Piney ever handed his mother money for rent. Of course, Gene, like the rest of them, knew better than to question his mother, and so Piney remained in their lives making them feel uneasy on a good day and scared on a bad one. And as Gene watched Piney sidle closer to his mother, he had a feeling today was a bad one.

Feeling nervous, Gene looked toward the house to again see Frank staring out the window. Frank looked in Effie's direction before looking back at Gene. Lifting his chin,

Frank gave his brother a slight nod. Gene nodded back before he turned toward their mother and the man who now held her attention, and, unbeknownst to them, her fate.

Used to waiting for Frank's direction, Gene stayed put and listened, as Piney demanded, "So woman, you gonna make me some of that Poor Do?" Piney smiled through a row of yellowed teeth crookedly spaced around the missing ones.

Effie shook out a wet sheet and pulled pins from her pocket. Then, without once looking at him, she answered, "I ain't making you nothing, Piney Boyer."

Stepping closer, Piney hissed, "Oh, I don't know 'bout that. You and me, Effie, we can make some fine things."

Effie smoothed the freshly hung sheet, picked up another, and snapped it straight. Sharp and wet, the cloth came close to Piney's face.

Ducking, he snapped, "Whoa, woman, you fixin' to take off my nose?"

Effie slung the sheet over the line, turned toward Piney, and said, "I'd settle for poking your eyes out."

Piney snickered, "Oh Effie, I always did like your sass even if you ain't got no right to have it." Then, tucking his dirt-stained finger under Effie's small chin, he whispered, "You enjoy sittin' on that high horse of yours, girl, 'cause some day you gonna get knocked down." Running his finger across her cheek, he hissed, "Real hard."

Hearing every word, Gene still did nothing. As if daring him, Piney stared hard at Gene until Gene dropped his head. Piney snorted, "I guess we know who's the man and who's the boy." Goading him more, Piney said, "That's okay, Eugene, your mama can handle herself just fine."

Piney leered at Effie, his eyes wandering over her body. Effie shuddered as though she'd been touched. Ignoring Gene, Piney grabbed Effie's arm. "I'm goin' out back to take a piss then you and me, woman, gots some talkin' to do." Effie pulled away and looked at Gene, who never lifted his eyes. He stared at the ground, his cheeks reddening with shame.

Effie turned back to her basket of wet clothes. Gene sunk to the ground and anxiously wound a piece of grass around his finger as he watched his mother dig through the laundry. Effie pulled out shirts, pants, and underwear, carelessly tossing them on the ground. It wasn't until he saw his favorite Harley Davidson T-shirt emblazoned with "I ride with pride" across the front that Gene realized all the clothes laying in a wet pile in the dirt were his; everyone else's clean clothes were in the basket untouched.

Angry, Gene abruptly stood. With tightened jaw and fists set, he was ready to fight Piney as he came around the corner. But before Gene could throw one good punch, Piney cuffed him alongside the head, putting Gene back on the ground where, holding his aching ear, he stayed.

Proving nothing and feeling weak, Gene muttered under his breath, "Screw her."

Sneering at Gene, Piney leaned close to Effie and said, "I put that sissy son of yours in his place and now I gots the mind to do the same to you."

Squaring her shoulders, Effie faced Piney. Then she cocked her eyebrow and tightened her fists at her sides. Watching, Gene knew this was his mother's fighting stance, but he also knew that Piney fought to win and he didn't fight fair.

True to form, Piney took the first swing by snidely saying, "Don't you worry, Effie, it ain't your fault Eugenie is a slick-faced pansy boy." Piney placed his right hand flat against the side of Effie's left thigh. Sliding his hand up slowly, he said in a deep, guttural voice, "Can't 'spect much good to come out from between these legs."

Effie swiftly raised her hand and smacked him hard across the face.

Without flinching, Piney pulled his hand from her thigh and grabbed her hard by the wrist, twisting her arm until she shrieked in pain. "You know, Effie, in all these years you ain't got a bit smarter." Piney pulled her arm farther up her back until her fingertips grazed the top of her shoulder blades as he shouted over her screams, "You ever—ever—hit me again, woman, you won't have a hand no more." Wrenching her arm a bit more, Piney again shouted, "You understand?"

Gasping, Effie choked out, "Yes. Yes. Just let go."

Piney didn't let go, but loosening his grasp, he said, "'Cause we such good friends, Effie Boyer, I'll forgive you." Squeezing her arm tight, he added, "This time." Piney let go and gave Effie a small push, causing her to stumble. This time Effie didn't raise her hand or her voice, instead she stood quiet.

Satisfied he'd put Effie in her place, Piney took a few steps back, and smirking, said, "Now why you gots to go and get me all riled up, Effie? 'Specially when we gots such a good thing goin' here." Piney lit a cigarette he took from his pocket and took a long drag. Slowly blowing out a puff of smoke, he said, "Now where did that girl of yours go?"

Effie said nothing.

Nodding toward Lottie, Piney said, "I ain't ever seen that baby without a handful of her mother's skirt, so you best think hard before you start spinnin' your lies."

Effie still said nothing.

Cocking his head, Piney said, "Better just tell me, woman, 'cause we both know I'll find a way to get it out of you."

Quickly glancing at Lottie, Effie said, "Sarah ain't my concern no more." Settling back on her heels, she added, "So, get off my land."

Piney snickered and said, "Your land?"

Rising up on her toes, Effie leaned forward and hissed, "Yes, my land. Fair and square."

Then, leaning in closer still, Effie whispered, "You ain't right about much, Piney Boyer, but you're right about one thing." With disgust, she looked him up and down before saying, "There ain't nothing good come out from between a whore's legs." Before Effie could step back, Piney clenched his hand into a fist and swung, knocking her to the ground with one swift hit to her cheek.

Gene was on his feet before his mother was knocked off of hers. In a blind rage, he ran toward Piney, legs flying, fists swinging. But Gene's flailing right hook missed as Piney adeptly ducked. Piney hooted with laughter as he clenched his fist and swung, walloping Gene in the stomach. The blow buckled Gene, who fell in a heap next to his mother, who now sat holding her cheek.

Sniggering, Piney mocked, "Like mother, like—"

But before he could finish his sentence, Frank, screaming and running at top speed, charged. He pushed hard against Piney's chest with the flat of his palms, and Piney was knocked to the ground with a loud thud. Then, still whooping loudly, Frank drew back his right leg and gave a swift, hard kick to Piney's groin.

Grabbing between his legs and doubling over, Piney moaned and swore, "You son of a bitch. I'm gonna kill you, you bastard!"

Frank snickered then kicked up a cloud of dust that caused Piney to choke and wheeze, trying to catch his breath.

Gene felt a hand grab his wrist. "Come on. Get up." Frank pulled on Gene's arm.

Still gasping for air, Gene wriggled loose from Frank's grasp and choked out, "I got it, Frank."

As Gene rolled onto all fours before trying to stand, Frank again reached to help. Shaking off Frank's hand, Gene barked, "I said I got it!" Holding his stomach, Gene stood unsteadily. Nauseous, he swayed before grabbing Frank's arm.

"Yeah, you got it," Frank said, smiling. Then he wrapped his arm around Gene's shoulders. Grateful, Gene allowed him.

As Frank and Gene stood staring at Piney groaning loudly as he writhed in the dirt, Effie sat staring at her boys—her sons—as though they were strangers. And in that moment, each seemed unable to recognize the other, because although they had often fought with each other, they had rarely fought for each other. Briefly they were drawn together, but just as the greatest defeat can follow the greatest triumph, it wasn't long before they were again torn apart.

Chapter Nine

Curtis didn't move a muscle other than the ones in his arm as he pulled Lottie close to him during the commotion. Frozen, he watched his mother, who sat on the ground holding her cheek. She stuck the tip of her tongue to the corner of her mouth, licking at the small stream of blood that trickled down her face. "Damn ring," she muttered to no one in particular.

Effie slowly pushed her unsteady legs beneath her and stood. No one held out their hand to pull her up, but Curtis knew she would have refused their offer anyway. Effie always told her children that she didn't take a hand out or a hand up. She often said that help came at a price she couldn't afford.

The Bilfreys stood silent while Piney, biting into his lower lip, moaned in pain. His stringy black hair fell in greasy strips across his forehead, which beaded with sweat. Long, deep groans filled the space between heaves of breath, which first rattled in his lungs before being pushed through his mouth, rank with the smell of whiskey and cigarettes.

Piney Boyer spent half of his days either drunk or working on it and the other half gambling. The youngest of six boys, by the time Piney was born there wasn't much hope that he would be any less wild than his older brothers, but he was different. He was angrier, crazier, and a grave disappointment to his mother, Louise. She'd believed that this son could be the one to save her from her gutless, gambling husband, from her other rotten, unloving sons, but, most of all, from herself. Louise's life was filled with hard work, lots of pain, and little else. Of course, she needn't look further than herself to see the creator of this hell.

Many considered Louise Boyer, once Louise Cantwell, beautiful. She had long flaxen hair, which often fell around her full cheeks in delicate tendrils. Her smooth, milk-colored skin was flawless, and her teeth, untouched by the common ravages of poor eating and mountain life, stood straight and shone white. Louise, however, was completely unaware of her beauty, making her not only more desirable but also an easy catch.

Louise Cantwell was sixteen when she met Cletus Boyer, who had recently moved to Talon Ridge. Having never lived in the same place his whole life and being five years older, he seemed worldly and wise. Young and sheltered, Louise was captivated. With rapt attention, she listened to his stories born more from imagination than truth. No matter how outlandish or boastful his tales, Louise was charmed.

The Cantwells were distrustful of strangers, but Cletus's determination won him enough time to prove to Mr. Cantwell that he had a gift with horses. Impressed, Mr. Cantwell, who owned fifteen Rocky Mountain horses, hired Cletus immediately. In exchange for his labor, Cletus stayed in one of the many small cabins that sat on the Cantwells' large plot of land. Any additional pay wasn't much, but Cletus was more than compensated when he met Louise.

Having been beaten as a boy by his father and coddled by his mother, Cletus became a cowardly and gutless man. Louise saw none of this, at least not at first. Every day she watched him from her bedroom window, which was in the direct sight line to the stable. She liked how he was kind and gentle with the animals. Seeing him sweat-covered as he hefted bales of hay made Louise think that he was strong and hardworking. Seeing him catch her gaze and smile made Louise think he could love her. Louise Cantwell, on all counts, was wrong.

All the weeks that Louise had watched Cletus from her window he had pretended not to notice. Every time, however, he brushed the horses' flaxen manes he thought of Louise's honey-hued hair. He also often pictured his hands resting gently on her delicate shoulders as he dreamed of kissing her full red lips. While tending to the animals, Cletus would often turn his head to catch a glimpse of Louise framed by the window. It could have been the sunlight striking the glass, but Cletus had never seen a girl who shone with so much light, and with pride he saw that this light was directed at him.

It was mere months before stolen glances and secret meetings turned to loving gazes and passionate kisses snuck behind the cover of barn doors and hay bales. Louise avoided her parents' suspicion by always having a reason to be in the barn. She would bring Cletus a drink or help with the grooming, so that she could freely listen to his stories. Wanting these same thrilling adventures, Louise believed the surest way to have them was to be with Cletus. Being young and naïve, Louise mistook excitement for love.

After one awkward night of naked bodies intertwined and quickly parted by the rustling sound of footsteps, Louise was pregnant, and Cletus was trapped. They had each imagined a life with the other, but even after all their talking and dreaming they didn't really know one another. Neither had any idea of the role each would play in the other's ruin.

Broken-hearted and with no other option, Louise's father agreed to her marriage to Cletus. Small and hurried, the service was attended only by Louise's parents and the pastor. Mrs. Cantwell's tears dotted the front of her church dress, as she never once cast her eyes up to meet those of her daughter. Mr. Cantwell, however, solemnly stared at his only child, his face visibly crumpled with the deep despair he felt—an image that would forever haunt Louise.

Four years and three children later, Louise felt utterly suffocated living in a small two-room shack with three toddling boys. Her days were spent wiping mouths, cleaning spills, and hanging loads of laundry that mounted with each new baby. The girl who wanted to see more than the reaches of Talon Ridge now saw no farther than her parents' yard.

By Louise's twenty-third birthday, she had five children and a life she no longer recognized or wanted. With no one to talk to, Louise bore her heartache alone until, like a pebble in a shoe, her sadness rubbed and wore at her soul, fading the beauty of it. Soon, ugliness formed.

Although angry at the part Cletus played in his daughter's sadness, Mr. Cantwell never ceased being impressed with his son-in-law's gift with horses. Because of Cletus's uncommon talent and Mr. Cantwell's failing health, Mr. Cantwell entrusted Cletus with the financial responsibility of the farm. But for as good as Cletus was with a horse was as bad as he was with money, and soon the farm was failing.

Loath to be discovered as weak and useless, Cletus lied. He hid the billing, forged signatures, and faked financial records. Cletus worried that his dishonesty and cowardice would be discovered, but it wasn't. Weeks turned to months, and Cletus's deception only won him more of his father-in-law's trust, and even some of his respect.

A year of untruths told and spun into tangled webs found Cletus struggling to keep a failing farm and Louise believing her husband was worthy of love. The sudden and tragic deaths of Louise's parents unraveled both these lies. The first string pulled loose when an orphaned Louise became a land owner at the age of twenty-four.

Louise's love for her parents stirred her desire to learn how to work their land, but her husband proved an unwilling teacher. Every question she asked and every attempt she made to learn more was met with Cletus's dismissal. Undeterred, Louise, dry-eyed and determined, demanded to know the particulars of every business deal made and broken. With grief deferred and unwavering resolve, Louise became stronger as her husband, fearful of being caught and kicked out, became weaker.

The sudden and striking imbalance put the already-mismatched couple at greater odds. Louise now demanded answers while Cletus continued to lie. Soon debt collectors came, and Cletus was forced to confess his lies and admit his failings. He didn't, however, offer his wife a confession without a plan. Angry, Louise listened. Disheartened, she agreed.

Bonded together only in their determination to put the farm right, Louise reluctantly agreed to Cletus's plan to win the needed money by gambling. Although Louise believed gambling was a sin, a cursory glance at papers outlining their debt caused her to cast off another piece of her morality. And Cletus, skilled at spinning wild tales, convinced her that he could not only play cards—he could win.

Five card games, four losses, two fights, and little money won, Louise refused to allow tears to streak down her face as the first ten horses were sold. With five animals left and even less hope, Louise clung to the loosely held conviction that Cletus could still save them with a good poker hand. A black eye, a swollen lip, and wounded pride saw the last five horses sold. Louise still refused to cry.

The money from the horses and some luck with un-skilled card players from a neighboring town saw the Boyers through a lean winter. During the other seasons, their needs were provided for from gardening, canning, and Louise's innovation. She no longer dreamed of faraway places and exciting trips; she wanted for no more than the comfort of an hour's rest or the sturdy shoulder of someone who cared.

Dinners for seven spreads thin and laundry for seven spreads wide, causing deep wrinkles not commonly seen on a young woman's forehead. Heartbroken and worn, Louise put away her little girl dreams and desires. A life of caring for uncaring boys caused her to believe that she would never feel loved until she did. His name was Everett Keefer.

Cletus Boyer spent most of his days in town, mostly to hide from his wife than to find a way to feed his family. Louise was grateful to have him gone, but she was lonely. Lonesomeness made Louise vulnerable. She ached for human contact. Although she had her boys, their only touch was to pull her arm or tug her leg with demands. Louise had for-gotten how it felt to have a touch given with no expectations other than it returned. So when Everett Keefer came into her life, bringing unbridled passion freely given for her pleasure, Louise drank it up.

For months, Louise found refuge in the empty barn stalls and beneath the knotted, twisted oaks where she would lie in Everett's arms. They told no one of their affair, but secrets, even closely kept ones, weren't kept long in Talon Ridge.

Cletus Boyer heard the whispers, saw the looks, and felt the pity. He didn't ask because he already knew. A prouder man would have been angry, and a more loving man would have been hurt, but Cletus was neither of these—he was a weak man. Weak men ignore what they can't change or fix. In time, his disregard of his wife's affair made him a fool to others, shameful of himself, and small to Louise.

In the time that Louise loved Everett Keefer, she saw little else in her life. She didn't see how her sons wandered lost with no direction from their mother, and she didn't see that Everett Keefer didn't love her. Months into their affair, Louise, used and abandoned, discovered she was pregnant. Once more she was trapped in a life she despised—a life she'd created.

Louise knew every time Cletus looked at her bulging belly he wondered whose child she carried. She enjoyed his suspicion and his pain, but after eight months Louise realized that no matter how much pain she inflicted on her husband, it didn't stop her own. So in a rare moment of compassion for him, Louise assured Cletus the baby was his.

Louise knew her husband had doubts, but she didn't care to convince him. She did, however, wish to stop the shame of gossip both vicious and rampant. She told everyone that she was carrying a boy, and that he would have his father's name. When questioned why her first sons didn't have his name, Louise simply explained that this child would be her last and finest—the one most deserving of his father's name. Louise was right about the baby being a boy, but she was wrong about him carrying his father's name.

She was exhausted by a pregnancy gone on too long, and five little boys underfoot paid little attention to the signs of impending birth. Louise ignored the pains as she dished out stewed cabbage to her sons, and she ignored the tightening of her belly as she wiped the table.

It was only after she put the younger boys to bed that Louise finally started on her way to the midwife's house, but she had waited too long for a baby who refused to wait.

So beneath a grove of pine trees, Louise lay down and had her son alone. She pulled his small slippery body from her own, and as she wrapped her arms around her new baby she felt as though she were wrapping her arms around a new hope.

She lay back with her new son nestled at her breast. Caressing his soft cheek, she whispered his name, "Cletus Boyer Junior." It was the name she would tell his father and everyone else in Talon Ridge, and it was the name that would be printed on his birth certificate, but it was not the name he would be called. This boy, her final son born beneath a grove of pine trees, would always be known as Piney Boyer.

Like snakes that slither across it and worms that burrow beneath it, Piney Boyer was born in the dirt, raised in it, lived in it. His soil-stained soul was fated, a man muddied with the imperfections of one born low and kept low. And whether coincidence or destiny, lying in the dirt was where Piney Boyer was most comfortable and most often found.

Watching Piney writhe on the ground, Curtis suddenly felt a sick bile rise in his throat. The way Piney thrashed and grunted was unsettlingly familiar. This wasn't the first time Curtis had seen Piney lying in the dirt. The first time Curtis had been five years old and picking blackberries.

He remembered being alone in the thick bush with only the sound of the soft thud of berries hitting the bottom of the metal bucket until he heard another sound, strange and upsetting. Even now, as he concentrated, Curtis could hear it ring in his ten-year-old ears.

The echo of it reverberated into a memory of his younger self peering through looping vines to see Piney lying facedown with his legs splayed. Underneath him, Curtis had seen a curl of long hair tumbled across a slender pale arm and a thin neck with tendons pulled tight, but he'd never seen a face.

Even now, Curtis shuddered. Cracker crumbs from Lottie's tight fists dusted Curtis's shoes, but he hardly noticed as he focused on Piney, trying to place the memory, connect the moment, and make sense of his sinking feeling.

Little Lottie spun in circles until Curtis stooped and caught her gently by the shoulders, turning her to face him. He carefully studied her upturned nose and delicate chin, which were his sister's likeness. Then he looked into her eyes, dark brown and deep as though chocolate-dipped. In Lottie's eyes, Curtis had always seen Sarah, but this time he saw something previously unseen—subtly insidious but unmistakable. The shock of Curtis's realization brimmed up like boiling liquid, causing him to turn abruptly on his feet.

Facing Piney, he studied *his* face, *his* eyes. With a heavy ache in his chest, Curtis slowly turned back toward Lottie and whispered with hushed horror, "Oh, Sarah. No."

PART TWO

Chapter Ten

Lottie lay in the grass staring up at the blue swept skies dotted with clouds. Her brown eyes, wide and focused, watched as these wisps of white drifted and swirled, morphing into dragons, monkeys, and tropical islands. As the clouds quickly changed into different shapes, Lottie's head spun a bit. She closed her eyes, trying to tame the dizziness even as the images still pressed and danced against the backs of her eyelids. She took a deep breath, exhaled sharply, and whispered, "Twelve. Today I am twelve."

With eyes still closed, she slowly slid her hands from her sides onto her thighs. She gave her legs, still thin and coltish, little regard as she quickly moved her hands to her abdomen, flat with only the protuberance of ribs. Taking another deep breath, Lottie allowed her palms to slide past her rib cage and to her chest; like her stomach, it was flat. Shyly at first, she felt for any hint of change. Nothing. Her collarbone still rose higher than her much desired and anticipated breasts. Dropping her hands in disappointment, Lottie muttered, "Still eleven."

Lottie looked up at the large oak tree at the edge of her granmom's yard. The same tree, knotted and gnarled, which she had climbed atop and lay beneath for as many years as she could remember. "Of course," Lottie huffed under her breath. "Nothing else is different today, why should I be?" Sitting up, Lottie leaned back on her hands, crossed her ankles, and furiously rocked her foot back and forth, waiting.

Lottie was always waiting; waiting on her body to change, her world to change. It seemed like all the girls at school had a mother to braid their hair, hear their secrets, and give flight to their dreams. Effie was, in Lottie's estimation, a poor substitution. As easy as it was to cherish the memory of her absent mother was as easy as it was to hate her mother for abandoning her.

If Lottie closed her eyes for long enough, she believed she could remember her mother. Although nothing much remained of Sarah, apart from a few photos of her as a child and a baby blanket she had knitted for Lottie, it was enough for Lottie to remember her mother or rather create imagined memories of her. Days when Lottie loved her mother, she saw a woman who baked better biscuits than her granmom, a woman who spun stories like yarn, a woman who loved deeply and freely, and days when Lottie hated her mother—she ceased to see her at all.

Celebrating Lottie's birthday was something else Lottie knew her mother would have done better than her granmom. After all, not much was celebrated in her granmom's house. After age five, Lottie stopped asking for dolls and pretty hair bows. The disappointment of not receiving them soon outweighed the hope of asking. But on her tenth birthday, Lottie got up the courage and told her granmom her birthday wish.

Late May two years ago, Effie, who was trying to scrub tough stains from her boys' shirts, didn't hear her granddaughter slip onto the porch beside her. Startled, she snapped, "Damn it, Lottie! You know better than to sneak up on people."

Her grandmother's unusual harshness with her caused Lottie to step back and lower her head. Effie dropped the soaked shirt onto the board and took a seat on her rocker. Pulling Lottie close, she soothed, "Ain't no reason to get upset. You ain't ever gonna survive these mountains with all that emotion."

Lottie did her best snarl as she stared her grandmother in the eye.

Laughing, Effie said, "Now that's better. So tell me, girl, why you sneakin' up on me?"

Lottie pulled back from Effie. Stuffing her hands deep into the pockets of her jeans cut crookedly into shorts, Lottie looked past her grandmother.

"Well, come on out with it, girl. Those shirts ain't gonna wash themselves, and the sun don't wait on the lazy."

Lottie mumbled a few words, which Effie couldn't hear.

"Now you know I can't hear you when you're talking to your feet."

Lottie took a deep breath, and with the exhale quickly spit out, "Tomorrow's my birthday."

Effie sat back in the rocker and pushed off with her feet, setting the chair into a rhythmic motion. "Well, it's also Wednesday, clothes drying day and a good day to snap peas." It was also the same day that Sarah had left Talon Ridge, her family, and the little girl who now stood before Effie looking scared and determined. But Effie didn't say that; no one ever did.

Lottie finally turned to face her grandmother. "I know, but it's my birthday."

Effie nodded. "I understand that, child, but what's your point?"

Lottie's face was now flushed with frustration as she cried out, "It's my birthday. People get presents on their birthdays. It's what they do; it's what everyone does."

Effie shook her head and said, "Well now, I don't think you can say everybody does. I know for certain I don't."

Lottie took her hands out of her pockets and placed them on her hips as she squared her body toward her grandmother. "That's not true. I made you a picture. It had grass and an old barn, and some birds and you said it was pretty."

Effie smiled at her granddaughter's unyielding spirit. "So you did. And it was pretty. But you got to understand, Lottie, things like dolls and hair bows cost. They cost a whole lot."

Lottie cautiously stepped closer but courageously spoke louder, "Not this. It don't cost nothing."

Effie cocked her head to the side, considering this possibility. "Really? So what do you want? You want me to draw you a picture?"

Lottie waited a moment and then pushed her hair back from her shoulder. Her likeness to her mother was startling—and it made Effie wince with the pain of her loss.

"I am going to be ten years old. I'm not a baby anymore," Lottie said firmly.

Effie grinned. "So you asking for some moonshine? Because it ain't free neither."

Lottie protested, "Granmom, I need you to be serious. This is serious."

Effie's smile faded as she recognized a familiar intensity in her granddaughter's face. "You're right, go on."

Lottie continued, "Like I was saying, I'm not a baby anymore. There's lots of things I can know. There's lots of things I should know."

Effie leaned in and whispered, "Is this about the birds and bees?"

Lottie pulled back. "No, Granmom. It's not about hair bows or dolls or moonshine or sex. I want to know about my mother." Effie froze, feet planted flat, rocker in midstride.

The shock of hearing the word "sex" roll off her granddaughter's tongue was overshadowed by Lottie's bold demand to know about her mother.

Seeing her grandmother's tight jaw and furrowed brow, Lottie explained, "Please, I don't need to know everything, but something—anything."

Effie rocked back and exhaled loudly. Gripping the arms of the chair, she tightened her fingers over the smooth wood until her knuckles whitened with the pressure. Then, as calmly as she could, she said, "But you see, child, what you wanna know is also not free. It may not be the price of a doll or a pair of shoes, but it's costly." Taking a deep breath, Effie added, "And I can't afford it. Not now." With that Effie closed her eyes, and softly set the rocker back into motion.

Lottie turned and stepped off the porch, believing that all she would ever know about her mother was what she imagined. Walking away from her grandmother, Lottie knew she would never get the birthday gift she truly wanted, not now, not ever. What Lottie didn't know was that she only needed to wait until she was twelve.

Lottie lowered herself onto her elbows and tilted her chin toward the sky, consumed by the clouds once again. She allowed the sun to cast across her face, gently warming her skin. Lottie was grateful for the summer sun, which thawed the chill that had settled in her fitful body. Although a bit more relaxed, Lottie never stopped rocking her feet back and forth.

"If you're not careful, you'll rock that thing clear off your leg," Curtis said.

Startled, Lottie turned to see her uncle grinning as he walked toward her. "Don't need it. Ain't nowhere to go anyway," Lottie said, tossing the words over her shoulder.

Curtis dropped the canvas bag he was carrying and flopped down next to his niece and bumped her shoulder with his. "You want to go somewhere, Lottie-Pops?"

Lottie smiled and said, "Anywhere be better than here."

Curtis, staring straight ahead, asked, "How do you know if you never been anywhere but here?"

Lottie gave him a sideways glance and snapped, "Because what I do know is this place really sucks and there has to be a place that don't suck as bad."

Curtis, quiet for a moment, replied, "Maybe, maybe not."

Lottie turned to face her uncle. "Don't you ever want to get out of here?"

Curtis shrugged. "Sure. I guess sometimes, but mostly I've found everything I would ever look for right here."

Skeptical, Lottie, with raised eyebrows, asked, "Really? Here? What have you found?"

Turning, Curtis looked at her. "You."

Embarrassed by her uncle's kind words and her own snarky ones, Lottie whispered, "Thanks, Uncle Coot." Hearing the name that Lottie once called her uncle when her toddler's tongue mangled most letters and sounds made them both laugh. Lottie so rarely used the name, so that when she did it warmed both their hearts.

Feeling less agitated, Lottie slowed her foot to a steady sway as she and her uncle watched a feral cat stretch and claw at the ground. "I see Boots is back," Curtis said.

Lottie nodded and asked, "You named it?"

Leaning back on his hands, Curtis replied, "Naming an animal helps you feel more for it. Like it belongs, you know?"

Disagreeing, Lottie said, "Just because you name it doesn't mean it belongs."

Curtis nodded. "Maybe but it's easier to claim something if you know what to call it."

Suddenly angry, Lottie shot back, "Really? Because my mother named me, but she didn't do much claiming, did she?"

Curtis said softly, "She loved you, Lottie. She did."

Lottie dropped her head and whispered, "I'm not so sure."

Without another word, Curtis and Lottie watched Boots until he bounded away into the bushes.

Finally breaking the silence, Curtis asked, "Shouldn't you be gettin' to school?"

Lottie answered dryly, "No. It's Saturday."

Curtis said, "Hmm, I forgot."

Hurt, Lottie snapped, "It's also my birthday. Not that it matters."

Leaning close, Curtis slung his arm across Lottie's shoulders. "I know it's your birthday, Lottie-Pops. I was just teasing." Giving her shoulder a squeeze, he added, "And it does matter."

Although Lottie didn't pull from his embrace, she said sourly, "Sure, it matters a whole lot." Bitterly blowing the last words across her lips, she added, "Nobody cares."

Curtis rubbed his fingers back and forth across his forehead as though trying to pull the right words from his head before he said, "Come on, Lottie-Pops, you know we all care. Doesn't your granmom always make you a big chocolate cake with icing blobs?" Hearing "icing blobs" made Lottie smile. Encouraged, Curtis said, "And she will get you a gift." Seeing Lottie's raised brow, Curtis added, "She did the last two years."

Lottie's smile slipped as she remembered those past two birthdays.

On her tenth and eleventh year, Lottie had received a beautifully gift-wrapped box with a wide pink bow. She knew that the drugstore perfume and sweet cakes were her grandmother's way of making up for not answering her questions about her mother, but Lottie also knew that there wasn't a gift her grandmother could buy or bake that would make her forget her mother. Every colored ribbon and each tightly tied bow only made Lottie ache more with the missing of her.

Trying to drive away Lottie's sudden dark mood, Curtis said, "What do you think you will get this year for your birthday?"

Lottie huffed and said, "Probably something stupid like cheap perfume."

Curtis smiled. "Well, I'm glad I didn't get you perfume."

Feeling ungrateful, Lottie said, "Perfume is nice. It's just not what I want."

Sitting up, Curtis rubbed the grass from his hands and asked, "What would you like?"

Lottie shrugged. "Something I won't ever get."

"Did you ever tell your granmom what you wanted?"

Lottie nodded. "Yes, but she won't give it to me."

Curtis thought for a moment then asked, "Does it cost a lot?"

Suddenly indignant, Lottie said sharply, "No! It don't cost nothin.'"

Curtis shook his head. "That's weird. Mama is usually all in if it's free."

Lottie, nearly shouting, said, "She said it's not free! She said—"

Interrupting, Curtis said, "Whoa, Lottie. I think I'm confused. How is it free and not free?"

Lottie straightened her back and said firmly, "I want to know about my mother. I want answers and Granmom won't tell me."

Curtis sighed, and with it a small "Oh" escaped his lips.

Lottie leaned back onto her hands resting behind her as she whispered, "I have right to know."

Curtis brushed some grass from his pant legs and said, "She's stubborn, Lottie."

Lottie argued, "That don't make it right."

Agreeing, Curtis said, "I know, but she has her own way of doing things. It ain't always right, but I believe she does most of it out of love."

Unsure, Lottie murmured, "I guess."

Looking into his niece's eyes, he said, "Right or wrong, she just wants to protect you, Lottie."

Lottie sniffed. "I know." Looking away, she added, "But I have a right to know."

Taking a deep breath, Curtis said, "So do I." Then he pulled the canvas bag, which he'd dropped on the ground earlier, onto his lap. He reached inside and pulled out a shiny pink book with purple and yellow flowers scattered across the cover and carefully handed it to Lottie.

Curious, Lottie turned the book over in her hand then asked, "What is this?" Curtis pointed to the single word scrawled across the book and said flatly, "Diary."

Lottie asked, "You got me a diary?"

Before he answered, Curtis gently took the book from Lottie. Holding it in his trembling hands, he considered again what he was about to do. He knew that giving Lottie her mother's diary was like opening a box that could never be closed again, and once the secrets spilled from the page none of it could be untold or unknown, and his part in it couldn't be undone. With this burden now heavy on his back, Curtis handed the book back to Lottie and said, "No. I'm not giving you a diary." Taking another deep breath, he continued, "I am giving you your *mother's* diary."

Holding the book tightly in her hands, Lottie barely breathed for a full minute before she tentatively asked, "Really?"

Lightly squeezing Lottie's hand that held the diary, Curtis said simply, "Yes."

Cautiously, Lottie smiled. Seeing the ache in her eyes and the desperation in her tightened fingers grasping the diary, Curtis knew he made the right choice—or at least he hoped.

Curtis watched Lottie as she traced the curly, swirled letters with her finger just as he had done ten years ago. She didn't open the cover; she didn't turn a page. Instead, she pulled the book close to her chest and wrapped her arms around it.

Sitting silently, Lottie softly rocked back and forth, holding on to the diary as though she were holding on to her mother. Soon aware of her uncle watching her and feeling foolish, Lottie laid the book back on her lap and gently rested her hands on top of it. Still uncertain of her windfall, Lottie asked, "Is it really mine?"

Curtis nodded.

Hesitantly, Lottie asked, "To keep?"

Curtis stood, then leaning down, he gently pressed her shoulder and said, "Of course."

Lottie's eyes welled with tears, which she quickly brushed away with the back of her hand. Pretending not to notice, Curtis slung the bag over his shoulder, but before he turned to walk away, Lottie looked up at him. The noon sun forced Lottie to cup her hands over her eyes to shield them from the light. Her uncle, caught in the frame of her fingers, was all that Lottie could see, making him in that moment her center, her focus, her answer. Truly grateful, Lottie said, "Thank you."

Curtis smiled then walked away, but he hadn't taken more than a few steps before he said over his shoulder, "Happy birthday."

Chapter Eleven

Effie stood alone in her kitchen. Slowly she looked around the small space as she took inventory of what she needed: bowls, large spoons, baking powder, sugar. She didn't, however, need a recipe for she kept every ingredient and every measure in her mind. Effie always had command in the kitchen, but today this familiar space was no longer her place of comfort. Instead, the empty counters and flour-dusted table was her battlefield; the frontline where she would fight again for Lottie's trust and love.

Effie opened cupboards, pulling out pans and canisters filled with flour. Setting each item on the table, she carefully considered and planned. Then, from the back of a drawer, she took out a bag of expensive dark chocolate. She dumped the pieces into a bowl and winced when she thought of the price she'd paid for it. Inhaling the rich smell, Effie shook her head, but then quickly reminded herself that price didn't matter, not this time. This time the cake had to be better than good—it had to be perfect.

Falling like soft snow, specks of flour landed lightly on the counter as Effie sifted it through a rusted strainer. After dusting her greased cake pan, Effie mindlessly wiped her powdered hands on her shirt, leaving little white dust prints on her favorite red blouse. Irritated by her foolishness, Effie murmured, "Damn," beneath her breath as she roughly brushed off the flour.

Effie then meticulously measured the salt and vanilla before stirring in the milk, sugar, and chocolate, which she'd whipped into a sugary confection. She licked the spoon and sighed, wondering if the deliciously sweet taste would be enough to make up for a missing mother and too many unanswered questions.

Pouring the thick, syrupy batter into the buttered pan, Effie knew no matter the taste and no matter how beautiful the swirled letters of icing, it wasn't what Lottie wanted. The girl wanted answers. Answers Effie didn't have, and answers she didn't want to give. Distracted by her thoughts, Effie pushed the pan into the oven without setting the timer before she settled heavily onto the closest chair.

Effie stared until her eyes fluttered softly closed, darkening the world as it brightened her memories. In them, Effie could see Sarah as plainly as her bones could feel the missing of her. It wasn't in Effie's nature to say how she felt, but there were moments when she wished she could tell Lottie how a piece of her heart was ripped away when Sarah left.

Effie also wanted to tell her granddaughter how much she loved her child and how she spent every second of every day missing her, but Effie believed it wasn't right to give the weight of her pain to a little girl to bear. So, she stayed silent.

Feeling a familiar ache, Effie slowly stood and shuffled over to the counter. She picked up the unrinsed mixing bowl, swiped the thick, gooey chocolate with her finger, then stuck it into her mouth. As granules of sugar touched her tongue, her taste buds awakened with the sweetness of the syrupy liquid. Alone, she stuck all four fingers into the bowl, scooped up the remaining batter, and hungrily shoved it into her mouth.

Staring trancelike, she enjoyed the rare indulgence. The creamy, warm chocolate was a bit of sweetness amid the bitter of Effie's every day. For a long time, she had never known the joy of eating candy or a well-baked cake. With no mother to make one and with a father who didn't care to try, every birthday for Effie went unmarked.

The only notice taken was by her grieving father, who, with each passing year, only blamed his daughter more for the loss of his wife. And so, in turn, Effie never felt happy on her birthday, only guilty. As Effie wiped the bowl clean, so, too, did she wipe clean the memory of lost birthdays from her mind, at least until she baked another cake. And since Effie baked cakes only for Lottie's birthday, she had another whole year before she had to tamp down the bitterness in the sweet.

Effie opened the oven door to check the cake. Seeing it start to rise, she slowly closed the oven, careful not to cause the cake to fall. She needed the center to be flat and high so that she could clearly write her birthday message to Lottie across the top. Effie never wrote, "Happy birthday," instead she always scrawled in icing, "Another year, we survived."

Effie knew it wasn't very cheerful, but it was honest, and Effie was determined not to lose her girl to lies. Effie never reasoned that the untold truths were just as dishonest. Instead, she cooked her secrets in biscuits, baked her unanswered questions in cakes, melted memories in chocolate, and hoped that one day Lottie would just stop asking.

Effie set the mixing bowl and dirty spoons into the kitchen sink. She was going to wash them while the cake finished baking, but she decided to first check to see if Curtis and Lottie were still sitting together. Careful not to be seen, Effie ducked to the left side of the window and, through the slit of the curtain only slightly parted to let in the light, watched Lottie, who now sat alone.

Standing quietly in the doorway, Curtis asked, "Who you looking for?"

Startled, Effie abruptly turned on her heel, faced Curtis, and said coolly, "Lottie. I want to make sure she doesn't come in and see her cake."

Grinning, Curtis said, "Sure. After all, she has no idea you're going to bake her a cake." After pausing a second, Curtis added, "On her *birthday*."

Ignoring Curtis's sarcasm, Effie said, "Well, she don't know it's chocolate." Flustered, she added, "And she don't know it's pink icing."

Continuing to tease his mother, Curtis said, "No, of course not. You've never made her a chocolate cake with pink icing before." Curtis exaggeratingly scratched his head and said, "Except for the last two years."

Grinding her top teeth into her bottom, Effie snapped, "You're late for work, Curtis."

Knowing he'd gotten under his mother's skin, Curtis chuckled. "It'll be fine, Ma."

Effie threatened, "It won't be fine when you don't have a job." Leaning closer, she warned, "No job. No home."

Curtis knew as well as his mother that her threats were idle.

Teasing again, Curtis swept his arm in front of him and said mockingly, "You mean I could be kicked out of this paradise?"

Effie snorted. "It'd seem like paradise, boy, after you been sleeping on a trash pile."

Curtis grinned. "Not sure I haven't been, Ma."

Before Effie could say another word, Curtis took three quick steps toward his mother and kissed her lightly on the cheek.

Effie frowned and said, "You got to eat more, Curtis Bilfrey. I can see your bones."

Twenty years old and over six feet tall, Curtis seemed to thin more with each inch added. "It's muscle, Ma." Seeing the concern on her face, Curtis said, "I'll eat more." Rubbing his hand over his stomach, lean and concave, he added, "Your cake will fatten me up a bit."

Effie gently pushed Curtis toward the door. Swatting him on his backside, she playfully scolded, "Get out! And don't come back until you got some change in your pocket and a growlin' in your belly."

Effie gripped the edge of the kitchen table as Curtis's hand gripped the doorknob.

Before he turned it, Effie blurted, "Curtis! Wait." Curtis looked over his shoulder at his mother. "What were you and Lottie talkin' about?"

Curtis shrugged. "Nothing really."

Effie's fingers whitened as she held on tighter to the table. Trying to stifle her panic, she asked, "What is 'nothing'?"

Not knowing the cause but clearly seeing her fear, Curtis answered, "We talked about birthday gifts and cakes. Stupid stuff like that."

Uncertain, Effie nodded then asked, "Did she ask about…" Effie stopped short; the rest of her sentence hung expectantly in the air between them.

Understanding, Curtis said, "I'll be home in a few hours. We'll have cake." Curtis opened the door. Standing in the threshold, neither inside or out, he quietly said, "It'll be fine, Ma." With those words, the screen door slammed shut.

Staring at the closed door, Effie again stood alone in the kitchen. Replaying Curtis's words in her mind, Effie wondered if it truly would be fine. The acrid smell startled Effie from her thoughts. She opened her eyes to see the oven breathing out thick puffs of black smoke. "Damn!" Effie shouted as she grabbed an oven mitt and threw open the door. Effie choked and gagged as more smoke billowed from her burnt cake. She threw the scorched pan into the sink and opened the window as she fanned the smoke with a tea towel. Furious, Effie snapped the towel against the kitchen table a few times as she swore, "Damn! Damn cake! Damn birthday! Damn Sarah."

As if surrendering, Effie dropped the towel and slumped against the counter. Peering into the sink, she took a knife and poked the deflated burnt cake as she muttered once more, "Damn." Then Effie, without shedding one tear or uttering one more curse, tossed the knife into the sink and walked to the cupboard where she pulled down the flour and then the sugar.

Again, Effie measured, sifted, and stirred. Each ingredient was considered and poured as though for the first time. Although tired from hours spent in the small, hot, and now smoke-filled kitchen, Effie refused to be distracted from baking her best cake yet. After all, Effie was used to starting over. She had learned at a young age how to take the broken bits and glue them back together.

After shutting the oven door and setting the timer, Effie sat down and watched as it slowly ticked off each minute. Focusing only on the cake, Effie refused to allow this one to burn. Sharply attuned to her granddaughter's movements, Effie's ears perked at the faint sound of Lottie's soft footfalls as she entered the house.

Chapter Twelve

Two weeks had passed since Lottie's uncle had given her the greatest gift she had yet to receive in her twelve years. Sitting alone on the steps of her mother's empty cabin, Lottie balanced her mother's pink diary on her reedlike legs as she stared straight ahead.

During these past couple of weeks, Lottie sometimes caught her uncle watching her as he tried to weigh out whether she'd read her mother's words. Lottie hadn't told him, but she hadn't read a page, a sentence, or even cracked the cover. She'd slept with the diary tucked beneath her pillow, she'd held it, cradled it, pressed it against her cheek, but she hadn't read it.

Lottie picked up the diary and held it in her trembling hands. She'd waited her whole life for even one word from her mother, and now she had a book full of her mother's words, yet since the day her uncle had given it to her, Lottie struggled to open it. She knew that opening the book would be like opening a window into her mother's life. And as Lottie flipped the diary over and ran her finger down the unbroken spine, she feared that she wouldn't like what she saw when she looked.

Her curiosity, however, outweighed her fear. Lottie read her mother's first diary entry and smiled. Her mother, twelve, same as Lottie, filled the entire page grumbling about the foolishness of writing in a diary. Lottie felt as though every word could have easily been her own. Feeling a connection to her mother, Lottie turned the page and read the next entry.

October 29, 1976

I haven't written nothing for two weeks. There ain't no reason since my days are all the same. I have to wake up too early, wash with water that's too cold, and walk too far to school, where Ms. Prindle says the same thing over and over. I guess she thinks we're stupid. Of course, living on this here mountain, there ain't much chance of being smart especially since we all have to share the same old, torn books.

I share a book with Cathy McQuinn. She smells bad and chews her hair. It makes me sick. I missed a whole chapter last week because I didn't want to sit closer to her.

Today, she pushed back her hair, and a big wet piece hit me in the face. I thought I was going to throw up. Ms. Prindle didn't say nothing but she moved my desk. I sit next to Dallas Cutler now. It's better.

Ms. Prindle is nice. She listens. I ain't sure but I think she cares too.

Lottie never would have thought that she could be grateful to a stranger, but after reading the first pages of her mother's diary, she was grateful to Ms. Prindle. Because although she didn't know the color of Ms. Prindle's eyes or the sound of her voice, Lottie knew that she had given her back her mother, if only a small part.

Lottie continued reading, trying hard to hear her mother's voice.

October 31, 1976

Today is Halloween. I love Halloween! I love that you can be someone else—anyone else—even if it is only for a day.

This year I borrowed Mama's only pair of heels and put on my best dress. I did my hair up high and rouged my cheeks bright pink. My younger brother Gene asked who I was supposed to be. I told him it didn't matter. It only matters that it ain't me.

I was ready real quick, but I had to wait on Mama, who kept fussing with Baby Curtis's costume. She cut eye holes in an old sheet, threw it over his head, and spun him around. She said he was a ghost. My younger brother Frank said he looked like he was fixin' to burn crosses.

Quick as a cat, Mama took two steps and slapped Frank across his face. His eyes filled with tears, but he didn't cry. He just balled up his fists and ran out the door.

Frank is only ten, but it don't stop him from trying to be a man. But since there ain't no man, at least no good man, for him to see how it's done, he ain't very good at it. Frank tries to be good, but lately all I see is a lot of mean. Mama thinks yelling and smacking will take out the mean, but I think every hit and hurtful word just takes out more good.

After the door slammed shut, Mama ripped the sheet off of Baby Curtis's head and said we weren't going. We stood there, quiet, for only a few minutes before we heard pounding on the door. Thinking it was Frank, Mama swung it open. But it wasn't Frank, it was Mrs. Royer.

Mrs. Royer looked at me and then told Mama that she could see the devil was working his ways on me. Mama just told me to take Baby Curtis to my room.

Our house is small and the walls ain't much thicker than paper, so I heard every word Mrs. Royer said. Most of them was about Mama inviting in the devil. Mama didn't say nothing. She never does. She just listens and waits for the rent money.

I asked Mama once why Mrs. Royer was so crazy. Mama said that when Mrs. Royer found God, she lost her mind. Then I asked her why she rented to a crazy woman. Mama said that no one survives on pride. I didn't tell Mama, but I think that having pride is sometimes the only way to survive.

Baby Curtis fell asleep hours ago. Trying not to
wake him, I took off my dress and wiped off my makeup.
Without the rouge and lipstick, I was again—sadly—
just me.

Lottie closed the diary and set it next to her on the step. Maybe, she thought, she and her mother weren't so alike. After all, Lottie hated Halloween. She hated that once a year everyone pretended to be someone else, especially since it seemed in her family to be that way every day.

Lottie reached for the diary but then quickly pulled back her hand, remembering the promise she'd made to herself to read only a page a day. She was determined to savor the pleasure of getting to know her mother but having read the first three entries her heart ached, and her fingers tingled with the anticipation of turning another page.

Lottie opened the diary. Allowing the pages to fan past her fingers, she reasoned that one more page would make it an even four—a good place to stop.

November 18, 1976

Next week is Thanksgiving so Ms. Prindle asks a
different one of us each day to say why we're thankful.
Today was my turn. I said I was thankful for my family.
Truth is I'd be most thankful if I could get off this here
mountain.

Lottie turned the page. Seeing it was blank, she flipped it back again. She couldn't believe it. Four sentences. "Well, that hardly counts," she whispered to herself as she turned the page and read another entry.

November 25, 1976

Today is Thanksgiving. Mama has been in the kitchen cooking since before the sun came up. She promised to teach me how to make her special stuffing this year.

Even though Mama is good at canning and keeping food, there's still some days when we feel the pinch of hunger but never on Thanksgiving. Mama makes sure of it.

Right now, Mama's baking biscuits. We all know to stay clear because Mama ain't herself when she's baking. Her hands shake when she cracks the eggs and her eyes turn glassy when she kneads the dough. But what worries me sometimes is how she stares out the window like she's looking for something she can't seem to find. She also hums. I never know the tunes, but they're always real slow and sad.

I'm also staying clear because Mama said that Piney Boyer is bringing over a turkey. And there ain't no way I'm gonna be anywhere near him when he does. He's always staring at me.

Piney is one of Mama's renters even though none us ain't ever seen him pay rent. But we know better than to

ask Mama about this. I told Mama that I didn't think a
free turkey was worth having him in the house. Mama
said it ain't free, nothing's free.

Free or not, I ain't eating nothing that Piney Boyer's
touched. There ain't nothing that could be any good
once his dirty hands touched it. Nothing!

Without closing the book, Lottie turned slightly and stared up at her mother's cabin. Years of storms and neglect showed in the cracked windowpanes and splintered wood. Yet strangely, in some ways, the cabin remained unchanged. Even as it stood empty, it was in Lottie's heart still her home.

Lottie again shifted on the step. Looking out across the small yard, she could see the rest of the cabins, which formed a large semicircle. Lottie and her mother's cabin sat on the end corner with the first three also empty for as long as Lottie could remember. Across the way stood four more cabins.

The closest to theirs was Mr. Goodwin's. Lottie smiled at her memory of a man whose existence was distilled to a sweet smell and baritone voice. He'd died when she was only five, so any further recollections were lost. Since his death, his cabin, too, sat empty. A problem that her Uncle Frank tried to fix by parading in potential renters, all of whom Effie refused without so much as a word as to why. But Lottie didn't think her grandmother needed a reason. After all, even as a small child Lottie knew Mr. Goodwin couldn't be replaced.

Next Lottie turned her attention to the cabin next to Mr. Goodwin's, where she saw Ms. Keefer standing in her yard hanging dingy sheets on a bowed clothesline. Ms. Keefer, spotting Lottie, waved. Lottie quickly popped her own hand up and waved back before her attention was once again pulled to the page she'd just read, but no matter where she looked her eyes focused only on *his* name.

Piney Boyer was a name Lottie knew well. His cabin was the farthest from theirs, but it never stopped him from slinking over and peering inside. Lottie wasn't sure why, but seeing him on her mother's porch always made her stomach turn. Her Uncle Curtis often warned her to keep a good distance from Piney, but Lottie never had to be told. The sick feeling she got every time he came near her told her all she needed to know, and now her mother's words confirmed it. Piney Boyer was no good.

Lottie swatted her leg, squishing a tiny gnat. Flicking the remains from her shin, she slowly looked up and peered across the yard. Relieved that Ms. Keefer had gone inside, Lottie now had the freedom to get a better look. Tucking the diary under her arm, Lottie stood and leaned forward so that she could see the cabin that sat between that of Ms. Keefer and Piney.

The small yard was fenced with crisscrossed boards crudely nailed and painted to form a barrier on either side. It was obvious that Mrs. Royer was trying to keep out both neighbors, but it was only on the side that joined with Ms. Keefer's yard that hung a huge cross. Scrawled across it in jagged handwriting were the words "sinners repent."

Lottie was only eight years old, but she still remembered the day that her grandmother decided to single-handedly tear down the sign. After all, it was hard to forget the day that two plank boards crudely crossed and nailed together caused her grandmother to challenge God and stare down the devil.

Lottie, of course, couldn't remember every detail of the day, but she did remember the heat of her grandmother's hand as it wrapped around her own and the determination in her voice when she told her granddaughter that it was a day for learning.

Lottie also didn't remember if the day had been sunny and warm or cloudy and cold, but she did remember the feeling of being judged and condemned before she even knew the meaning of the words. Four years later, standing on her mother's porch, Lottie still felt the sting. She also, however, felt pride remembering how her grandmother had stood up not only for herself that day but for those she loved.

With a slight smile, Lottie recalled how her grandmother, whose backside had never touched a pew bench, expertly recited Bible verses with the skill of a seasoned preacher. She and Mrs. Royer cited book and verse in turn until Effie ended Mrs. Royer's pious rant with John 8:7. Lottie could see Granmom even now, standing up on her toes leaning close to Mrs. Royer's face as she said in a low clear voice, "He that is without sin among you, let him first cast a stone at her."

Of course, Lottie also still remembered the look on her grandmother's face when Mrs. Royer venomously spat back, "Knowing a few Bible verses don't make you a godly woman,

Effie Bilfrey. You ain't nothing more than common trash raising mongrels with no one to claim them. Your daughter is the
worse of all of 'em, laying like a dog in heat then leaving her
mutt." Lottie instinctively touched her face as just the memory
made her cheek sting as though slapped.

Lottie grabbed the porch rail, bracing herself as she
relived the moment her grandmother tried to take down the
cross and God with it. Effie had abruptly pushed Lottie to the
side and stormed off Mrs. Royer's porch steps. Although Effie
Bilfrey was a slender woman with slight shoulders and a thin
waist, when measured in strength and determination, she was
a formidable figure.

And that day, Lottie could clearly see it as she watched
her grandmother pull and yank at the cross until her fingers
were full of splinters. Breathing hard and howling like an
injured animal, she jerked and ripped and tore at the wooden
planks, but the cross still hung. With bloodied fingers she held
tightly to the edges, looking up she shouted at God, "You don't
exist! Not for me. Not for Sarah!" Falling into a heap beneath
the cross, Effie plaintively called out, "Where are you?"

Lottie and Mrs. Royer watched motionless until Lottie
heard what she thought, for a moment, was the voice of God.
"Did God's little lamb lose her way?" Slowly he came into
view. Smirking, Piney Boyer mocked, "I know a way you can
find God, Effie Boyer, and you ain't even have to get up."

It may not have been God's voice, but it brought Effie
to her feet faster than if it had been. Looking up again, she
shouted, "There is no God! Only the devil dare come here."

Effie marched back to the porch and grabbed Lottie's hand. They were almost home before Effie said, "Ain't ever going get learning like that in school." Lottie looked up at her grandmother, who stared straight ahead before adding, "And this is the kind of learning you need to know."

Lottie sank back onto the porch step. Drained, she laid the diary next to her. She didn't want to read or think or feel anymore. Tearful, she took a deep breath and looked up. Standing at the edge of the yard was the person who had always been Lottie's source of comfort, her soft place to fall even if Lottie hadn't realized it until that moment.

Chapter Thirteen

Effie was careful to keep her distance. She had been watching her granddaughter, unseen, for several minutes. Effie knew by the way Lottie cradled her head as it hung low that she was hurting; Effie knew that hurt all too well. Even after all these years, Effie keenly and sharply felt the pain of loss.

Lottie had been gone most of the morning, but Effie hadn't worried because she knew she would find her on Sarah's porch. Effie wished the girl wouldn't try to hold on to something that had long slipped through her fingers, yet Effie also understood. She, herself, would sometimes sneak away and sit on those same steps, trying to capture the smallest sensation of her daughter's presence, but Effie was always disappointed because, in truth, it wasn't the feeling of her daughter that she sought, it was her daughter.

There were moments when the memories of Sarah and the pain of them pushed from deep within Effie's cells to the surface of her skin. The reasons that Sarah suddenly flooded her thoughts were usually simple and often unexpected, like the way a smell curled beneath Effie's nose or the way a flower danced in the breeze. Some days Effie allowed these memories of Sarah to flow freely, filling her mind with still framed moments of her daughter as a stubborn toddler or a restless teenager.

Effie could never understand why her brain chose to keep some memories and abandon others. But what Effie did understand was that in order to remember the good memories, she also had to remember the bad—she just wished there weren't so many bad ones.

Often, Effie longed to recollect the feel of her mother's arms around her or the smell of her mother's skin, but her infant brain was neither able to form nor keep these memories. Instead, her mind held tightly to the memory of her grieving father's unskilled hands and the sour smell of his gin-soaked breath.

Over the years, Effie had become so skilled at locking away the times in her life that were terrifying and heartbreaking that she feared there would be an unexpected moment when these memories would rush like water over a broken dam and drown her.

One such memory washed over her now as she stood watching her granddaughter pluck a violet and inhale its sweet scent. As a young girl, Effie loved wildflowers. She loved finding, gathering, and arranging them. Some days she would walk several miles in pursuit of a particular color or type of flower. With her, she took a small metal pan, sharp scissors, and her mother's botanical book, *A Lady's Companion to Wildflowers*. After carefully matching her finds to the illustrations, Effie would clip and collect the flower.

Effie wasn't sure if she loved wildflowers because of their sweet smell and simple beauty, or if she loved them for the connection they gave her to her mother. She tried hard to remember but couldn't recall if she had found her mother's book before or after she started picking flowers. What she wished she could forget was the reason for putting so many inside the house. Every three days, Effie filled soup and coffee cans full of field pansies and violets.

She put them on the kitchen table and on the small slat of wood used for a counter and in any other space she could find. Sometimes she even placed a few cans on the floor. There were so many bundles and batches of flowers that the fragrant smell seeped into every crack and crevice. Effie kept placing cans even after her father grumbled that the house smelled worse than a cheaply perfumed whore. Effie didn't care. A house thick with the smell of lavender was much better than a house thick with the smell of whiskey and grief.

Effie's father, who had worked in the mines since he was thirteen, often came home after a ten-hour day, soot-covered and exhausted. Ignoring Effie, he would sink into the couch where his attention was completely focused on the bottle in his hand. Effie's father had always enjoyed a swig or two of beer, but it wasn't until his wife died that he started drinking whiskey. Gene Bilfrey took to drinking spirits in hopes that they would chase away the memory of his wife, but instead they chased him down into the hell he slowly built one drink at a time.

Even as a little girl, Effie did what she could to make sure her father didn't drag her down, too, by putting beauty where there was ugliness, and when she couldn't, she simply closed her eyes to it—the hard drinking and the rage that followed. Slowly the parts of her that were trusting and innocent fell away.

Effie loved her father, and she believed that her father loved her. Maybe it was because in those rare moments, when the moonshine drained from his blood, he did love her. In those times, he would awkwardly wrap his arm around Effie as he told her in a soft voice that she had her mother's beautiful eyes. Gentle words and loving embraces, however, were uncommon in Effie's world and never enough to provide her with all the love a little girl requires.

When Effie turned the age when girls understand how to catch a boy's eye, she finally found love. It wasn't in the arms of a local boy, but rather in the deep chocolate eyes of a russet-colored Irish setter. A tender-natured animal whose missing left ear and furless scarred legs attested to the abuse he'd suffered in a life before knowing one with Effie.

Effie had found him lying on Mr. Goodwin's porch. A man whose inexhaustible patience and boundless attention often brought Effie to his steps; it was the reason she was standing on his porch the day she found the dog.

The dog lay on its side, panting hard. His breaths were labored and his eyes blank as he stared. Effie took a tentative step forward, causing the bowed wood of the porch to creak. The dog's ear twitched at the sound, but his body remained motionless. Without lifting his head, he rolled his eyes in Effie's direction. Recognizing the fear and sadness in his eyes, Effie climbed the porch steps and knelt beside the animal. Effie gently placed her hand on the dog's head and scratched under his ear as she softly talked to him. Effie sat petting and whispering to the injured animal until Mr. Goodwin finally came home.

Curious, Mr. Goodwin bent down to have a closer look. Without a single question, he reached his hand toward Effie, helping her to stand. "Go on inside and get a pot to boil. We have some work to do." Effie, also without question, went into the house and did as she was told. Mr. Goodwin and Effie spent the next three hours cleaning, bandaging, and feeding the beaten animal. During that time, neither one said much. When they'd finished, Mr. Goodwin carefully laid the dog on his bed.

Seeing Effie's surprised look, he smiled and said, "He needs it more than I do." Then he added, "You get on home, girl, and come back tomorrow. If he dies, I'll bury him. If he doesn't, you can name him." By the time Effie reached home, she knew his name.

"Sunset? Are you sure?" Mr. Goodwin asked as he and Effie petted and coaxed the dog to eat. Effie nodded. Mr. Goodwin ran his fingers through Sunset's red fur. "Hmm, makes sense, I guess," he agreed.

For the next three weeks, Mr. Goodwin and Effie fed, walked, and cared for Sunset. Although the animal was always at the side of one of them, it didn't take long before it was obvious that Sunset favored Effie. The dog's tail wagged when Effie arrived in the morning and his tail drooped when she left at night. Mr. Goodwin, knowing Gene Bilfrey well, never offered for Effie to take the dog home, and Effie, knowing her father even better, never asked.

Effie's days were happy as she spent them caring for, playing with, and loving Sunset. Sweet-tempered and loving, the dog stole Effie's heart as quickly and as easily as whiskey had stolen her father's soul. And as Gene Bilfrey held tighter to his bottle, Effie Bilfrey held tighter to her dog. Soon neither noticed the other, or so Effie thought. She became so comfortable in her invisibility that she no longer took pains to hide Sunset. Instead she allowed him to lie at her feet while she ate and lie at her side while she slept.

Gene noticed. Even in his drunken haze he saw the mangy creature curled next to *his* daughter on *his* coach, saunter through *his* house, and eat *his* food. Gene was angry, but he was madder still that his daughter seemed to love this worthless stray more than him.

Effie awoke late on a hot mid-July morning with her constant companion curled beneath her arm. Petting his soft fur, Effie said, "Come on, boy, It's my birthday, and there is lots to do." Hurriedly, she pulled a T-shirt over her head then slid on some shorts. Seeing Effie turn the doorknob, Sunset bolted from the bed to her side. With adoration in his eyes, he looked up at her and loyally waited for her next step.

It was Wednesday, which meant Gene was at work, so the house was silent and still. Effie walked into the kitchen, already stifling from poor ventilation and the hot sun. Either from habit or wishful thinking, she quickly scanned the empty counters even though she knew there would be no cake or gifts.

Effie grabbed two slices of plain bread, and taking one and giving the other to Sunset, she said, "No time for a big breakfast." Sunset cocked his head then stayed close to Effie's heels as he followed her outside. After nearly tripping over a coffee can on the porch, Effie picked it up then squealed as she lifted it to her nose. Arranged beautifully was a big bouquet of wildflowers. Stuck between the stems was a small slip of paper with the letter "G" scrawled on it. Showing the flowers to Sunset, Effie exclaimed, "They're from Mr. Goodwin. He remembered my birthday!" Effie didn't allow herself to think of her father; she chose to forget him as he'd forgotten her. Effie stepped off the porch and whistled sharply for Sunset to follow.

After their daylong adventure of running and swimming, Effie was tired when she finally walked into the quiet house, so she headed for her bedroom as Sunset obediently followed. Exhausted and hungry, she quickly removed her wet clothes and put on her soft nightgown. Effie and her dog then headed to the couch, where they curled up together before quickly falling asleep.

Effie wasn't sure what woke her—her growling stomach or her own intuition waking her body to what her mind already knew. Someone was in the room. Effie slowly opened her eyes. Still drowsy, Effie fought hard to focus, her limbs hanging limp. Effie, trying not to disturb the dog, slowly lifted her head. She knew what it was to feel afraid, but until that moment she'd never known real fear. Overwhelmed by the terror of what she saw, Effie froze, her eyes locked with his.

Threatening, Gene stood in the doorway. Effie knew he was drunk by the way his body unsteadily swayed back and forth. She also knew by his clenched jaw and furrowed brow that he was angry. Effie didn't know how angry until she saw the gun he uneasily held in his unsteady hand, cocked and pointed at her head. Swallowing hard, Effie choked out, "Daddy?"

Gene took a step forward and stumbled. Bracing against the doorframe, he steadied himself. He shifted his feet and straightened his back. Never once did he take his eyes off of Effie.

Gene Bilfrey's rage was palpable. "Don't you call me Daddy. Don't you act like you love me when you don't."

Effie wanted to shout that he was wrong, but the words didn't come, because in that moment, they both knew he was right.

Trembling, Effie wrapped her arm tighter around Sunset's neck. The dog, sensing her fear, growled. Low-pitched and guttural, the sound didn't stop Gene from hurling more hateful words at his daughter. "You think I care whether you love me? I don't! I don't give no shit. I had someone to love me. I had your mother until you killed her."

Gene raised his right hand, which had dropped with the weight of the gun. Effie could clearly see the gleam of the metal and her father's finger pressed tightly to the trigger. Gene stepped forward. Cowering, Effie buried her face into Sunset's back. Hackles up, fur bristling, and eyes narrowed, Sunset growled. Startled, Gene took a quick step backward.

Gene's eyes flashed with rage and closed to slits. "Shut up! Shut him up! Shut that damn dog up right now!"

Effie petted and cooed to the dog. "Shh, boy. It's okay. Be quiet. Please be quiet." Effie's small voice did nothing to calm the animal who understood too well the severe and deep pain of undeserved and unrelenting abuse. Now up on his front legs, Sunset bared his teeth as he snarled at Gene.

Wobbly and nauseas, Gene clamped his left hand against the side of his head as he tried to block out the dog's barks. Each one, sharp and staccato, snapped against Gene's eardrums until it felt as though his head would crack. Again, Gene shouted at Effie, "I mean it, girl. Shut him up, or I will!"

Effie reached for Sunset, but only a slight tickling of fur across her fingers could be felt before the dog was off the couch and on his feet. Loyal and protective, Sunset was ready to fight, but before Effie could reach her feet to stop him, he lunged at Gene, who aimed his gun low and shot twice.

The dog fell into a heap on the floor as a small stream of blood trickled from the wound in the side of his head and the one in his chest. Effie let out a scream, primal and gut wrenching, as she screamed as she sunk beside her dog. Wrapping her arms tightly around him, she rocked back and forth as she petted his fur, dampened and matted with blood. Whispering in his ear, she pleaded, "Stay, Sunset. Please stay.

Please. I'll get Mr. Goodwin. He'll fix you just like before." Woozy from the sight of blood, Effie stood on unsteady legs and staggered toward the door.

With his hand still gripping the gun, Gene Bilfrey didn't move as he stared at the dead dog at his feet. Gene didn't stop Effie from getting Mr. Goodwin; instead he sat down the gun and told her he would go. He knew it was pointless, but he also knew that he owed her a bit of hope. After all, he had spent her lifetime stealing it.

Effie looked up into a blue sky etched with white clouds. Squinting in the light of the fierce sun, she saw nothing yet felt everything. She closed her eyes as she tried to force the memories to recede once more, but even behind her closed eyelids she still saw what she couldn't face—the regret, the pain, the past. Opening her eyes, she saw her granddaughter, and in Lottie she saw what she must face—the regret, the pain, the future.

Chapter Fourteen

Frank stopped at the broken fence post and leaned against it, trying to regain his balance. Holding his aching head, Frank cursed the drink. Trying to stomp but managing only a stagger, he headed toward his sister's porch where his mother sat. Hungover and angry at the world, Frank glared at Effie.

Having ignored Lottie's existence for so many years, Frank was surprised when out of the corner of his eye he saw her sitting next to his mother. Lottie fidgeted uncomfortably before whispering, "Granmom, I'm going to head back home." Frank watched as his mother nodded and patted her granddaughter's back. The gentle touch filled with warmth and affection was one that Frank couldn't remember ever feeling from his mother. Jealous, he glowered at Lottie, hoping she could feel his hatred, but Lottie simply stood and stepped off the porch. Never once looking at Frank.

"What are you doing here, Frank?" Effie demanded.

"What? You ain't happy to see me?"

Effie shifted her body on the steps. Frank was surprised by how his mother, small boned and slight, easily filled in the space left by Lottie. Suddenly her presence seemed larger, making her words seem louder and sharper.

"What I mean, boy, is that you come and go as you please. You never tell no one where you're going and when you're coming back. Then you show up expectin' us all to be pleased as punch. It don't work that way."

Refusing to shrink from her, Frank leaned down and pushed himself into Effie's face. "I'm a grown man. Twenty-six years old. And I don't need to be telling no one shit about shit."

Effie snorted before snapping, "Shit, Frank Bilfrey, you're a man all right. You're a grown man still living with his mama."

The hair on the back of Frank's neck bristled. He stood straight and took a step back before hissing, "You want me out? 'Cause I can leave today. I never needed you or that shit shack you call a house."

Now also on her feet, Effie, standing toe to toe with her son, who now towered above her by several inches, shouted, "Shit shack? Shit shack! Well, I tell you what, you ungrateful son of a bitch, that shit shack kept you warm and dry for more years than I want to count. And I don't remember hearing you complain when hot food was put on the table or clean clothes put on your bed."

Standing his ground, Frank volleyed back, "You're right, Ma, and I don't remember hearing you complain when you took my money."

Effie said nothing.

Thinking he'd gained ground, Frank snapped, "That's what I thought. It's easy to sit up on that high horse until you see that the only way you got up there was by crawling over other people's backs."

Thinking about how her son always underestimated her, Effie smiled. "You're right, Frank. I took the money because it was mine. It was my payment for housing you, feeding you, and putting up with your shit." Lowering her voice, she added, "But I ain't taking the money no more."

Effie sank back onto the steps, but far from finished, she said, "I don't need your dirty money."

Standing about a foot from his mother, Frank bent down and hissed, "Oh it's dirty now, huh? And why's that, Ma?"

Effie shook her head. "You know damn well why it's dirty."

Frank leaned back and again rested against the porch railing. He always found his mother difficult, but his hangover and the rising heat were making her seem insufferable.

Frank wiped away a bead of sweat that trickled down his temple before turning his attention back to his mother. "Gettin' my money selling pot ain't no worse than gettin' it shoveling shit. The only difference is I don't get my hands dirty and my clothes don't stink."

Sneering at her son, Effie snapped back, "You never got your hands dirty, Frank Bilfrey, no matter what you done. You talk about crawling over other people's backs. Well, I don't think there's a boy in this town, including your brother Gene, who don't wear your footprints."

Defensive, Frank shot back, "All I ever done is help Gene out. Besides, he's a grown man who can make his own damn decisions." Frank knew by the distrust that furrowed his mother's brow that she didn't believe him, which made sense to Frank, since he hardly believed himself.

Protective of Gene, Effie said, "Maybe Gene can make his own decisions, but he don't. You make them all for him and not a one of 'em has been a good one. Shit, Frank, you got your brother selling drugs for Christ's sake."

Frank snickered. "It ain't drugs. It's just pot."

Frustrated, Effie said, "God, Frank, I didn't raise you to be this stupid. And I sure as hell didn't raise you to rot in a jail cell."

Frank snorted. "No, Ma, you didn't raise me to be much of anything. All I got, I got on my own."

Straightening her shoulders, Effie said, "Ain't much to be bragging about, boy. And let me tell you another thing, you can also get yourself out of jail, because I ain't never going to bail your ass out."

Frank shrugged his shoulders and said quietly, "Never thought you would, Ma."

Feeling suddenly dizzy and nauseous, Frank slid down the porch rail and sat on the first step, surprised that his mother quickly made room before saying, "I ain't an idiot, Frank. I know there's folks who grow and sell pot in these hills, but they're protected by family and friends. But you ain't got much family and you ain't got no friends."

Frank's face hardened and his voice tightened as he said, "So you'd turn my ass in?"

Effie shook her head. "No, Frank. I wouldn't turn you in, but I can't say that I'd be able to protect you neither." Effie took a deep breath and said, "I know you, Frank. You've always been a schemer and a show-off. You take risks without ever considering who might get hurt."

Sounding more plaintive than he intended, Frank asked, "You ever think that maybe the only person getting hurt is me?"

Without considering her son's words for more than a second, Effie answered, "If only that was true I wouldn't have to spend my nights worrying that when I lose one son, I'll lose two."

Angry again, Frank spit out, "So that's it, huh? You're just worried about Gene?"

Effie folded her hands, and without looking at her son, she said, "I was once told that a drowning man will take under the person trying to save him." Looking up at her son, she whispered, "I know this to be true."

Frank clutched at his neck as bile rose in his throat. Facing his mother, he demanded,

"Why do you make it so damn hard?"

Effie shrugged her shoulders slightly and asked, "What?"

Frank sighed and answered, "To love you."

Effie stared out across the yard and said flatly, "I don't know."

Refusing to let it go, Frank asked, "You think *I'm* a drowning man?"

Effie again shrugged her shoulders. "I think you're headed for a bottom."

Frank laughed sarcastically. "I'm already at the bottom."

Effie shook her head and said, "There's always a new bottom, Frank, just waiting underneath."

Effie slowly stood, stretching the tightness from her legs. She groaned a bit as she kneaded her fist into her lower back, trying to release the ache that had settled into it. Squinting from the sun, she cupped her hands over her eyes as she looked at the small hill that sloped up toward her house. Turning back to face Frank, who sat cast in shadows, she never dropped her hand. She no longer needed it to shield her eyes, but she kept it perched above her eyebrows with her fingers and thumb slightly squeezing her temples. As her palm dipped low to hide the hurt in eyes, she said, "I know all about hitting bottom. I've hit quite a few." She finally dropped her hand, and Frank could see his mother's eyelids flutter nearly closed as she said softly, "And I'll tell you again, there's always a new one right underneath."

Saying nothing more, Effie walked away. Dropping his head, Frank didn't watch her leave. It was only in the silence that Frank could really hear his mother's voice. He knew she was right. He knew there were other bottoms. He'd seen others hit them, and he feared them, but he also couldn't see any way to avoid them. Not here, not in these hills. Talon Ridge was a place where ignorance was inherited and poverty a birthright, and Frank knew there was no escaping it no matter how great his plans and schemes.

Chapter Fifteen

Struggling to walk up the small hill to his sister's empty cabin, Gene stopped, wheezing and gasping to catch his breath. His head throbbed, and his sweat-soaked T-shirt clung to his back. Every time, following a night of liquor, cards, and the occasional fistfight, Gene would swear that he would never again join in his brother's drunken benders. But even as he slumped into the grass, once again retching, he knew that he would be sitting beside his brother, mason jar of moonshine in his hand, two days later.

Gene knew that following Frank would only lead him to the gates of hell, but the way he figured it, he would probably end up there anyway. At least by going with Frank the trip would be a lot more fun. Gene sat up. With the back of his hand, he wiped saliva and the remaining vomit from his mouth.

Then, searching his pockets for something to take away the rancid taste, Gene pulled out some lint and a few quarters. Absently, he dropped them on the ground as his stomach lurched. Vomiting again, Gene knew he should have blamed Frank for mixing all the booze into a cocktail that was now threatening to kill him. But he didn't blame him. He never did.

Having finally made it up the hill, Gene stopped. Trying to find his footing on the ground, which now seemed to move beneath his feet, Gene stumbled forward. Dehydrated and hot, he longed to lie down on the cool riverbank and sleep until his body no longer ached, but he knew he had to find Frank and soon.

The last time he'd seen his brother, he was passed out on Susan Lowry's couch with Susan stretched out across him. Although Gene admired Frank's easy way with women, he also envied it and was often reduced to taking Frank's scraps. Last night those scraps were Susan's cousin, Shelby.

Under the haze of four beers, Shelby's frizzy blonde hair looked perfectly curled, and her slightly crossed eyes sparkled blue. Gene shuddered as he relived the awkward hour they spent together fumbling and apologizing. Even though the memory of every touch and kiss made Gene cringe, he was already creating a better version of the story to tell his brother. Remembering what he needed to tell Frank, Gene muttered, "Shit," as he pressed on, even though every part of his body screamed for him to stop.

Finding Frank sitting on Sarah's porch steps, Gene tried to gauge his brother's mood. Well acquainted with Frank's unpredictable temperament, Gene always approached him carefully. As Gene slowly stumbled toward Sarah's house, Frank called out, "Where the hell you been?"

Reaching the porch, Gene tried to sit on the bottom step but missed. Watching him clumsily fall over, Frank snickered.

"I thought I was in bad shape but, shit, at least I can walk." Leaning close, Frank sniffed Gene before he quickly pulled back and said, "Whew, Gene! You stink. What did ya do? Puke all over yourself?"

With a swollen tongue and a dry mouth, Gene just nodded. Laughing, Frank shook his head. "You really can't hold your liquor, can ya?" Frank slapped his brother on the back and jeered, "I know a skinny little white trash whore who could drink you under the table and still not have enough whiskey in her to spread her legs for ya."

Gene smirked and shot back, "I guess you got just the right amount of whiskey into Susan Lowry." Gene's grin quickly slipped when he saw the darkness that suddenly clouded his brother's eyes.

Stiffening his back, Frank snarled, "What are you saying, Eugene? Are you saying that I have to get a girl drunk before she'll fuck me?"

Gene stammered, "No…no, Frank. I was just…"

Frank pushed his face close to Gene's and hissed, "At least the girls I fuck, and there's been a lot, don't look like they were beaten with a fence post."

Stung but wanting the storm to pass, Gene gently pushed Frank away and said, "You're right, Frank. I'd be better just to fuck the fence post."

Frank bumped Gene's shoulder with his own and snickered before he said, "You just might want to try that, Genie. There'd be less hassle."

The brothers sat without saying another word for about ten minutes before Frank, feeling Gene stare at him, snapped, "What? What the hell are you looking at?" Without taking his eyes off of Frank, Gene nervously rubbed his hands together. Irritated, Frank hissed, "Seriously, asshole, what are you looking at?"

Cautiously, Gene said, "Do you ever worry, Frank? You know, about what we're doing?"

Annoyed, Frank said, "What the fuck are we doing, Gene?"

Gene said, "Selling weed."

Frank shot back, "No shit, Gene." Slapping Gene's hands to stop his nervous habit, Frank asked, "What's going on, Gene?"

Gene said, "Nothing, man. Nothing. I was just thinking that we have a really good thing going selling weed, and it's because of you."

Easily flattered, Frank grinned. "So why the fuck are you so nervous?"

Gene jammed his hands under his legs. "I was just wondering what would happen if we couldn't do it no more."

Cocking his eyebrow, Frank asked, "What the hell are you talking about?"

Shaking his head, Gene said, "Nothing. I was just thinking, I guess."

Frank chided, "Well stop. Your thinking never did no one any good."

Again, both brothers fell silent.

It was a full five minutes before Frank, furiously rubbing his shin, exhaled and asked, "Why the hell wouldn't we be able to sell anymore?"

Gene shrugged. "I don't know. Lots of reasons."

Frank snapped, "Name one, asshole."

Gene sputtered, "Maybe Ma finds out and she's pissed or maybe people lose interest or…I don't know."

Rolling his eyes, Frank said, "Look, Gene, Ma already knows, and who gives a shit if she's pissed? She's always pissed. And people ain't ever gonna lose interest. Getting stoned ain't like some shit hobby."

Gene agreed, but still uncertain, he asked, "But a good thing can't last forever, right?"

Frank huffed, "If you got something to say, Gene, then just fucking say it!"

Gene quickly explained, "I heard that Billy Kinsey and Matt Dancy have been talking about how they're going to take over our share. I mean it could just be rumor but—"

Cutting Gene off, Frank demanded, "Kinsey and Dancy?"

"Well, yeah, that's what I heard."

Frank's laugh, short and humorless, punctuated his words as he said, "Those stupid assholes couldn't find their dicks with both hands on it and a sign pointing to it. There's sure as shit no way they're gonna find our stash."

Disagreeing, Gene said, "They've been doing this longer than us, Frank. They may be dumbasses, but they're pissed dumbasses who are looking to get back at us for cutting into their share."

Frank snorted, "So? What are they going to do? Steal it?" With a devious laugh, Frank sneered, "Let 'em try."

Shaking his head, Gene said, "It ain't gonna matter how many snake and nail pits we got if they decide to turn our asses in." Agitated, Gene added, "Shit, Frank, we keep going, we ain't going to be able to hide the patches no more. We get up over five hundred plants, where we gonna stick 'em?"

Frank snickered. "We'll stick 'em up your ass if we have to."

"This ain't funny, Frank."

Frank gripped his knees until his knuckles turned white, then without a shadow of a smile, he said through gritted teeth, "You think I'm stupid? You think you have to *tell* me this ain't funny?" Pressing his face close to Gene's, Frank hissed, "Tell me, Eugene, who the hell was the one who came up with this idea? Grew the fucking plants? Put the money in your pocket?"

Dropping his head, Gene said quietly, "I know, Frank, and I appreciate it. I really do. I'm just worried. I mean if Kinsey and Dancy get a mind to screw us over—"

Frank cut in, "How they gonna do that? Rat us out? To who? That stupid little pissant, Roy Radley?"

Gene said, "Frank, he is the sheriff."

Frank snorted, "Not fucking here, he's not."

Gene argued, "No, but he can make arrests here."

"Sure, if he can find anything, but we got those patches buried so deep ain't no one gonna find 'em."

Lifting his head slowly, Gene looked at Frank. "Maybe Roy ain't so smart or powerful, but it don't have to be Roy who stops us. Jack Bardon told me that federal agents were all over Loletta looking for patches."

Frank sniffed, "So? Loletta ain't here."

Gene said, "I know, but Loletta ain't that far. And if they're willing to go there, Frank, they're willing to come here."

Frank stood up. Holding on to the porch rail, he tried to steady both his feet and his anger before he growled, "So, Gene, what's your fucking point?"

In a rare act of boldness, Gene stood and faced his brother. "My point is that maybe it's time we do something else."

Enraged, Frank sneered, "You think because I allow you to be a part of this that you can tell me how it's going down? You, little brother, don't tell me shit. I run this. I own this." Through gritted teeth, Frank hissed, "Got it?"

Trying to escape Frank's hot breath, Gene leaned back and said, "I ain't trying to tell you nothing, Frank. I know you run things. I just...I don't know. Forget I said anything."

Frank nodded his head before slumping back down onto the porch steps. Feeling satisfied in his win, he let it go.

Still standing, Gene considered his options. He looked at his sister's empty cabin before casting his glance up to his mother's house. Then, just as inevitable as the sun rising, Gene slid down onto the porch step next to his brother. After all, it was the only place he knew to go, the only place he belonged.

Even though Gene didn't look at his brother, he could feel Frank's stare boring into him.

Feeling as though his skin would blister from it, Gene, unconsciously, rubbed his arms. Finally looking away, Frank said quietly, "It's just that this mountain soil ain't much good for anything other than growing weed." Glancing down at himself, Frank said, "God knows it don't grow nothing else worthwhile."

Gene could have argued that Talon Ridge grew the biggest oak trees and the most beautiful mountain laurel, but knowing that wasn't what Frank meant, he just nodded.

Frank turned. Facing Gene again, he said with determination, "I just ain't gonna let two pissant nothings screw up what we've worked for."

Gene said cautiously, "That's all I was trying to say, Frank. I just don't want nothing or no one to screw this up for us."

Frank snapped, "Well, they ain't because I ain't going to let 'em." Stomping his boot against the step for emphasis, he added, "And if one of those assholes tries, I'm going to bury 'em." Frank talked tough, but catching his brother's eye, Gene could clearly see that Frank was more scared than angry. More than his rage, it was Frank's fear that terrified Gene.

Frank slid forward on the step before leaning back so that his entire body stretched across the full length of the steps. His head, which awkwardly rested against the top one, swayed slightly from side to side as he stared up at the sky. Gene knew by the intensity of his brother's gaze that he was scheming and planning.

Frank closed his eyes and said with quiet conviction, "No one ever shoots the bear that's already been bagged. They hunt for a bigger and better one." Slowly opening his eyes and rolling his head to the side, Frank looked at Gene and said, "We need to go hunting, little brother."

Confused, Gene asked, "What are we hunting?"

Turning his head and closing his eyes again, Frank answered softly, "Something better, Genie. Something better."

Chapter Sixteen

Curtis stood in front of his sister's empty cabin. Sarah's house seemed to hold on a sadness that made Curtis want to both never leave and at the same time never come back. But no matter how painful, he always did come back. Searching for clues, searching for other diaries, and even though he couldn't admit to himself, searching for her. In the past few weeks, Curtis had snuck into the quiet corners of Sarah's house. Running his fingers under loose floorboards, sliding his hands beneath cupboards feeling for something, anything, only to find nothing.

Curtis had hoped to come sooner, but with work and little time to himself, he wasn't able until now. Standing in the same spot again with a new plan and a new determination, he peered under the porch. Rubbing his index finger across his chin, he wondered how he was going to slide his body underneath the small space. Determined to find what he'd come here for, he walked to the side of the porch and squatted down close to the open space beneath it.

Cocking his head, he took measure of the narrow gap and his lanky body. Then, lying flat on his back, Curtis slowly slid until he was completely under the porch with the exception of his feet, which he nervously rocked back and forth while his hands reached, searched, and felt every floorboard. Finding nothing, Curtis dropped his hands to his sides and slowly exhaled.

Agitated, Curtis inched his body back from beneath the porch. Abruptly, he stood and shook his head as he cursed, "Goddamn it, Sarah!" With balled fists, Curtis drove his boot into the dirt. With three hard stomps, he muttered, "You just leave? You just fucking leave? And what do we have? Fucking nothing." Resentful, Curtis took loud, staccato steps in rhythm to the rage he felt blistering his insides. Upon reaching Sarah's door, he angrily swung it open and allowed the screen door to slam shut behind him.

Curtis forcefully exhaled, his eyes darting around the cabin, never landing on any one thing for long. With anger-fueled intention, he stamped across the room. There was no plan, only pointless raging as he yanked open cupboard doors, jerked open drawers, and shoved back the table, but every empty corner and bare shelf only infuriated him more until he was no longer looking—he was destroying.

Turning on his heel, he headed back to the other room. Stepping to the dresser, he pulled every drawer, from top to bottom, wide open. Although he knew each would be empty, their vacant space maddened him. Wrenching the top drawer from its runner, he dropped it. The sound of wood splitting could barely be heard as the drawer loudly crashed to the floor.

Breathing hard, Curtis stood in the destruction for a moment. Drained of his anger, he surveyed the damage. Guilty for what he'd done, he picked up the broken drawer. He gingerly ran his finger across the unscathed front, relieved. Certain that it was the bottom that cracked, Curtis turned the drawer over, and that was when he found it.

Folded several times, stuck, and nestled next to the wooden runner was a small piece of paper. With shaking hands, Curtis reached in and carefully pulled it from its tight makeshift tomb. He then wiped the sweat from his forehead, took a deep breath, and opened it. Although it was wrinkled and yellowed, Curtis could clearly see his sister's familiar flowery scrawl in purple ink across the page. Curtis's lips moved soundlessly as he read.

June 5, 1982

I took Lotus to see Mama. She finally held her after a
year of barely looking at her. It was nice watching Mama
rock her and stroke her hair. Maybe it was holding
a baby again, my baby, which got Mama to talking.
Whatever it was, Mama told me about the day I was
born. She said that I fought hard against coming into
this world. She labored for over eighteen hours. She said
it was only when she screamed loud enough to almost

burst the midwife's eardrums that the poor woman
finally pulled me out with a big pair of metal tongs.
Mama said my first breath was a shriek. She said I
screamed like I knew the world I was leaving was much
better than the one I was coming into. Mama seemed to
feel bad about this.

I don't fault Mama that I was born on this moun-
tain and bred in these hills. But God knows I blame her
for not helping me escape.

Curtis balled his fist, crumpling the paper between his
tightened fingers. Again, he was angry, but not at Sarah. This
time he was angry for her. Pounding his fist onto the top of
the dresser, he asked the question that always haunted him,
"What could we have done?" The answer echoed off the walls
in silence. Curtis crumpled to the floor. The page fluttered
onto his lap as he pinched the corners of his eyes to stop the
sting of tears that were never enough to drown the pain of
losing his sister.

Looking down at the paper, Curtis tried to smooth
out the wrinkles before reading his sister's words again more
slowly and thoughtfully. He gave each word consideration but
found his eyes drawn back to her painfully penned phrase,
"I blame her for not helping me escape." Curtis didn't need
to give much thought to all the reasons someone would want
to leave Talon Ridge. After all, no one got much more than a
raw deal and a hard life in these hills. No one knew that better
than the Bilfreys, but Curtis knew after reading Sarah's torn

journal entry that she didn't just want to leave Talon Ridge—she *had* to leave.

Curtis pressed his sister's diary entry against his chest and allowed the image, which he kept carefully buried, to surface. The long pale limbs trapped beneath the sinewy arms that forcefully pushed and shoved, and legs twisted together in a distressed tangle. The sickening sounds of moaning and screaming that had sounded more animal than human. Even now, Curtis covered his ears against the reverberation of it. Unsettled, he opened his eyes and shook loose what he was no longer sure was a nightmare or a memory.

Curtis folded the paper into a tiny square that fit neatly into his shirt pocket. Satisfied it was safe, he leaned forward to stand but stopped suddenly when he heard faint footsteps. Keenly aware of the sounds around him, Curtis quickly determined that the light quick steps were Lottie's. Panicked, he grabbed the broken drawer and rushed out to the porch.

Standing on the steps, Lottie, puzzled, asked, "Uncle Curtis, what are you doing?"

Curtis stammered, "Uh, nothing. I was just, uh, making sure…" Unable to quickly come up with a reasonable explanation, Curtis sidestepped. "What are *you* doing here?"

Lottie shrugged and said softly, "I like to come here sometimes."

Curtis nodded. "Yeah, I could see that. I guess I also like—"

Seeing the drawer, Lottie interrupted, "What's that?"

Looking down at his side, Curtis was surprised to see

that he'd absentmindedly grabbed the broken dresser drawer. "It's from your mother's dresser."

Lottie smiled. "I knew that much. I wanted to know why you have it."

Curtis blurted, "I got it for you."

Confused, Lottie asked, "You got me a…" Taking a closer look, she finished, "A broken drawer?"

Thinking more quickly this time, Curtis said, "Yes. Well, no. I thought that we could make something out of it." Seeing her forehead wrinkle and the slight tilt of her head, Curtis explained, "I know you don't have much of your mother's, so I thought we could paint it and maybe you could keep special things in it."

Lottie lit up. "That's nice." Heading up the steps, she said, "I'm just going to get one that isn't broken."

"No!" Curtis nearly shouted as he blocked the door with his body.

Confused, Lottie stopped. "Why?"

Trying to convince his niece that he'd chosen this one specifically, he said, "It's the perfect size to keep the diary."

Satisfied, Lottie smiled. They stood awkwardly together for a few minutes before Curtis said, "I going to head home and get started on it. You coming?"

Lottie shook her head. "Not yet. I want to stay for a bit."

With the drawer tucked under his arm, Curtis started across the yard. "Uncle Curtis!" Lottie shouted. Curtis turned. "I always wanted a hope chest."

Scrunching his forehead, Curtis asked, "What's a hope chest?"

Lottie answered, "It's a chest where you keep all your hopes."

Curtis smiled as he nodded. Placing his hand gently over his shirt pocket where the diary entry lay tucked, he called back, "Of course, where else would you keep hope?"

Chapter Seventeen

Stepping off the porch, Lottie could easily hear the hushed sounds of the mountains as they whispered in her ear. The murmurs made from the rustling of delicate leaves in the gentle wind and the chatter of twigs snapped by the scurrying of small animal feet.

Finding the perfect spot to sit by an old hickory tree, Lottie pulled her mother's diary from her bag. She opened it to the page she'd carefully marked by laying an old yellow hair ribbon across it. Taking the silky strand of material in her hand, Lottie wound it and pulled until the slip of fabric slid across her fingers. Lottie had formed this habit after her mother left, rubbing the silk trim of a blanket across her cheek to fall asleep. Even now the feel of softness against her skin soothed and comforted her. Lottie lifted the book and reread the same page for the third time.

January 2, 1977

I haven't been writing in my diary. I guess it's because there ain't really been nothing worth writing about.

Ms. Prindle says, "New year, new start." So, I'm going to start writing again. I guess I also wanted to try out the new purple pen Ms. Prindle gave to me. Purple is my favorite color. I wanted to paint my room purple, but Mama said we don't have the money. I told her we'd have more money if she made that rat, Piney Boyer, pay rent. I thought for sure Mama was going to slap me, but she just said that getting what we need is more important than getting what we want.

Maybe Mama's right, but I think what we need is for Piney to pay rent. Of course, even if he did pay rent, it still ain't worth having him here. There ain't no amount of money that makes putting up with him worth it. His rotted teeth and stinking breath make me sick. The way he stares at me makes me sick.

January 3, 1977

There always seems to be someone sniffing around my stuff. If it's not Mama, it's the boys. I don't want them to find my diary, so I've been working on a safe place to hide it. I finally figured it out after watching Mr. Goodwin's crazy dog.

You don't hide something in a place you think no one would go. You hide it in a place no one thinks you would go.

Lottie repeated the last line out loud. "A clue," she murmured. A clue that Lottie hoped would lead her to her mother's other secrets and possibly, she prayed, to answers. Lottie reread the last two lines again. Trying to work out what her mother meant, Lottie muttered to herself, "A place Mama wouldn't want to go." Up on her feet now, Lottie paced as she said softly to herself, "Go. Go. Where would you go, Mama?"

Lottie stopped pacing and began rocking from one foot to the other. Crossing her legs, she swore, "Damn. Why didn't I go before I left?" With her bladder full to bursting, Lottie realized she wouldn't make it to her grandmother's house in time. Groaning, she wiggle-walked her way over to the outhouse. Slowly she opened the door, which, hanging at a severe slant on its hinges, creaked loudly.

Carefully, Lottie peered in, making sure that no sharp-clawed animal had made its way inside. Other than a few spiders dangling from thick webs, the outhouse was empty. Relieved, Lottie stepped inside. With still a fair amount of hesitation, she closed the door so that the only light coming in had to fight its way through the slats. Trying to get her bearings, Lottie held on to the door handle as she pulled down her pants. Refusing to allow any part of her body touch the filthy seat covering the hole in the center of the raised wooden platform, she gripped the sides to brace herself as she squatted.

Lottie felt instant relief, which soon turned to impatience as her slow-to-empty bladder forced her to stay, with shaking legs and gripped hands, crouched over the toilet. Readjusting her body, Lottie moved her hands a few inches over on either side. As she slid her fingers under the boards, she felt something strange.

Lottie jumped, causing a bit of urine to splash her shorts. "Damn," she muttered as she looked down at the wet spot. Quickly pulling up her shorts, Lottie turned and stooped down. Then, with her foot, she nudged open the door to allow in more light. Leaning sideways, Lottie bent her head down and looked underneath the boards. Unable to see, she ran her fingertips under the splintered wood until she felt something hard but smooth.

Grasping the edge of it, Lottie pulled, but it was wedged in so tightly that she had to brace her feet against the base of the wooden seat. Lottie yanked and tugged until her prize was pulled free. However, the force of her determination catapulted her backward causing her to tumble, feet above head, out the door and onto the ground.

Dazed, Lottie lay still for a moment. Smelling the fresh air, she inhaled deeply then stretched her legs, which were tender from the fall. Then, slowly rocking her head from one side to the other, Lottie saw that in her right hand she held a small sunflower-yellow book. Lottie knew what it was even before she opened the cover, but still her fingers trembled as she flipped to the first page.

Inscribed on the inside was, "Sarah Bilfrey's Diary, 1978." Lottie smiled as she looked from the grass to the trees to the sky. Then, to whatever unknown force held her mother, she whispered, "Thank you, Mama."

Sitting up, Lottie straightened her T-shirt and pushed back her hair without ever letting go of the diary. It wasn't until she leaned forward to stand that she saw it and let go of her tight grasp of the book, causing it to fall softly to the ground.

Only a moment ago, Lottie would never have believed that there would be anything greater than finding her mother's second diary until she found the third one. The edge of the book's spine stuck out ever so slightly from underneath the boards of the toilet, but its existence was undeniable.

After a couple of hard jerks, the third diary, small and sky blue, was pulled free. Lottie flipped to the inside cover. Gone was the flowery script of childhood, replaced by the cursive letters of a young woman. But still, it was there, plain and simple: "Sarah Bilfrey's Diary, 1981."

Lottie turned and picked up the other one so that she held both diaries between her slender fingers. Squeezing them tightly, she whispered, "Two. There are two." Then, remembering the one that rested safely at the bottom of her bag, Lottie giggled and said in disbelief, "Three. Three diaries."

Lottie took the first diary out of her bag, and then piled each one on top of the other. After carefully rationing every page so that she could spend weeks, maybe even months, wrapped tightly in her mother's words, her mother's world, Lottie now had a stack.

The temptation to feed the desire after weeks of deprivation was too great. Lottie clutched the diaries to her chest, slung her bag over her shoulder, and ran back to the hickory tree, where she settled back into her shaded spot. Leaning her back comfortably against its trunk, Lottie opened her mother's first diary. Taking in a deep breath, she slowly exhaled and began to read.

January 21, 1977

It's finally Friday. This week was so long. And the cold weather and Mama made it feel even longer. Mama is always looking at me like she's trying to figure something out.

Yesterday, she said that all of me ain't in the mountains no more. When I told her that I'm here more than I want to be, she looked sad and said that's how she knows I ain't.

At least today Mama won't be pestering me too much. It's Gene's tenth birthday, so Mama will be busy making him his favorite dinner of fried chicken livers. Gross.

Mama just stomped in my room and told me that Gene ain't getting his special dinner on account he got into a fight with Thomas Bain after school. Mrs. Bain wasn't happy. Mama had to stand in the yard and hear her out for over twenty minutes, so now Mama ain't happy.

I'm happy I don't have to eat liver, but I am sad for Gene. I know it wasn't his fault. Not really. It's

Frank. Lately, his hits have been coming harder and faster than the reasons. And Gene just follows along like he's following Jesus. I don't know where that will lead Gene, but I know it sure won't lead to his salvation.

Lottie placed her finger between the pages and paused for a moment as she thought about her uncles. They were grown men and not much had changed. Gene still followed Frank, and Frank still got them both into trouble. Lottie sighed and mumbled, "I guess nothing ever does change in these mountains." Lottie turned the page and read.

February 14, 1977

Today is Monday. Not much good ever happens on a Monday. It's also Valentine's Day. Nothing much good ever happens on Valentine's Day. Except for today.

Ms. Prindle, unmarried Ms. Prindle, loves Valentine's Day. She filled the whole classroom with pink and red paper hearts. She even put a bowl of small candy hearts on her desk. Then she gave each of us a piece of paper with a quote she said she'd picked especially for each one of us.

Mine said, "We know what we are, but know not what we may be." —William Shakespeare. I don't think this fits me since I pretty much know all that I am is all that I'll ever be.

Anyway, the day was fine enough until Cathy
McQuinn told Jimmy Russell that I liked him, and I
don't! He grinned at me then licked his fat lips and
said something I couldn't hear. Whatever it was, Dallas
Cutler rammed his shoulder into Jimmy's and told him
I was too pretty to give him a second look. Cathy and
Jimmy looked mad. I tried hard to hide my smile.

So, the day was good until I got home.

Scanning the page, Lottie whispered, "What happened,
Mama?" With little regard to time, Lottie turned the page and
kept reading.

February 15, 1977

I couldn't write about what happened yesterday after
school until today because Mama has been pressed
closer to me than my shadow.

It started after Mama saw me on our porch holding
a wooden heart that I'd found on the step. Because
it had my name carved on it, I picked it up and was
holding it when Mama walked out. She didn't say
nothing. She just grabbed it and asked me where it
came from. I said I didn't know. She got so angry. She
shoved it back at me and told me to think hard.

As I snaked my finger over the crooked curves
of the "s" then the "a," I remembered seeing Piney
standing at the edge of our yard last week whittling a

flat piece of wood. I remembered how his thin, wet lips pulled back over his yellow teeth as he grinned at me. I also remembered how it made me sick.

I don't know why, but I didn't tell Mama. I just shrugged then looked down at my feet. When I finally looked up at Mama, she didn't look angry anymore—she looked scared.

She told me to go on inside, and as I walked past her, I handed her the heart. She pressed it between her hands and whispered to herself, "It's nothing."

As the screen door shut behind me, I thought to myself, "I'm not so sure."

"Neither am I, Mama," whispered Lottie before turning another page.

March 6, 1977

It's Sunday, and I'm still in bed. Baby Curtis is curled up next to me sleeping. He doesn't take up much space, so I don't mind. Besides, it's easier to keep an eye on him when Mama is gone. She leaves every Sunday morning. She's never told me where she goes, and I don't ask.

I don't want to get up. It's so cold this morning that I have just been lying here thinking about Dallas Cutler. Dallas has been so nice to me. He doesn't just talk, he listens. Not that I've had much to say, but it's good to know that if I did, he would listen.

I wish I had a pretty dress to wear to school tomorrow.

Before Lottie turned the page, she traced her finger over Dallas Cutler's name. She wondered if he was her father. Missing a mother served as enough pain, but there were times when Lottie thought about him. Running her fingers over her jawline, too sharp to be her mother's, or catching a glimpse of her profile in the mirror and seeing someone else caused Lottie to consider him if only briefly. She had always resisted treading down that painful path, but now there was a possibility, real and reachable, and so Lottie kept reading.

April 21, 1977

I walked home real slow today, some because the air was sweet but mostly because I walked with Dallas.

We stopped for a bit at Culver's Creek, where we skipped stones. He's really good. He showed me how to get more than two skips. I showed him bloodroot and told him how it's good for ailing skin.

I learned about a whole bunch of flowers and plants in Mama's book, "A Lady's Companion to Wildflowers." I found it in a cupboard tucked behind the flour. I have had it for over a year now and Mama still hasn't noticed it missing.

We were almost home when Dallas grabbed my hand and wrapped his fingers around mine. It was nice.

I felt safe. Something about Dallas Cutler makes my feet feel like they've grown roots. Thick and wide, stretching across these old mountains pulling me into them. And, strangely, I don't mind.

May 15, 1977

Since it's Sunday, I was in the yard this afternoon watching Baby Curtis when I saw Dallas walking up the road. I made sure to run in the house quick and brush the tangles out of my hair. I also used a dab of Mama's lipstick.

We were sitting on the porch when Mama got home. She was wearing her best dress, but she didn't look as pretty as she did this morning. Her dress hung funny, and her lips were wiped clean of the bright pink color she'd put on before she left. She looked tired.

She stepped onto porch then she flattened her dress before putting her hand on her hip. It's Mama's fighting stance. I waited, but Mama didn't say a word to me. Instead she looked at Dallas like he was some stray cat I found.

She stared for about a minute before she told him he best be heading home. His foot hadn't hit the bottom step before she said that we'd see him next Sunday afternoon. I couldn't believe it.

After he left, Mama pulled me down onto the step and sat beside me. Then she told me that I was never to have Dallas here when she wasn't home. She told me that's how good girls don't stay good for long. I told her Dallas is a nice boy, and she told me there ain't no such thing. Then Mama grabbed my arm and said that I need to be real careful when it comes to men because it ain't a game.

I don't know if it was the look in her eyes or the way she squeezed my arm too tight, but I got this weird feeling that Mama wasn't talking about Dallas Cutler.

June 27, 1977

Dallas and me have been seeing each other almost every day since school ended. Mama's come around a bit. She even helped me with my hair this morning. She combed out all the tangles and twisted it into a long braid. She hasn't done that since I was little. I liked it. I think she did too.

Today Dallas and me walked to Culver's Creek where we thought it would be a good idea to go wading, but since it was so cold we just sat on the bank, holding hands as we dipped our toes in.

We talked about school and his family and mine. What I really wanted to tell him was how my feet always felt like running until I met him, but I didn't. Instead, I told him the day was nice, and it was until Piney showed up.

I saw him hiding behind an oak tree. Some low branches covered his face, but I knew that it was

*twisting up like a storm as he spit out meanness with
his tobacco. Seeing he'd been caught, he nodded at me
and said that I was getting real grown up. Then he
glared at Dallas and said that I should be with a man
not a boy.*

*I never like when Piney talks to me, but something
about how he sounded today really scared me. I pushed
closer to Dallas then told Piney to go away. Piney just
laughed and told me he ain't ever going to go too far
from me. Dallas stood and pulled me up. As we were
walking away, Piney started laughing and calling for
me to come back. Dallas told me to ignore him. He said
Piney is just a dirty, old fool.*

*I didn't say nothing, but the truth is that Piney may
be dirty and old, but he ain't no fool, and that scares
me. It scares me a whole lot.*

July 16, 1977

*Yesterday was Mama's birthday. I forgot. She reminded
me this morning. I told her that I was sorry, and I am
sorry. I'm sorry that I can't remember nothing anymore
except for the one thing I want to forget.*

*It sticks to my brain like a sore, oozing and seeping
into all the other parts until it feels like that's all there is
but I can't tell Mama. I can't tell no one.*

*Mama asked again this morning to braid my hair.
Again, I said no. She said I seem like I don't care about
nothing anymore. Not about her birthday. Not about*

how I look. Nothing. Mama's right, I don't. Caring costs too much.

Dallas came by today to give me a letter. He wants to know what's wrong. He wants to help, but how do I tell him that any roots that I grew have been cut? Sliced and ripped from me, caught and tangled, and tossed like garbage. There's nothing to hold me still and safe anymore. Now I'm just twisted and tied down to these mountains and ain't no one can do anything about that—no one.

August 19, 1977

These mountains have a hold of me and I'm so tangled that I can't find a place to cut loose. But I know...

"What? What do you know, Mama?" Lottie asked as she hurriedly flipped through the remaining pages, all of which were blank. Exhaling deeply, Lottie laid the diary in her lap. Pinching the corners of her eyes, she tried to clear her focus, now clouded from reading her mother's fine, small script.

Seeing how the sun cut low across the sky, Lottie knew she was late for dinner. "Damn!" she muttered. Picturing her granmom's clenched jaw and flared nostrils, Lottie jumped up, and as she did, the diaries tumbled to the ground. "Damn. Damn," Lottie grumbled as she quickly gathered up the books.

Frantically looking around, she whispered, "Where? Where?" Although Lottie desperately wanted to take the diaries with her, she knew that she could never keep them secreted from her grandmother's watchful eye. Taking a couple of quick steps forward, Lottie hesitated. She hated to put her greatest treasure in an outhouse. She knew her mother's words deserved better; her mother deserved better. She also knew her mother had been right; it was the best place.

Lottie swung open the outhouse door and carefully tucked the books, including the first one, back where she'd found them. After shutting the door, Lottie placed her hand on it and whispered, "I'll be back." Then, turning in the direction of her grandmother's house, Lottie ran home—the whole way.

Chapter Eighteen

Effie tapped her foot and clamped her hand on to her hip until her fingers dug into her skin. She was angry with the girl for being late, for being disrespectful, for scaring her. There wasn't a moment when Lottie was even a few minutes late that Effie didn't think it, worry about it, dread it, and pray it wasn't true. There were moments that Effie didn't take full breaths until her granddaughter walked through the door.

Effie paced. Short strides were all the tiny space of her kitchen allowed, so she moved in tight circles, waiting, wondering, and worrying. She stopped only to stir her now-bubbling stew and to glance at the clock, which seemed to taunt Effie with its quickly moving minutes. At the turn of her tenth lap, Effie abruptly changed direction and headed for the door. She stopped short of grasping the handle when she heard the unmistakable sound of Lottie's light footsteps. It was a soft and simple sound, which always caused Effie to inhale deeply as she realized, with great relief, that she could once again breathe.

Effie's fear and even her anger disappeared with the gentle breeze that blew in when the door opened, revealing an anxious Lottie, brow furrowed with worry and beaded with sweat. Seeing her granddaughter, Effie felt only relief and love. She wanted to extend her arms, pull the girl to her, and tell her that she loved her. Effie had wanted to do this many times, but she always steeled herself against the urge to do so, fearful that too much love would weaken Lottie's spirit. Effie knew the strength a woman needed up here in the mountains, not just to live here, but also to survive. So Effie chose to do what she always did—the best she could for Lottie.

Lips pursed and anger in her voice, Effie stomped her foot as she spit out every word, "Where have you been, girl?" Without allowing Lottie a chance to answer, Effie demanded, "Well? Where you been?" With barely a breath, Effie kept on, "You think you can just come and go as you please?"

Saying nothing, Lottie shook her head.

Encouraged by Lottie's silent agreement, Effie continued, "I'll tell you what, girl, it's best you be knowing right now that the sun don't rise and set on you." Even as Effie said the words, she knew in her heart that for her it wasn't true. For Effie, the sun didn't just revolve around Lottie, Lottie was the sun.

"Well, come on in. Dinner ain't going to get no better the longer it sits." Effie firmly placed her hand on Lottie's back and gently pushed her inside. "You go on now and get washed up."

Lottie took only two steps forward before turning back around to face her grandmother. "I'm sorry, Granmom. I really am."

Effie accepted Lottie's apology with a small nod and slight smile. Effie appreciated her granddaughter's words, but she found more reassurance in Lottie's sad eyes, because in them Effie saw that Lottie was still her girl. What Effie refused was that Lottie was quickly becoming more of a woman than a girl.

Lottie quietly came into the kitchen to see the table set with mismatched chipped bowls and different-sized spoons laid neatly beside them. A lopsided breadbasket filled with Effie's biscuits was placed in the center. Lottie sat down and waited for her uncles, who scrambled in from the porch at the sound of Effie's call to dinner. Frank, Gene, and Curtis took their places at the table, an order that hadn't changed since Lottie was old enough to sit among them.

Lottie's place was between her grandmother and her Uncle Curtis, for which she was grateful. What she hated was sitting across from Frank, whose glare so often bore into her that many nights Lottie saw more of her lap than the dinner table. Tonight, though, Lottie refused to look down. Instead she looked, carefully and deliberately, at each of them.

Lottie watched her grandmother, who, like a seasoned conductor, orchestrated the entire meal with only her ladle, her casual comments, and her quiet, indeterminable command. It was Effie's authority that Lottie had always admired, if not feared a little. "Stop staring. Start eating," Effie said.

Lottie took a sip as she watched Effie's hand gracefully dance back to her own spoon.

Watching Lottie, Frank turned his fork between his finger and thumb, over and over again. Slow, deliberate movements, movements that mirrored the twisting and turning he often felt inside. In his other hand, he gripped his butter knife too tightly, the cheap metal pressed into his palm, but he felt no pain; he felt nothing except anger. "Stupid girl," he hissed under his breath. Catching her eye, he scowled. Lottie quickly looked away. Frank grinned. He liked that she was afraid.

Feeling an elbow nudge his side, Frank jumped slightly and dropped his knife. "Damn it, Gene!" Frank muttered. Frank accepted his brother's apology even though with every "sorry" Gene uttered, Frank lost more respect for him. It was perhaps part of the reason that Frank didn't face him when, through clenched teeth, he demanded, "What the hell do you want?"

Even over the din of Effie and Curtis's conversation, Frank could hear Gene whisper, "I'm worried." Frank snorted with disgust.

In Frank's opinion, Gene worried when he thought the sky wasn't the right shade of blue. "We're fine," Frank said through gritted teeth.

Although it was a sure sign that Frank was finished talking, Gene rarely recognized it when his own fear gripped too tightly. "I'm serious, Frank. I ain't sure this was such a good idea."

Tired of his brother's hysterics, Frank hissed, "It's gonna fucking work. Now shut up!" Frank's words silenced everyone at the table.

It was a full two minutes before Effie, who had simply stared at Frank, spoke. "What's gonna work, Frank?"

Frank's eyes darkened. He said nothing.

Knowing the volatility of her son, Effie kept her voice steady as she asked again, "What's gonna work?"

Frank shrugged and casually offered, "Nothing, Ma."

With a mocking laugh, Effie returned, "Yep, that's usually what works. Nothing."

Looking down, Frank said under his breath, "Maybe for you."

Having the sharp ears of a mother, Effie scoffed and shot back, "I known you your whole life, boy, and I ain't see what's worked out so good for you."

Keeping his head low, Frank rolled his eyes up to meet his mother's and asked, "And whose fault is that?"

Feeling the sting of Frank's accusation, Effie stiffened her back and spit out, "The only back that should be hurting from carrying any burden of blame is yours, Frank Cashel Bilfrey. And I'll tell you what else. You start acting like the man you supposed to be instead of a whining little boy and maybe life gets a bit better."

Frank bit his lip.

Another victory, Effie thought, before quickly realizing how hollow both the win and the feeling of it were. Sipping her soup, she enjoyed the warmth that passed over her tongue, down her throat, and spread across her body, which felt cold from Frank's icy stares. Effie simply averted her eyes and wondered when it happened. When did speaking to her son become like a gunfight that only ended when one person was left standing? Only in the rare moments when Effie didn't look at Frank as an adversary to be fought and beaten but rather as a son to be protected and loved did she wish that it weren't so often it was she who was left standing.

Leaning close to his brother, Frank whispered, "Look, Genie, you can't go hunting bear and then get scared when you see one." Gene looked at Frank, who leaned back and shoved another spoonful of stew into his mouth, clearly indicating that was the only words of assurance he was going to give. Gene wasn't reassured.

Looking up, Gene locked eyes with Curtis, who shrugged his shoulders and awkwardly smiled. Suddenly Gene felt guilty for always rejecting Curtis, but by the end of the night Gene would realize that it was only in rejecting his brother that he saved him.

Even after Gene looked away, Curtis stared at his brother, closely studying his pinched face and glassy eyes. Gene was a curiosity to Curtis, because though he liked him far better than Frank, he understood him far less. No matter how he tried, Curtis couldn't work out how Gene, who was kinder by nature, willingly waded in the wreckage of Frank with no visible regard to himself. Curtis also couldn't understand how Gene never learned that the only way to truly stand is to stand on your own.

Lottie looked around the table. She studied her granmom's deep frown lines and her Uncle Frank's furrowed brow. She watched her Uncle Gene nervously tap his fingers on the table and her Uncle Curtis rub his thumb across his chin. Lottie knew these expressions and behaviors well, yet the familiarity of them now seemed strange. Each one no longer appeared to Lottie as her family but rather as butterflies caught in a net. Suddenly uneasy from the almost imperceptible feeling of change felt in the discordant quiet, Lottie keenly felt the fetters of her family as well as her own desperation to be free.

"I want to see the bottom of your bowl, girl," Effie said as she handed Lottie another biscuit. "You can use this to sop up what's left." Grateful for the interruption to her thoughts, Lottie took the biscuit without complaint. Surprised, Effie offered the butter. Lottie shook her head. "Well," Effie scoffed, "you ain't going to put any meat on your bones without some butter."

Effie was in a constant battle against the nature of Lottie's figure, which stayed thin regardless of the food Effie forced upon her granddaughter. Again yielding, Lottie held up her biscuit so that Effie could swipe a bit of butter on it.

"That's real good. You'll be real glad we plumped you up when it comes time to find a man. Men don't want no skinny girls with hard edges and sharp bones." Frank snidely added, "Ain't never seemed to hurt you none, Ma."

Trying to sound convincing, Effie flatly said, "No, ain't nothing can hurt me, Frank."

Always the peacekeeper, Curtis said, "I think both Mama and Lottie are real pretty."

Lottie smiled. Effie beamed.

"Kiss ass," Frank hissed. Gene laughed.

Ignoring his brothers, Curtis added, "She's only twelve. She don't need to worry about finding a man for a long time."

Lottie added, "If ever."

Snickering, Frank said, "Well, at least she knows it."

Boldly, Lottie looked right at her uncle and asked, "What is it that I know, Uncle Frank?"

Taken off guard by his niece's daring, Frank didn't answer.

Emboldened even more by his silence, Lottie said, "If I don't get a man it will be because I don't want one, not because some man don't want me." Lottie glanced admirably at her grandmother before adding, "Granmom's done just fine without a man."

Sarcastically, Frank shot back, "Having a man and keeping a man are two different things, little girl."

Fed up with Frank for hurting his mother and Lottie, Curtis pushed back his chair and growled, "Come on, let's go."

Frank, amused by his little brother's challenge, laughed and said, "Settle down."

With his chest puffed out, Curtis took a step forward and snapped, "I will not settle down, Frank, not this time. You always push too far."

Frank pushed back his chair and stood, but then he did what none of them expected. Frank looked at his mother then his niece before he said, "Okay. I'm sorry, okay?"

Effie leaned forward and asked, "How'd that feel?"

Frank grinned in spite of himself. "Rough. Real rough."
Then, in a rare but not completely uncommon moment in the
Bilfrey family, they all laughed.

Each was awkward at first, unaccustomed to the sound
and inexperienced at the action, but it wasn't long before the
room filled with their laughter, genuine and loud. The teasing
followed. "So, little brother, you was going to whip my ass,
huh?"

Curtis returned, "Yeah, I was. I still can."

Frank smirked, then elbowing Gene asked, "What
were you going to do? Pretend you weren't here?"

Gene stammered, "I had your back, Frank."

Lottie joined in. "My money was on Uncle Curtis."

Frank sniffed, "Well, that ain't no surprise. I always
took you for making a poor bet."

Lottie shrugged.

Pushing back Lottie's hair, Effie patted her granddaughter's shoulder and said, "Well, I know what was my
best bet."

Hearing his mother's rare words of praise reserved
only for Lottie, Frank looked at Effie. She could see the flash
of hurt in his eyes, but she chose, like always, to ignore it.

Frank turned back to his brothers and taunted, "You
know, Curtis, the last ass that got kicked was yours." Curtis
balled his fists and mocked taking a swing at Frank, whose
exaggerated duck bumped into Gene, who nearly toppled out
of his chair. Soon each brother tried to best the other with
hard pushes and quick swings.

Effie watched as her sons turned back to the boys she remembered. Once again, they were pups—tugging at one another, pushing, teasing, laughing, and loving. Effie smiled.

The boys, a mass of tangled legs and arms, didn't hear it at first, but Effie did. To her the loud knocking sounded like rapid gunfire. A familiar feeling gripped Effie's chest. Instinctively she placed her hand over her heart. Swallowing hard, she choked down her fear before she said, "Shush. Be quiet!" But there was no need for Effie's words, because no one made a sound as a fist again thudded against the door. Frank, Gene, and Curtis quickly untangled themselves from one another. Stumbling, each stood straight and still—waiting.

The next voice they heard was Roy Radley as he shouted, "Open up this damn door, Frank Bilfrey. Right now!"

Frank groaned, "Oh shit," as the color drained from Gene's face.

Before Curtis could open the door, Roy broke it down so that it swung open, nearly missing Lottie, who stood too close.

Curtis swiftly pushed his niece toward his mother before yelling at Roy, "What the hell are you doing? You could have hit her."

The door, which now hung crookedly on its broken hinge, framed the local cop, who the Bilfreys had known since he wore leg braces and stuttered. "This ain't none of your damn business, Curtis. I'm here for your brother." Pushing past Curtis, Roy glared at Frank before hissing, "You're under arrest, Frank Bilfrey." Roy took a step toward Frank, who took a step backward.

Effie, clutching Lottie, turned to Frank and shrieked, "What have you done, Frank?"

Never taking his eyes from Roy, Frank said, "It's okay, Ma. It's nothing."

Roy snickered, "That's a far way from the truth, Frank Bilfrey." Roy pulled his handcuffs from his belt. Effie gasped.

Shaking off Roy's attempt to cuff him, Frank, through gritted teeth, said, "You ain't gonna cuff me, you little shit." Still seeing Roy Radley as the weak boy he'd made cry on the playground for years, Frank underestimated Roy's power as he aimed his gun directly at Frank's chest.

Roy's fingers, white from clenching the grip too tightly, trembled, as did his voice. "We ain't seven no more, Frank. Now I'm gonna make *your* life hell, you son of a bitch."

Frank impulsively knocked his hand against Roy's arm, causing the gun to drop, sending a stray bullet flying. Lottie screamed. Frank forced Roy onto the ground, knocking over the table, as Effie shouted for him to stop. Her words hardly heard over the sound of dishes crashing to the floor. Gene, seeing his brother struggle, jumped on top of Roy, who thrust himself up, shouting, "Back up, back up," before Frank pushed him back down, laughing.

Frank didn't laugh long before three large, broad-backed policemen from Fayette pushed him hard to the ground and shouted, "Get down and stay down, asshole!"

Frank didn't move. No one moved. Pressing his knobby knee into Frank's back, Roy cuffed Frank's hands together.

The click was all anyone could hear until Effie, like a wounded animal, screeched, "What are you doing?" Her eyes wildly searched each cop's face. "Why? Why are you cuffing him?"

Roy grinned. Frank tried to answer, "It's a mistake, Ma. It's all a…" but his words were strangled by Roy, who placed his black boot across Frank's neck and pressed down.

Leaning over, Roy hissed, "Well, what do you make of this, Frank Bilfrey? Now it's me who's got my boot on your throat, you son of a bitch." Roy's shrill laughter filled the room for a brief moment before one of the Fayette cops pulled him up and shoved him toward the door. "We got this, Radley. Go home."

Humiliated, Roy kicked Frank in the ribs before storming out the door. Groaning, Frank grabbed his sides and rolled over. Again Effie shouted, "Why the hell are you arrestin' him? We got a right to know." Frantic, Effie screamed, "Someone tell me. Now!"

One of the bull-necked men roughly pulled Frank to his feet and said, "Frank Bilfrey, you are under arrest for the possession of marijuana and methamphetamine with the intent to sell."

Frank's rights were read, but no one in the room heard even one word above the sound of racing thoughts and pounding hearts.

Even though she shouldn't have been, Effie was shocked when another barrel-chested man turned to Curtis and growled, "You Gene Bilfrey?"

Wide-eyed, Curtis didn't get the chance to answer before Gene nervously said, "I am."

The cop roughly grabbed Gene's arms, pulled them up behind his back, and cuffed his wrists together. Effie's eyes shone with tears as she whimpered, "No! Not Gene."

Pushing Lottie from her arms, Effie ran toward him, pulling Gene to her as she glared at Frank. Looking to the man closest to her, she pleaded, "Don't take Gene. It's Frank's fault, just take Frank."

Frank, who had been struggling against the cop's tight grip of his arm, stopped. Dropping his head, he relented. Having taken his final blow, Frank no longer fought.

As Gene was led out the door, Frank shuffled behind his brother. Although he tried not to, Frank couldn't help taking one last look at his mother, who stood silent, offering him no words of comfort. Her arms stayed limp at her sides as she refused to reach for him. He knew by the shattered look in her eyes just as Effie knew by the dimmed look in his that she had extinguished the final bit of light in her son. Neither broke the other's gaze until Frank was pushed completely across the threshold, and it was only then that Effie fell to her knees.

Lottie ran across the glass-littered floor to her grandmother, falling beside her she wrapped her thin arms around Effie's neck. Effie, like a weak child, collapsed into them, and her head lolled on Lottie's tiny shoulder. "It's okay, Granmom. It's okay." Lottie soothed. In a singsong voice, Lottie repeated the words, but as she sat on the floor surrounded by broken dishes, staring at the overturned table, she didn't believe them.

Curtis ran after his brothers. Trying to crawl into the police car, he felt a boot kick against his head. With his eyes shut in blind determination, he kept pushing until one swift kick knocked him to the ground, where he lay panting and cursing. Looking up through teary eyes, he saw the boot belonged to his brother. Frank pulled his foot inside the car before the cop slammed the door shut, leaving the last Bilfrey boy alone in the dirt.

Squinting in pain, Curtis tried to focus on the car, but the spinning tires created a cloud of dust that cloaked all but the bumper. Seeing the sliver of silver fade from his sight, Curtis shook as he sobbed uncontrollably. Turning on his side, he spit out the thick dust choking him.

Pushing his now-exhausted body up, Curtis slowly stood.

Standing unsteady, he stared at the dark and empty road—the one that wound its way off this mountain. Taking a tentative step forward, Curtis whispered his sister's name as in a prayer for bravery, but no courage came. Turning toward the house, Curtis saw the dim light from the kitchen cast a soft glow across the worn path to the porch. Heaving a deep sigh, he turned and took it. His choice made, Curtis, sure-footed, climbed the three wooden steps. Picking up the broken screen door, Curtis laid it against its cracked frame before heading inside to try to put the rest of the pieces back together.

PART THREE

Chapter Nineteen

He stood behind the cover of a crooked oak, watching. He was always watching, waiting. Hiding in the shadows, he could, unseen, see her, and he liked what he saw. His eyes traced up her coltish legs of childhood, resting on her new womanly backside. The round softness teased him to seek out the other curves of her body with his eyes, which he greedily did. Imagining his mottled skin pressed against and into the whiteness of hers, he wiped away a thin line of sweat that beaded above his lip.

Even in the cool October air, his rawboned body felt hot. Pulling off his damp T-shirt, his fingers shook as he thought about what it would be like to pull off her clothes. Taking his eyes off of her for a moment, he closed them and pictured how he'd do it. His smile, thin-lipped and cruel, exposed the vulgarity of his thoughts. Staring at her once more, his gaze lingered on her body's hollows secreted by her clothes and a young girl's modesty. He hungrily smacked his lips—a sound that echoed to her ears, causing her to turn.

"Hello?" Lottie cautiously offered to the otherwise stillness of the afternoon.

He quickly hid his body, angular and gaunt, behind another tree. Keeping his gaze fixed on her, he was determined to do it right this time. Right meant biding his time; right meant not getting caught. He quivered with anticipation as his heart raced and his head ached with too many thoughts, bad thoughts that tormented him even as they excited him.

He pressed his dirty hands against the trunk of the tree as he tried to steady himself, willing his feet to stay still, even as the curves and bends of her body begged him to run forward. Then, watching as she wrapped her delicate arms around her small waist, he was tempted to feel those arms around him. His breath caught as he choked down his desires, his needs. Having to swallow his cravings caused bile to rise from his stomach, burning his throat and filling his mouth with the taste of rage.

He could clearly see her games. The way she baited him just as her mother had, both pretending that they knew nothing of their beauty, leading him on with a turn of their shoulder or a hint of a smile. It sickened him. She sickened him. His hand tightened and clenched into a fist. Determined to show her what happens to little girls who play grown-up games, he stepped out from behind the tree and walked into the clearing, where she stood unaware.

As he stepped closer, the memory of the time he'd touched Sarah flooded over him. Remembering the soft feel of her skin, young and smooth, calmed him. He stopped suddenly as the scent of lavender filled his flared nostrils. It was soothing but not near as sweet as the smell of her fear that fed his hunger more than any caress of her body ever could. He wondered if Lottie's fear would smell the same.

Startled by the sound of his footsteps, Lottie gasped. Turning, she said, "Piney?"

He grinned. It was neither kind nor reassuring. "Yep," he answered, his voice guttural and his eyes dark.

"Wh-what are you doing here?" Lottie stammered, taking a tentative step back.

Piney shook his head, his smile sinister as he hissed, "I could ask you the same thing, girl."

Lottie took another step away from him as she said timidly, "I was just talking a walk."

Piney sneered, "Next to your mama's old shit house?" Stepping closer to her, he added, "What you up to, girl? You hiding something?"

Fearing he knew her secret, Lottie faltered as she tried to answer, "N-no."

Piney slithered closer, and pressing his mouth close to her ear, he whispered, "You don't sound so sure, girl."

Feeling his hot breath against her ear, Lottie turned her face, but Piney just moved closer. Then he raised his boney arms and pressed his palms against the outhouse wall so that Lottie, much to her horror, was trapped. The stench of corn whiskey and stale cigarettes filled Lottie's nose, causing her stomach to turn.

Feeling like she was going to retch, Lottie twisted and ducked beneath Piney's arms so that she was temporarily free from his reach. Her involuntary need to vomit caused her body to contort as she bent forward, feeling her stomach contract violently. Lottie dry heaved until her throat and eyes burned with the effort. Each failed attempt to expel the sick feeling caused Piney to howl with laughter. Lottie gasped, fresh air filling her lungs, taking away her nausea but not her fear. Exhausted, Lottie dropped to the ground and lay in the cool grass. Innocent, Lottie failed to understand that this was a position of weakness.

Piney, seeing her sprawled on the ground before him like an offering—a gift—ceased laughing. Lying before him, Lottie was a tangle of beautiful limbs with a delicate face framed by those familiar wild curls. Piney slowly licked his dry lips, feeling his mouth water. The same way it did when, hungry, he smelled food and longed for the first bite. Piney knew he needed to be patient; he needed to wait. But there were so few moments when Lottie was alone.

Piney gnashed together his remaining tar-stained teeth. "Never alone, always with that haggard bitch or that weak-ass boy," he muttered under his breath. He angrily thought of all the times he was forced to wait, only able to watch hidden in the shadows. Piney had spent months, years, not being able to satisfy his craving, and he felt it—the depth of it—now more than ever. Balling his hands into tight fists, rage reddening the deep hollows of his gaunt face, Piney decided he was done waiting. Taking a determined step forward, he loomed over the now-defenseless Lottie as she, like a helpless animal, lay waiting for what was now inescapable.

She was afraid. He knew it. He could smell it, feel it. Leaning over, he wanted to see it. He wanted to see her eyes, terror-filled and waiting. But when Piney looked, he didn't just see fear, he also saw fight. He knew in that moment that Lottie wouldn't give up easily, but he also knew that he wouldn't either. "You look real pretty lying there like that," Piney said.

More than his words, it was his honeyed voice that terrified Lottie, who instinctively sat up and wrapped her arms tightly around herself.

"What's the matter, girl? You afeard?" Piney taunted.

"No! I'm not afraid at all," Lottie lied. She pushed herself back, but Piney blocked her from standing.

"You think I'm just an old man, huh? And you not afeard of an old man?" Piney hissed.

"Wh-why should I be afraid?" Lottie asked, her stammering betraying her effort to seem brave.

"I can think of lots of reasons," Piney snickered. Then, with his bare foot, black from rarely being washed, he slowly ran the tip of his toes across Lottie's leg. She shuddered; the feeling of his touch repulsed her. Piney knew it, and it excited him more.

"I think me and you could have ourselves a real good time," Piney said as his body swayed slightly, somewhat from the whiskey, more so from his urges. Piney groaned as he bent his knees, stiff with arthritis. Now squatting close to Lottie, he could smell the sweetness of her, and he wanted a taste. Piney locked his eyes on Lottie. Her mother's eyes looked back at him, and in that moment, Piney knew that Lottie was his.

"My uncle will be coming real soon. He was gonna meet me here."

Piney's grin grew. "Oh, I don't think so."

Lottie's voice quivered as she said, "He *is* coming. He'll be here any minute."

Piney slowly rocked back and forth as he stared toward the sky for a few minutes. Then, taunting her, he said, "Still not here." Snapping his fingers, he said, "Not this minute." Snap. "Not this minute." Snap. "Not this minute."

Scowling, Lottie said, "Those aren't minutes. They're seconds."

Piney stopped abruptly. "You real sassy, ain't ya, girl? Your mama was sassy. But I gots myself some ways to take that sass right out of a smart-mouthed girl." Piney snickered then added, "Your mama found that out." Smirking, Piney sunk back onto his heels.

"Mama?" Lottie soundlessly mouthed as an intense fear gripped her entire body making her feel as though she couldn't breathe. Intrigued, Piney watched as Lottie tugged at her throat. So focused on her thin, delicate neck, he didn't see the small heel of her hard-soled shoe until it hit him. Instinctively grabbing between his legs, Piney pitched forward in excruciating pain. The agony, intense and far-reaching, rendered him helpless. For the next few minutes, he rolled back and forth while moaning loudly. In between the groans of pain, he shouted at her, "You bitch! You worthless little bitch!"

He didn't know when she managed to scramble to her feet, but he could see that Lottie was now standing, stock-still and tall, above him. All he wanted was to get to his feet and make her hurt like he did. He wanted to hit her, torture her, ruin her. While trying to get to his knees, a searing sensation swiftly sent him onto his back where he lay spitting out vulgarities and threats, paralyzing Lottie with fear.

Even through his red-rimmed and watery eyes, Piney could see that she regretted her bold action. Piney swayed unsteadily as he walked toward Lottie, wanting nothing more than to make her suffer, but with each step he made closer to her, she took another step back. Determined to catch her, Piney took two quick strides forward, causing him to nearly topple. Trying not to fall, he grabbed Lottie, who pulled away and pressed herself against the wall of the outhouse.

Turning so that her mouth was close to the rotted whitewashed boards, she whispered, "Help me, Mama."

Even over his curses, Piney heard. "That's right, girl." Piney snickered before adding, "If you was gonna find your mama anywhere, it would be in a shit house. She weren't never worth much more than that."

Hearing Piney's vicious words, Lottie shuddered and held tighter to the sides of the outhouse.

Finally righting himself, Piney moved toward Lottie with slow, predatory steps.

Frozen with fear and having no other choice, she stood still, holding her breath as she prayed. Again Lottie could feel Piney's hot, rancid breath on her cheek as he whispered, "I still don't see that uncle of yours." Wrapping a loose strand of her hair around his finger, he pressed his lips close to her ear and said, "Just me and you, girl. Alone."

With his body close to hers, Piney could feel Lottie's slight frame tense as every muscle tightened; her dread excited him. No longer able to control his lecherous impulses, Piney pinned Lottie against the outhouse before roughly running his hand up her thigh.

Lottie winced, but Piney didn't release the pressure on her shoulder, nor did he stop his hands from wandering over her body. Horrified and desperate, she pleaded, "Please, Mr. Boyer. Please. Please stop."

Even though Piney had touched no more than her trembling limbs, he did stop. He pulled back. Looking into her eyes, he saw the same flecks of gold that used to dance in her mother's.

Piney laughed. As Lottie demanded, "What's so funny?" Piney howled, holding his side as he laughed harder. Lottie screeched, "Why are you laughing? Tell me! Why are you laughing? Stop it!" Lottie's voice rose to a pitch that scared her more than the sound of Piney's wretched laughter. Abruptly, Piney stopped. His mouth became a tight, straight line drawn on a face now drained of any previous amusement.

"You want to know why I was laughing, girl? I was laughing 'cause I think it's funny how folks find their manners when they is afeard."

As Lottie shook her head, Piney roughly grabbed her jaw and physically stopped her protests as he hissed, "Don't you go disagreein'. You ain't ever called me Mr. Boyer." Looking around, Piney added, "But with no granmommy or uncle to protect you, I'm Mr. Boyer."

Scared and exhausted, Lottie begged, "Please. Please let me go home. Please just let me go home."

Now Piney shook his head. "No. I don't think so. I gots other plans for you, girl." Then, with his voice gravelly and his words vulgar, he said things to Lottie that caused her skin to crawl with disgust and her heart to race with panic.

Blood pumped fast through her veins, pounding against her eardrums so that she couldn't hear him. She couldn't hear the crackle of dried sticks and leaves or the primal scream as he ran toward her. All she heard was the low, guttural sound of Piney moaning as Curtis ripped him away from her. Pushing the old man to the ground, Curtis straddled him, fell to his knees, and beat him until his own fists became bloodied and sore.

"Stop it! Stop it! Stop it, Uncle Curtis!" Lottie screamed as she grabbed a fistful of her uncle's T-shirt, pulling and pleading until he finally relented. Worn out, Curtis leaned over and rolled onto his back so that he lay next to Piney who, knocked out, lay lifeless. Lottie cautiously stepped closer to him before nervously asking, "Is he dead?"

Turning to look, Curtis shoved the tip of his boot into Piney's ribs, causing him to groan. Lottie jumped. Curtis sighed and said, "Nope. Not dead."

Feeling her chest constrict with fear, Lottie grabbed her uncle's arm. Pulling hard as she stepped back, she said, "Come on, Uncle Curtis, let's go."

Aching and not quick to stand, Curtis pulled back on his arm, causing Lottie to panic.

Lottie shouted, "Please, Uncle Curtis. I want to go. I want to go now!"

Getting to his feet, Curtis carefully and loosely laid his arm across his niece's shoulders before saying, "Okay, Lottie. Okay." Turning slightly, he kicked Piney in the side one last time before saying quietly, "Let's go home."

Chapter Twenty

Curtis tried at first to dust off the dirt from his arm, but it stubbornly stuck smeared across his pale skin. Licking his palm, he furiously rubbed his skin, but still the thick red clay stuck. Distracted only for a moment, Curtis turned his attention back to Lottie, who stayed close to his side. "Are you okay?" With her eyes set forward, Lottie kept walking. "Lottie. Are you okay?" Again, she didn't answer. Panicked, Curtis grabbed her arm and, nearly shouting, asked, "Are you okay!"

Shaking loose his grip, Lottie slowly nodded and kept pace. Curtis quickened his stride, stepping in front of her to stop her. "Do you know what could have happened back there? Do you know how bad it could have been?"

Dropping her head, Lottie mumbled, "Yeah, I know."

Unsatisfied, Curtis said, "He's bad, Lottie. Piney Boyer is really bad and…"

Jerking her head up, Lottie yelled, "I know! I was the one underneath him as he tried to rape me! Just like he…just like…" Lottie stammered before collapsing into tears.

Curtis wrapped his arms around his niece. Shuddering, she folded into his arms and sobbed. Ashamed of his outburst, Curtis gently rubbed her back and said, "I'm sorry, Lottie. Please don't cry."

Pulling back from her uncle, Lottie sniffed, wiped her eyes, and straightened up. "It's okay. I'm okay."

Trying to hug her, Curtis reached out only to have Lottie sidestep away and start walking again. "Lottie?"

Without turning, Lottie said, "It's okay, I just want to go home."

The two walked together in silence for a while before Curtis softly said, "I shouldn't have let you go."

Without looking in his direction, Lottie said, "I wanted to go, Uncle Curtis. I wanted to sit on my mom's porch. I wanted some time alone. You and Granmom haven't left my side since the trial." The day Frank and Gene were sentenced—the day they were *all* sentenced—was jarred loose from Curtis's memory.

He'd sat on a hard wooden bench in the courthouse next to his mother pleading with God to save them, but after a swift deliberation, the judge sentenced them both to five years in a state prison without parole. The words, clipped and final, didn't just determine Frank's and Gene's fate; it determined the fate of all of them. Curtis no longer prayed.

"Uncle Curtis?" Interrupting Curtis's thoughts, she said, "Are you okay?"

Curtis nodded. "I was just thinking about that day."

Lottie sighed, "It was a bad day."

Curtis agreed, "A really bad day."

Lottie stopped. Pointing her toe, she made little circles in the dirt and asked, "Why didn't Granmom cry that day?"

Curtis shrugged.

Lottie said, "I know she never cries, but I thought for sure she would when they put the chains on them."

Curtis pictured his brothers, who had shrunk beneath the shackles looking ashamed and scared.

Walking again, Lottie asked, "Do you remember that old bailiff?" Curtis nodded. "What did he say to Granmom?"

Curtis shrugged again. "When?"

Lottie explained, "After Uncle Frank and Uncle Gene were taken away and everyone left. This old bailiff came over to Granmom and whispered something."

Curtis lied, "I didn't hear." But he had heard. Curtis was so close he could feel the man's neatly pressed pants brush against his arm as he told his mother that the pain would go away, but Curtis couldn't tell Lottie something he knew wasn't true—the pain never goes away.

Lottie fidgeted with her fingers before nervously asking, "Where were you?"

Confused, Curtis asked, "When?"

Taking a deep breath, Lottie said timidly, "Before. When I was...when Piney..."

Feeling guilty, Curtis mumbled, "I was at Ernest Weddell's. Frank set me up with a job." Knowing his reason fell short, Curtis explained, "I really thought you would be okay. I just went to get my check."

Lottie grabbed her uncle's arm. "Uncle Curtis, it isn't your fault. I'm not blaming you. It was my fault. I should have—"

Curtis interrupted, "No! Lottie, you are not to blame. Piney Boyer is a sicko."

Looking into Curtis's eyes, Lottie said, "He should be stopped."

Seeing the cold-edged determination in her eyes scared Curtis, who gently scolded, "Don't you even think it, Lottie. Do you hear me?"

Turning away, she nodded. Pulling her back around, Curtis pleaded, "Please, Lottie. Don't ever go near that man again, okay?"

Hesitating for a minute, Lottie said, "Okay."

After a few more minutes in silence, they neared home. Suddenly anxious, Lottie said, "Don't tell Granmom. Okay?"

"Lottie, I don't know. I think it would be good if—"

Frantic, she begged, "Please, Uncle Curtis. Please don't tell her. I just want to forget this, and if she knows then she is going to start asking questions and following me. I will never have a minute alone. Please!"

Not wishing to upset her more, Curtis agreed.

Still not reassured, Lottie said, "Promise."

Reluctantly, Curtis said, "I promise."

Taking a deep breath, she said gratefully, "Thank you, Uncle Curtis."

Curtis shuddered as the image of Lottie pinned against the outhouse flashed before him as if he were still standing at the edge of his sister's yard, looking past the clearing to see Lottie struggling, her long limbs flailing, helpless as Piney pressed against her. Soundless, inside his mind, Curtis asked himself why. Why were they each pulled back to that overgrown patch of land and crumbling shack over and over again? Maybe, Curtis thought, he and his mother and Lottie were not going to find Sarah. Maybe they were going to find themselves—the parts that were still good, unbroken, and worth saving.

As they neared the yard, Lottie's eyes widened when she saw her granmom pulling weeds. Grabbing her uncle's arm, she said, "You promised, Uncle Curtis." Curtis nodded, but he wondered silently if in giving Lottie what she wanted he was failing to give her what she needed.

His eyes darkened and his fists clenched as he thought of how he had failed her and her mother. Curtis looked at his own mother and then down at his arm. This time, however, he didn't try to scrub it clean, because he knew that this mountain mud had stained more than his skin—it had stained his soul.

Chapter Twenty-One

With her knees sunk deep in the dirt, Effie leaned back and stretched. Pushing her fist into her lower back, she tried to loosen the knots that tightened her muscles after more than an hour of pulling weeds. Even in the chilly October air sweat beaded on Effie's forehead, which she wiped with the back of her hand as she took in a deep breath. The musky smell of wet leaves and crisp earthy air filled her lungs. Exhaling, she admired her work. "You did good, old girl," Effie whispered to herself. Effie wasn't sure why she'd decided to weed now. After all, she could feel winter's bitter curl just beneath the warmer air, and she knew soon it would all be covered in snow, but she persisted.

Turning, she looked at the large pile of sow thistle at her side. For a moment, she admired its prickly and determined nature. Then, careful not to pierce her fingers, she gathered it into a loose bundle. Walking to the edge of the yard, she tossed it into the woods. Satisfied that she'd set order, Effie took quick, confident steps back to the house. She was almost to the porch when she saw Curtis and Lottie. Effie's stride instinctively slowed and her smile faded before it fully formed. She wasn't sure if it was the darkness that rested in her son's eyes or the emptiness in her granddaughter's, but something pulled at Effie's body so hard that every step forward became slow and painful.

Even with her leaden legs and heavy heart, she finally managed to stand before them. Wordless, she asked a thousand questions with a look they both knew too well. Lottie, unable to answer even one, simply turned and walked into the house; the soft bang of the screen door against the frame punctuated her silence. Without even the slightest effort to stop her, Effie watched her go inside. Then, turning to her son, she asked, "What happened?"

Her tone was even and calm, but just underneath was a panic untamed and boundless. She knew Curtis heard it when he answered, "Nothing, Ma. It's nothing."

Disbelieving and more fearful, Effie said, "It ain't nothing. I saw the look in that girl's eyes."

Curtis said flippantly, "Ain't no telling with girls that age."

Knowing it was an act, Effie stepped closer to her son and said softly, "I see the look in your eyes."

Curtis lowered his head and mumbled, "I'm just tired, Ma."

Recognizing her disadvantage, Effie was careful not to press too hard. Gently she said, "There's been enough pain, Baby Curtis."

Effie didn't know if it was with defeat or disappointment that Curtis shook his head before asking, "So why bring more?"

Effie now knew she had reason to be afraid; her fear wore at the edges of her calm and patience. Her voice rose as she answered, "Because I don't want none of mine suffering if I can help it."

Curtis's strangled laugh made Effie uneasy. "But that's just it, Ma, you can't help it. Frank, Gene…" Curtis paused before adding, "Sarah. You can't help it."

Effie's hand reflexively covered her cheek as though slapped. "Curtis?" Effie said, feeling desperate both for answers and now also for comfort.

Recognizing her pain, Curtis softened and whispered, "Let it rest, Ma. Just let it rest."

Stunned by her son's quiet determination, Effie said nothing as she watched Curtis turn and walk silently into the house.

Alone, Effie felt her panic take a sharp turn toward terror. Her breaths were rapid and shallow as her eyes darted from one flowerbed to the next. She was frantically seeking reassurance, which she surprisingly found in the neat rows of blooms unfettered from the thorny stalks and stems that threatened to smother them. No matter where Effie's eyes rested, she saw flowers pruned and perfect in their soil. She found order. She found calm. Effie's breathing slowed; her fear fell softly. She nodded proudly, knowing she'd created this. A slight breeze encouraged the pale colors to dance, and as each petal freely shifted in its desired direction, Effie felt ashamed. It wasn't enough. Guilty, Effie knew she hadn't helped—not with what mattered.

Laying her palm against her breastbone, Effie felt for it even though she knew it would be there; it was always there. The smooth stem lay softly against her chest even as the metal bit pressed small indents into her skin. Effie had worn it on a long, cheap chain since her father died. She was always careful to keep it hidden beneath her clothes. The effort to keep it secreted was outmatched only by her effort to hide the past it unlocked. Effie's fingers slowly slid up the chain, following the links until she felt the small clasp. She unhooked it, quickly cupped her hand, and caught the key before it fell. Grasping it tightly, Effie kneeled down by the edge of the porch and examined it. An old skeleton key, it was plain and slightly rusted. Effie smiled in spite of herself, thinking how she wasn't so different from it.

After thirty-one years of wearing the key, Effie had taken it off only in the few times that she'd needed to keep its existence a secret. Having rested in the hollow of her breasts for more than half her life, the key had imprinted itself onto more than Effie's skin, becoming a part of her. Suddenly Effie felt unsettled. Before she could have second thoughts, she slipped the key into her pocket and leaned forward until she lay flat on her stomach. Then, shifting her weight from one side of her body to the other, Effie slowly scooched until she was halfway under the porch. Stretching her arm forward, she blindly felt for the familiar steel box. Its discovery was met with Effie's small groan as the sharp edges cut her fingers. Carefully pulling the box to her as she shimmied her way from underneath the porch, Effie didn't notice the small droplets of blood that dotted the dirt. She saw nothing but the box.

Its small rectangular size belied its significance. Effie held it for a moment, inspecting the sides, the top, and the bottom. The one side was dented, but it always had been. The corners were corroded, Effie guessed from years of rainwater seeping through the porch slats and soaking the ground. After turning the box round several times, Effie was satisfied that it had not been found. Her examination of it ended in disappointment when Effie saw that the latch was perfectly preserved. There was no reason not to open it even though there were a thousand reasons.

Effie shut out each of these reasons as she slid the key from her pocket. Then she loosely held the key's bow so that it swung lightly between her thumb and finger. Even though the hypnotic swaying caused Effie's eyes to blur, she could still see that the key cast no gleam. Effie believed the setting sun or the tarnished metal was the reason the key didn't reflect the light but rather swallowed it until it was merely a small shadow hanging silently from her fingertips. Shrugging off the possibility it was more, Effie slipped the key into the lock. Before turning it, Effie thought how a skeleton key seemed most fitting to unlock the box that held the bones of her past.

The soft click of the lock reverberated through Effie's soul, shaking loose everything that she'd spent years keeping close. She lifted the lid slowly, then taking in the deepest of breaths, she closed her eyes and waited. She waited for her fear to pass; she waited for her courage to come. When neither happened, she simply exhaled and looked.

There wasn't much lying at the bottom of the steel box, but what was within held great significance, even if only to Effie. She lifted the first item from its cavernous home. Taking it gently in her hands, she turned it round and round, smiling as she remembered the first time she held the leather collar. He'd been so happy to give it to her yet so sad to let it go. She recalled how he held on to it even after he'd placed it in her hands. Uncomfortable, she'd kept her fingers loose until he gently released his grasp. It was only then that Effie traced her finger over the rough cuts made deep in the leather.

"Tom," she whispered as she slowly looked up at Mr. Goodwin.

His eyes glistened with the threat of tears as he nodded and said, "He was a good dog. Loyal. Strong. Better than most folks."

Effie understood. She knew that although seemingly ordinary, the collar was special, and so she treasured it beyond anything she'd ever been given.

Effie's fingers tingled with the remembrance of Sunset's downy fur as she put the collar around his neck. He didn't pull away or turn his head in protest, rather he stood still and allowed her to claim him. The dog seemed to know that the collar wasn't a means of owning him but rather a measure of loving him. And Effie did—with all her heart.

Holding the worn collar against her cheek, Effie closed her eyes and allowed thirty-five years to melt away. Behind her softly pressed lids, she was again the young girl, optimistic and hopeful, full of expectation and waiting, not the woman defeated and full of dread. Her legs twitched with memories of running up hills and across fields with Sunset in full stride beside her. Her arms relaxed as she remembered stretching them around the dog's warm neck. Effie didn't feel fear or panic, just love. She'd settled into that feeling of love when the memory—unexpected and terrifying—of her father killing her beloved dog ripped through her as though she, too, had been shot.

Overcome, Effie opened her eyes wide; she flung the collar back into the box. Its metal clasp clinked against the steel bottom. The low and simple sound hollowed out Effie's soul. Tentatively, she peered into the box and immediately saw the source of her pain. It wasn't the collar but rather what lay next to it—still, silent, deadly. Effie's fingers shook as she slowly reached in and picked it up. Her breaths shallow, her hands shaking, she studied her father's .22 pistol with both awe and disgust.

Carefully turning the gun over in her hands, Effie recalled her father's pride every time he held it. He loved the gun most when he was drunk. Unfortunately, he was drunk most of the time. Revulsion rose within Effie as she remembered how her father's unsteady hands would slip, causing the barrel to point wildly in all directions—even hers. Effie shook loose these thoughts as she examined this same gun, which now lay in her own unsteady hands.

The grip was a laminated wood that shone like a fine mahogany table, no chips or cracks. There were a few scratches, but Effie noticed only the one that ran down the side of the barrel to the chamber like a vein running to the heart of the gun. Tracing the deep line scored into the metal, Effie could feel the pulse of the gun's power to both destroy and save.

Effie gently wrapped her fingers around the grip then tightened them until her knuckles whitened with the pressure. Raising the pistol, she looked through the iron sights. Even though Effie's vision was limited to the scope of the gun's sight line, she suddenly felt as though she could see everything more clearly. She slowly lowered the gun and laid it on her lap. Smiling bitterly, she finally knew why she'd kept it.

So small, Effie thought as she looked down at the .22 pistol resting on her leg. Yet she knew that despite its size, it was deceptively powerful. She'd seen that firsthand when one of its bullets ripped through her dog, killing him and destroying the part of her that trusted and truly loved.

Effie's head throbbed with the memory of the loud crack in the silence as the gun was fired. Her leg trembled; the gun teetered. Setting it on the ground beside her, Effie held her head in her hands as she waited for the pounding to stop. As the memory receded, the pain subsided, but only in her head, never in her heart, which always ached.

She stared sideways at the gun, and fear once again coursed through Effie's body. Having lived with it for far too long, it was a terror she knew well. Familiarity with this panic formed when she was just a young girl watching in horror as this same gun dangled in the hands of her drunken father. Tortured almost nightly with the deadly possibilities, Effie cowered now as she had then against a force she couldn't fight. Older and stronger, Effie knew she could fight now if only she knew what she was fighting.

Effie picked up the gun once more and cradled it in her hands. The weight of it pressing against her palm sent a sensation like an electric current up the length of her arm. The strange feeling stretched across her chest and back, then ran to her head, which began to buzz with a new consciousness.

Entombed memories, shadowy and dark, swiftly unraveled from their tangled graves. Every cell in Effie's brain seemed to kindle with a painful remembrance that she believed she'd buried long ago. Her ears rang as though pierced with the sound of a gunshot. Effie's breath quickened, and her heart ached, as to her horror she was once more in that moment—that terrible, haunting, life-altering moment.

Curling her back so that her head lay close to her lap, Effie closed her eyes. Without option, she allowed herself to be abruptly and rapidly pulled back into the past. Years like seconds disappeared so that Effie was once again seventeen. Slight with a small waist and slender arms, a young Effie moved with an effortless grace. Her skin, unblemished and bright, appeared almost translucent against her raven-colored hair, which flowed in rivulets down her narrow back. She wasn't beautiful, but she was pretty.

She possessed the kind of loveliness that is easily afforded in youth and blossoms in innocence. Effie's girlhood had not been easy, but life's cruelty hadn't set upon her hard enough to rob her of her natural beauty. Effie was aware of her attractiveness but never so much as to forget her kindness. In the few times that she'd allowed herself to think of it, she'd wondered if it was because of this that he'd targeted her. Effie had caught the attention of men before, but it had always been the harmless smiles and winks of young boys. So, when he boldly flirted with her—held his hand on her arm too long, touched the small of her back—Effie wasn't sure how, but she knew it was wrong.

Charles Derrick wasn't grown in mountain soil and held little regard for those who had been, including Effie Bilfrey. To him, she was a flower—pretty and wild—to pick, to hold, and to disregard. She'd caught his eye only days after he settled into Talon Ridge. Twenty-three, arrogant, and with too much power, he'd been sent from North Carolina to work as a manager in the Ghost Creek Mines. His job was to oversee the miners who'd started to agitate over what Derrick called trifles like too little pay, too much work, and too many deaths.

Discord deep as the mines had always existed between the men and owner, Robert Jeffers, but fear of losing their jobs quieted the men's complaints. Tension like strings pulled too taut held the men together even as it tore them apart. In the moment when they could have divided, Euston Clarence, who feared being broken more than being broke, decided that they deserved more. It took only a few more brave or foolish men, including Effie's father, before they were united in their unrest and their determination. So it was Charles Derrick among others who were sent to settle the conflict, bring order, and restore peace. He did none of this.

The darkness of early morning shrouded Effie and her father as they sat at their kitchen table. With little food and even less to say, they sat in silence until Eugene laid his gun on the table and slid it toward her. Then, in a voice raspy from coal soot and smoking, said, "Take it."

Afraid, Effie shook her head and pulled back her hand.

Clearing his throat, Eugene snapped, "I said take it, girl. Now take it!"

Without picking it up, Effie slowly placed her hand over the cold steel and waited.

Her gesture was enough to calm down Eugene, who said more softly, "It's gettin' rough. You may need it."

Effie nodded and prayed to God she wouldn't.

On her father's orders, Effie walked two miles into town that afternoon. The sky was clear, and the air cold. The bare trees provided no protection from the November wind, which cut across them and through Effie. Pushing her hands deep into the pockets of her threadbare coat, Effie replayed her father's instructions in her mind. She didn't want to get it wrong. Under her breath, she repeated each step: "Go to the manager's office, and ask for Eugene Bilfrey's check, and then..." Effie crinkled the paper in her fingers before adding, "Hand him the paper." Nervous, she repeated, "Hand him the paper."

Effie was worried it wouldn't work, and she knew no paycheck meant no food. Even though Eugene drank most of his paychecks, he always set back some so that he and Effie could eat. Lately, though, the liquor seemed to be stealing more than just his soul, Eugene was now losing his sense. Effie wasn't sure where her father spent all the money; she only knew that she often had to make a potato and little else last for days. It wasn't until that morning that a sober Eugene, with an unlit cigarette wobbling in his unsteady hands, saw what he always missed when he was drunk—the hollows beneath his daughter's eyes and the sharp angles of her jaw. In that brief moment he felt what a father should feel, and in doing so he did what he thought a father should do. He signed a paper, giving Effie permission to pick up all his paychecks. Ashamed, all he asked in barely a whisper was that she bought him a few bottles.

As Effie neared the manager's office, she remembered her father's warning, and she knew from the talk in town that it was true. The miners had spent the previous few days refusing to work, which only fueled the manager's determination to keep them in their place. It hadn't become violent—yet. Effie worried that they would refuse her the check as another means of punishment. Trying to stay focused, she calculated the lost wages. Her stomach rumbled; she hoped there would be enough.

When she stepped inside the small building, she was briefly grateful for the warmth before feeling choked with the longing to leave. Standing behind the narrow counter, she waited patiently for a stout man, with bulging eyes and a dirty, cheap clip-on tie, to help her.

"What?" he snarled.

Pushing the paper toward him, Effie quietly said, "I'm here to pick up my daddy's pay."

The man snatched the paper. Taking a large mouthful of food, he looked it over as he chewed loudly. Then, without argument, he handed her an envelope. Relieved, Effie smiled.

"Don't get too excited, girl. It ain't going to buy you much."

Effie tucked the money into her pocket and quickly left.

As promised, Effie's first stop was Wilfred's Spirits and Drink. It was nothing more than a dilapidated lean-to run by an old man drunker than most of his patrons. Seeing the grizzled, white-haired man, Effie was surprised by his dirty coveralls and unwashed face. After all, Wilfred could own the town with the money he made selling corn whiskey and watered-down vodka to the miners every Friday afternoon. Wilfred, who was missing his front teeth, smiled and lisped, "What can I do for you, pretty lady?"

Pulling out a few dollars, Effie answered, "Two bottles, please."

With one gnarled hand, he took the cash, and with the other waved her toward the shelves, "Lots of choices, pretty lady. Pick 'em."

Effie stepped closer to the bottles and, with no experience, asked, "Which one is best?"

Comically tilting his head, Wilfred scratched his chin and said, "Hmm, ain't never been asked that before. Well, this here vodka make ya not care about your problems, and this here corn whiskey make ya forget ya got any at all." Wilfred snorted, laughing at his own joke.

Effie smiled politely then considered her father's life for a moment before grabbing the corn whiskey. "Good choice," Wilfred said as he dropped the bottle into a brown paper bag. "Now get yourself home, pretty lady. Gonna be dark after not too long and ain't no place for a young girl with all this foolishness going on."

Pulling her coat tightly around her, Effie nodded and headed outside.

Grateful for the fresh air, Effie walked quickly in the direction of home. She knew better than to count the cash now, but she was sure she would have enough to buy some real food. Daydreaming about fresh biscuits and eggs, Effie didn't hear him. It wasn't until his footsteps became so close, falling in time with hers, that she looked over her shoulder and saw him. He smiled; she didn't. In a few quick strides, he caught up to her and said, "I saw you walking down this here empty road all alone, and I thought you could use some company."

Tall and broad-shouldered with a chiseled jaw and a shock of black hair, Charles Derrick was handsome. There was something about him, though, that filled Effie with a fear not unlike what she felt when her father drunkenly held his gun too close to her.

Never losing step, she shook her head. "I'm fine. It's not far."

Leering at her, he said, "I know where you live. I am staying real near there."

Keeping her eyes straight ahead, Effie didn't answer.

"I'm staying at the Boyer place. I'm in the cabin closest to the woods," Derrick said. Then, laying his hand on Effie's arm, he suggestively added, "With no one around, I can do whatever I want."

Effie recoiled as though bitten. Not saying a word, she quickened her step.

Derrick walked faster to keep her pace. Winded, he panted, "Hey, slow down a bit. There ain't no reason to run."

Giving him a sideways glance, Effie saw the darkness in his eyes, and she knew she had every reason to run.

She knew enough about wild dogs, though, to know that doing so would only give chase, so she kept her steps steady even as her heart beat wildly. Derrick was now close enough for Effie to feel his hot breath on her neck. Effie's body tensed with a knowing her mind wouldn't yet accept even as Charles Derrick's unyielding fingers curled tightly around her wrist. Stopping short, she turned to face him. And although a suggestive smile slid across his face, all Effie could see was the rage in his eyes. Instinctively, Effie pulled back her arm, which only caused Derrick's grip to tighten and his eyes to darken. A drunken father and years of needless whippings had taught Effie that sometimes it was best not to fight but rather wait out the storm. Taking a deep breath, Effie steadied herself knowing she was about to endure a hurricane of tremendous hurt.

Derrick roughly pulled her into a thicket of trees then with his black boot swept her feet from beneath her so that Effie fell hard onto her back. Lying in a crumpled heap, Effie heard nothing but her own shallow breaths and trembling bones until the sound of Charles Derrick's hateful laugh pierced her ears. Then silence. Except for the blood rushing against her eardrums. Whoosh, whoosh, whoosh; rhythmic, it was almost soothing. Effie calmed for a moment until Derrick dropped to his knees, laid his full weight upon her, and putting his lips close to her ear, whispered, "I ain't never had a mountain girl."

A broken zipper and slipped seams caused Effie's tattered coat to easily fall open. Underneath she wore a thin dress, cornflower blue with small white daisies. It had been her mother's spring dress. Effie had foolishly made the sentimental, not practical choice when picking it out this morning. She'd believed that having the material that once touched her mother's skin next to her own would comfort her even in November's brisk air, but she felt no comfort now, only cold.

Effie clutched the collar of her dress with hands unsteady from shivering. She held tightly to the crumpled fabric as if keeping the dress close to her body would keep Charles Derrick from it, but it didn't. He ran his hands roughly up her legs before forcefully pulling the hem of her dress up, laying bare her naked body. Tattered lace sewn to the bottom of the dress fell softly across Effie's face, but to Effie it felt as though a thousand razor blades slid across her cheek. Squeezing shut her eyes, Effie focused on pulling all that she believed was truly good in her to her chest and held it next to her heart as all other parts of her were swiftly and savagely destroyed by a man who held less regard for her than an animal.

There was moaning—his. There was crying—hers. Then there was silence. In the quiet, Charles Derrick lay satisfied with what he had stolen. Effie Bilfrey lay shattered at what she had lost. The greatest part of her had been mercilessly taken. What was so cruelly robbed from her was not her virginity or her innocence or even her trust, but rather it was her faith—in others, in God, and most tragically, in herself.

Effie heard his panting and thought how his rapid breaths didn't sound human but rather like the sounds of a beast that cared for little more than satisfying its own fiendish desires. His actions, also inhuman, convinced Effie he was a monster, and so, in that moment, her greatest desire was to destroy him as he had so carelessly destroyed her. Her eyes, with tears still caught in the corners, stung, as did her now-tender and sore skin as the bitter wind cut across her body.

Effie pulled down her dress, covering all the painful places except for her heart, which felt exposed and raw. Then, sitting up, she shifted her coat back onto her shoulders and wrapped it tightly around her. Unsteady, she stood and pushed her frozen fingers deep into her coat pockets: Effie found more than warmth inside the soft folds of cotton lining. She felt the familiar steel against her fingertips. This time, Effie wasn't afraid. This time, she felt strong. As she pulled the gun from her pocket, she also felt very powerful.

Holding the gun tightly in her hand but loosely at her side, Effie stared at Charles Derrick, who sat leaning against the trunk of a large oak. As the day's last light cast across his face, Effie saw his satisfied smirk and in it the lack of remorse or shame. Any hesitation Effie held fell swiftly from her as she realized that she couldn't forgive someone who wasn't sorry. Lifting up her trembling arm, Effie steadied the gun with her other hand. Aiming, she peered through the sight.

In that moment, she saw in Derrick's eyes a flash of recognition or surprise or maybe fear. She wasn't sure which one; she didn't care. Effie didn't feel her finger tighten on the pulled trigger, and she didn't feel the kickback in her body. She heard only the sound—deafening—as it ripped through her ears and pierced her skull. She didn't see the gun drop to the ground. She saw only Charles Derrick's white T-shirt—pulled free from his unbuckled pants—turn crimson.

It was the vengeance Effie held in her eyes, not at her side, that Charles Derrick saw first; he thought little of it though. To Charles Derrick, Effie Bilfrey was as small and insignificant as the ants crawling beneath his boots. Her anger humored him; he smirked. It wasn't until she pointed a .22 pistol at his chest that she ceased being so small and he ceased finding her so funny, but he wasn't afraid. To him, she was a simple-minded mountain girl who he could easily charm, and he was going to try until he saw him standing behind her. It was only then that Charles Derrick felt fear. It lasted only for a moment before all he felt was pain.

Piney Boyer was the last man Charles Derrick saw before he saw nothing. Piney Boyer was the first person Effie Bilfrey saw when she thought she lost everything. Feeling a presence as soft as a whisper, she turned. He casually stood staring at Derrick's now-dead body before slowly facing her.

Piney—years older than Effie—was still very young. Although his sharp jaw and sunken cheeks belied his youth, his hair black as pitch and soft as down framed a face that still held the shadow of a boy. Small-framed, Piney seemed built only of bony elbows, knobby knees, and steely determination. Effie saw none of this. Looking into Piney's eyes, all Effie could see was the hollowness that rested not only beneath them but also within them. She searched for a glimpse of fear or courage. Instead, she saw an emptiness that gutted her.

With fingers interlaced, Effie wrapped her hands around her head, which she pushed toward her knees in an effort to coil her body into a tight ball. Softly rocking back and forth, a sound like that of a wounded animal escaped her lips. Effie slowly lifted her chin and saw she was back—no longer seventeen—she was safe. Yet, as she looked around, she knew that wasn't true. The familiar fear edged around her heart until all she felt was the fast pounding and the pain of its existence.

Pushing back, Effie sat up straight and stared at the gun. Squinting, she tried to hold back the tears that pooled in her eyes, causing the world around her to blur and soften. The ropes that held her to another time loosened, unmooring her memories. Each moment, like fine filaments of silk, floated far from her grasp. Effie mentally clutched at the strands, trying to remember how they'd been arranged, but every recollection only disintegrated into a haunting fog of vague memory. Cunning and quick, these memories slipped back into the recesses of Effie's cells, becoming once again a part of her that was both inextricable and unreachable.

Left with only pieces and parts that made little sense, Effie peered into the gray and saw, laying softly between the slivers of light, the gleam of the gun. She picked it up and cradled it in her hands. Her tears now flowed freely as she accepted what she had always known—she'd kept the gun not because it destroyed her, but because it had saved her. As she set it back into the steel box and looked up at her house and the hurt held within, she couldn't help wondering if her salvation was worth their destruction.

Chapter Twenty-Two

Lottie let the curtain slip back; she'd seen enough. After watching the lid of the steel lockbox snap shut on even more secrets she knew her granmom kept, Lottie was even more determined to uncover each one. She wasn't sure where she would find the answers, but she knew where she had to look. And she was willing, regardless of the cost.

It had been more than three weeks since Curtis had saved Lottie from Piney's attack. Afterward, Curtis vowed to never again risk Lottie's safety for her freedom, so he stayed close to her, which was too close for Lottie. She loved her uncle, but his constant presence was stealing her very breath and, slowly, her soul.

Her thoughts still her own, Lottie now kept them focused on her mother's journals. She even dreamed of them in recent days. Three years had passed since Lottie had carefully placed her mother's diaries, two of which still held untold secrets, beneath the wooden slats of her mother's outhouse. Three years, she'd waited as her fractured family tried to pick up the broken pieces. Three years, she tried to right her grandmother, whose every step seemed slightly unsteady to Lottie. With her uncles gone and money tight, the need to read her mother's diaries was pushed to the outer reaches of Lottie's mind but never her heart. When the memory of them would come to mind, she would whisper a promise to return to retrieve them only to have the day end with empty hands.

Lamenting the lost time, she prayed for the moment she could hold them once again and finally read them. Patiently, Lottie waited for this moment, which finally came two days before Thanksgiving. Curtis, working a short-term job on a turkey farm, was gone for the day. And Effie, distracted by making pies, never noticed Lottie, who silently slipped out but not before sliding a butcher knife into her pocket.

Even though the wind was cold and cutting, Lottie refused to tuck her head into her coat. Instead she endured her burning cheeks and stinging lips as she watched for Piney Boyer. It was her fear of being attacked again that kept her vigilant, but it was her fear of never holding her mother's journals again that kept her moving.

Bearing in mind her first failed attempt, Lottie was quiet and quick as she walked the narrow path to the front porch. She peered around the side of the small cabin before sprinting to the outhouse. Pressing her back against the sidewall, Lottie again looked around. Satisfied she was alone, she carefully opened the door, which swung heavy with a loud creak. Lottie jumped and pulled back her arm. Looking down, she saw a broken piece of wood, pulled free from the door, lying by her feet. After years of disregard, the tiny outbuilding, old and weather beaten, was crumbling. A sigh heavy with worry escaped Lottie's lips. She only hoped the outhouse stood long enough for her to rescue the remaining pieces of her mother that she could save.

Tentatively reaching beneath the wooden boards, Lottie felt for the small books. Finding nothing at first, she panicked. "Please. Please, God," she prayed. Sliding her arm in farther, she again prayed, "Please, God. I need this." Just as panic spread a blush of red across her body, Lottie felt the familiar smooth surface beneath the splintered wood. Pulling gently, the first diary slipped into her hands. "Thank you, God," she whispered. Sliding her hand back beneath the boards, she found the other two, which she tenderly stacked in her hands. Breathing easier, she whispered, "You're not lost." Pressing them close to her heart, she repeated softly, "You're not lost." Lottie slipped the diaries inside her coat and closed the outhouse door. Then she ran past the home she wanted to the only home she'd known.

Breathless and wind burnt, Lottie quietly opened the door. Effie's ears, which always perked to her granddaughter's steps, heard. Without turning, she asked, "What have you been doing, girl?"

Unable to hide the happy in her voice, Lottie answered, "Nothing, Granmom."

Effie turned to see a smile swept across her granddaughter's face. The rare sight of it caught Effie's breath and raised her suspicions. Pointing her rolling pin at Lottie, Effie demanded, "You got a secret?"

Lottie knew it was more an accusation than a question. And, although startled, she calmly answered, "No secret, Granmom. I'm just happy to feel the wind on my cheeks."

Suddenly concerned, Effie asked, "Is Curtis home?"

Feeling suffocated by the mere question, Lottie snapped, "No."

Undeterred by her granddaughter's rudeness, Effie asked, "You went somewhere?" Now worried, Effie continued, "Alone?"

Emboldened by her find, Lottie answered, "Yes."

Effie, surprised by her granddaughter's frankness, sputtered, "You know you can't just go roaming around alone, girl."

Frustrated, Lottie snapped, "I know, Granmom. I didn't go roaming nowhere. I was just in the yard. I...I..." Lottie stammered, "I needed some air."

With raised eyebrows, Effie argued, "We gots plenty of air right in here."

Feeling her mother's diaries pressed close against her skin, Lottie battled once more for her freedom. "The air in here is too thick, Granmom. I can't breathe."

Effie snorted, "You seem to be doing just fine now." Stomping her foot, Lottie snapped, "No! No, Granmom. I can't breathe with Uncle Curtis always sticking so close to me. Sometimes I just need to be..." Lottie stopped.

Finishing her sentence, Effie said, "Alone."

Teary-eyed, Lottie nodded.

Effie calmly said, "Well, you can't, because if your uncle thinks he needs to be sticking to your side then there's a reason."

Defiant, Lottie stepped closer to Effie and hissed, "Don't you want to know the reason?"

Leveled more by the implication of her granddaughter's words than her bold action, Effie looked down and said nothing.

Lottie stepped back and waited. "Granmom?" Lottie whispered. Effie looked up. Seeing the pain on her grandmother's face, Lottie, guilty for her harsh words, said sweetly, "Your pies smell real good. You know they are the best tasting in the county."

Grateful for the kind words and the forgiveness she chose to find in them, Effie let go of her hurt and teasingly shot back, "You've tasted them all?"

Lottie smiled. "Don't have to."

Even Effie wasn't immune to flattery, especially when given by Lottie, but she hid her pride and said, "Don't go feeding me pig slop and telling me it's steak, girl. I've been around too long for that." A shadow of a smile slipped across Effie's lips before she said, "Go on now. Get yourself warmed up before you catch your death."

Lottie obediently nodded. Then as Effie pulled the pies out of the oven, Lottie slid the knife, unseen, back onto the counter and quickly headed to her room.

After closing the door, Lottie went to the farthest corner of her room and sat. She didn't take off her coat nor did she pull the diaries from beneath it. She wanted nothing more than to read them, but for now it was enough to cradle them close to her. Their existence pressing against her skin was the most comfort she'd felt in years and she didn't want to let go. Ever.

Lottie spent the next hour trying to decide where to hide the journals. She put them in the bottom of her dresser drawer only to take them out a minute later. She put them under her mattress, then her bed. Walking in small circles, Lottie looked, debated, and questioned. Stopping short, she looked around her room and whispered, "There isn't a space." Turning slowly, she took a deep breath and exhaled. "Not a space that's mine."

Lottie sat. Resting her back against her bed, she considered her limited options. Then, while lightly tapping her fingertips on the floorboards, she thought of the perfect hiding place. She pushed her bed to the side, exposing the loose floorboard. She took one of Curtis's abandoned screwdrivers, lifted the board, and smiled. Gently, she slid the journals underneath the wooden plank and pushed back the bed. Sure of their safety, Lottie now only had to bide her time. She longed for the perfect moment when she would have the freedom to not only read her mother's words but also to live, uninterrupted, in her mother's world. This moment came later than Lottie hoped but sooner than she'd expected.

It had been two weeks since hiding her mother's diaries and Lottie now stood buttoning her threadbare coat. These diaries, which were not only hidden in the floor but also in Lottie's heart, caused her to think of little else other than safeguarding the secret of their existence. Flinching every time Effie came too close to her bed, Lottie knew it was only a matter of time before her grandmother understood the fear in her granddaughter's eyes. Now careful, Lottie kept her eyes averted from her grandmother's watchful stare.

Looking out the window, Lottie traced her finger across the cold glass. Wet streaks snaked the frosted pane so that the figure of her uncle looked small and shrunken as he walked toward the house. Lottie imagined trapping him between the spaces of her fingers, keeping him still in the wintry gray light of December. She pictured him frozen. Caught inanimate in the triangular corners of a snowflake. With him safely kept and quieted, she would have a small space unencumbered by his constant presence, which shaped him into her shadow. One that grew larger in the dark, cold winter.

He was gone from her sight but rarely her side, and Lottie remained unmoved when she heard the shuffle of his feet on the porch. She didn't turn when she heard the groan of the door opening or when she heard his voice. Through chattering teeth, Curtis stammered, "It…it sure is cold." Rubbing his hands together, he repeated for emphasis, "Damn cold!"

Effie rolled her eyes and chided, "What was you expecting in December?"

Curtis shrugged, then, turning to Lottie, said, "I'm going to grab a heavier coat and then we'll go. You ready?"

Never turning from the window, she shook her head and said, "No."

Before Curtis could say another word, Effie cut in, "What do you mean by no?"

Lottie pressed her palm against the window. Methodically moving her hand from side to side, she erased the watery streaks that cobwebbed the glass. "I mean I don't want to go."

Puzzled, Effie asked, "Don't you like learning?"

Lottie shrugged and muttered, "Maybe I've learned enough."

"Humph," Effie grunted. "Saying that just proves you don't know nothing."

Lottie slowly turned to face her grandmother. Then, with a defiance that shaped her soft spaces into the sharp edges of her mother, she snapped, "You always said that the best learning was done by living."

Refusing to be humbled by her own words, Effie asked sharply, "You think you've lived?"

Never taking her eyes from her grandmother, Lottie shot back, "Maybe I could live if you would let me."

Swiftly, Effie stepped closer to her granddaughter and, through gritted teeth, hissed, "You listen to me, *little* girl. I'm the reason you have a place to live, food to eat, and clothes on your back. I'm the reason you do live. You hear me?"

Unyielding and determined, Lottie answered, "Yes, Granmom. I hear you. You gave me everything." Stepping closer, Lottie said in a hoarse whisper, "And you took nothing. Not *my* home. My mom. My freedom."

Curtis caught Effie's raised hand midair. "Ma!" Curtis gasped.

Effie angrily wrenched her arm free from her son's grasp. Lottie reflexively laid her hand across her untouched cheek. Dropping her chin to her chest, she said nothing. Suddenly ashamed, Effie dropped her arm to her side and stepped back. She and Curtis exchanged a look that conveyed the other's worry and the painful familiarity of that feeling.

Effie's head spun with fear, making her dizzy. Stumbling while stepping back, she quickly steadied herself with the kitchen chair. After a few minutes of silence, she said quietly, "You don't have to go to school. You can stay home." Realizing the present insignificance of the word, Effie quickly withdrew it, saying, "Here. You can stay here."

Without a word, Lottie grabbed her scarf from the hook and wrapped it loosely around her neck.

Effie mistakenly interpreted Lottie's action as proof of her effect on the girl. Satisfied with herself, Effie said, "Well, it's good to know that you still have enough sense to do the right thing."

Lottie placed her hand on the doorknob. Turning, she looked at her grandmother and asked, "What's my choice?"

Confident she still had the upper hand, Effie answered, "You can go or you can stay."

Turning her back to Effie, Lottie said, "I don't want to go." Opening the door, she said over her shoulder, "But it's better than here." Lottie ran down the steps. Her skin felt raw, and her eyes, pooled with tears, burned, but she didn't stop. She didn't look back.

Effie and Curtis tripped over one another as they hurried to the door. Curtis rushed to catch up, but Effie, slower to move and barefoot, stopped at the doorway. Leaning outside, she hollered, "What is it you want, Lottie?"

Without answering, Lottie kept walking.

Determined, Effie hobbled on the sides of her feet down the snow-covered steps. Grabbing the rail, she forced a deep breath into her lungs and shouted, "What? What is it you want, girl?"

Lottie stopped. Effie stood up straight.

Standing with her uncle and grandmother at her back, Lottie looked across the snow-swept yard. Ice-tipped pines loomed and bowed around her. Lottie pulled at her scarf, ripping it from her neck as she fought to catch her breath. These mountains seemed to strangle her. Watching the red woolen scarf fall and lie like a streak of crimson blood across the white snow, she knew what she wanted. She wanted freedom.

Lottie turned to see her grandmother standing on the steps, shivering but steadfast. She watched as her grand-mother's warm breath caught in the cold and curled around her face. She looked unreal, ethereal. Lottie thought of her mother, who had become nothing more than wisps of broken memories, whispers of half-truths and words kept in secreted diaries. In that moment, Lottie knew what she needed, and, for it, she traded what she wanted.

Walking in quick strides, she reached the porch as Effie, unable to tolerate the cold any longer, slipped up the steps. Standing in the doorway, framed by the splintered wood, she appeared suddenly small to Lottie, who said, "I want a day. A whole day to myself with nobody checking on me." Giving a sideways glance to Curtis, she continued, "Or following me." Again, looking back at Effie, she said, "Or bothering me."

Suspicious of the simple request, Effie carefully asked, "Is that all?"

Lottie nodded.

Giving it more consideration before striking the bargain, Effie added, "You can't go traipsing around by yourself."

Through gritted teeth, Lottie assured her that she wouldn't go anywhere.

Effie thought for a moment then, double-checking, asked, "You're just going to stay in your room?"

Again, Lottie nodded.

"How long?"

Considering her limited possibilities, Lottie answered, "One day. I just want one day."

Effie laughed. It was a joyless staccato sound that stuck in her throat. Disbelieving, she once more challenged her granddaughter. "One day? That's all you want? *That* is what is going to fix all this fussing?"

Lottie answered, "Yes."

Effie snorted, "Well, hell, girl. That ain't no big deal. You could have that any old time."

Just as Effie settled into the simplicity of granting an easy wish, Lottie leaned close and added, "Christmas."

Pulling back as though slapped, Effie asked, "Christmas?"

Lottie stood her ground and answered, "Yes."

Effie put her hands on her hips and demanded, "Why does it have to be that day?"

Recognizing her grandmother's fighting stance, Lottie didn't back down. "It's the day I want. You said yourself, it isn't much to ask."

Regretting her words, Effie tried backtracking. "Well, that was before I knew you was planning to hide from us on Christmas."

Trying to appeal to her granddaughter's sensitive nature, Effie, in a plaintive voice, added, "It's Christmas, Lottie."

Unwilling to bend, Lottie said, "It's just a day."

Effie shook her head. "It's not just a day. It's special. It's time for us to be together." Effie stammered, "It's…it's—"

Lottie cut in, "If it helps, you can consider it a gift to me."

Effie argued, "It's not the gift I want to give."

Unwilling to hear her grandmother's protests, Lottie returned, "It's the gift I want." Without allowing Effie another word, she said, "It's that day or nothing, Granmom."

As her granddaughter, strong and determined, stood before her, Effie saw the same gold flecks dance in her eyes that she saw in Sarah's all those years ago when she, too, stood before her on this same porch. Sarah—eighteen, stubborn, and soon to leave her baby girl at Effie's feet—was gone. Knowing she couldn't bear it again and knowing she was bested, Effie nodded and reluctantly agreed, "Okay. Christmas."

Lottie started down the steps then, turning, said, "The whole day."

With the regret of striking another bad bargain, Effie sighed and conceded, "Yes. The whole day."

Happy in her victory, Lottie skipped across the yard with Curtis close behind. Effie watched until they were nothing more than dark dots in the distance. Closing the door to the cold air and a nameless fear, she slid to the floor. Cradling her head in her hands, Effie closed her eyes and thought about how she'd just traded what she wanted for what she needed.

Walking at a pace fast enough to keep a few feet in front of her uncle, Lottie was winded from trudging through the thick snow, which curled in folds around her legs. Pulling her feet up from its frigid grasp became increasingly difficult, but Lottie knew that if she stopped, even for a moment, this mountain would keep her tethered here. Refusing, she moved forward.

With the oaks stripped bare and the sun set high, a glare bounced across the white-washed landscape. The sharp gleam that cast across Lottie's eyes still couldn't blind her to the bleakness of winter and the knowledge that her life was now limited to the narrow scope of her mother's words and the fading hope that she would find her own way.

Chapter Twenty-Three

Lottie hadn't counted down the days until Christmas since she was ten years old. After receiving socks, two pairs of underwear, and a plain hair comb that year, she never thought she would have reason to do so again, yet at fifteen she was again drawing thick black crosses across each day as she wished the next one away. Each inked day soon disappeared into the next until she was sitting in her bed, wide-awake and excited on Christmas morning.

For a long while, Lottie didn't move. Instead she stayed still, listening. She loved that silence had a sound, especially in this house. She could hear soft snoring, the creak of worn boards settling under new snow, and the pounding of her heart.

Slowly, she slid from beneath the covers and swung her legs over the side of the bed, allowing her toes to lightly graze the icy floor. Even though a chill snaked up her legs and across her chest, Lottie didn't pull back. Instead she pressed her feet firmly into the cold. Lottie was determined to *feel* everything today—the pain, the discomfort, and, she hoped, the joy.

The morning's light hadn't yet streamed through the slats of her shutters, but Lottie didn't turn on her lamp. She didn't need to. She knew from memory and by touch where to find what she'd so carefully closeted.

She retrieved her precious gift from where it rested, waiting for her hands, her eyes, her heart, and crawled into bed. Pulling the covers gently over her, Lottie clicked on a small flashlight she'd saved for this moment, opened her mother's second diary to the first page, and began to read.

September 21, 1978

Ms. Prindle has given me another diary. I didn't tell her that I never finished writing in the first one. I just thanked her and told her that I didn't feel like I had much worth saying.

She said that all my thoughts and feelings were important. I don't know why, but when she said that I felt like I was going to cry, so I told her I had to go.

It wasn't until I got to go outside that I really looked at the book. It's a real pretty bright yellow color. Cheerful. I like that.

October 17, 1978

I've never really liked school. The walk is too long and so are the days. But lately school is even harder.

Ms. Prindle kept me after class today. She asked if I'd been writing in my diary. I told her I had, but I'm not sure she believed me. She told me that lately she sees me daydreaming a lot. She said writing those dreams in my diary might help me to pay attention better in class, then she smiled at me so sweetly that I wanted to tell her that these aren't dreams. These are nightmares.

But how could I tell her? She still believes in the pretty stories she reads to us. I can't tell her that these stories aren't my story. I wish I could tell her, because maybe then she would understand why I stopped listening.

October 31, 1978

It's Halloween and Baby Curtis is mad at me because I ain't dressing up. I didn't dress up last year, so I promised him I would this year. I didn't mean to break my promise. I just thought a year would make a difference. It didn't.

I told him fourteen is too old to dress up. He was sad. I didn't know what to say to make it better, so I said nothing. He just dropped the old rubber face mask he's worn for the last three years at my feet and walked away.

Maybe it's better that he stops dressing up too. After all, ain't no dime store mask or pretty dress going to change who you are, not even for a night.

December 17, 1978

Christmas is next week. Not that it matters much. Christmas in Talon Ridge just reminds you of what you don't have, what you need, and what you ain't ever going to get.

Baby Curtis quit being mad sometime in November, but things still ain't right between us. I've wanted to build him a little wagon out of scrap wood, but I don't know what I'm doing. I thought about having Frank help, but I can tell by the way he looks at me that I best not ask.

Seems like no one is right with me. Makes sense, I guess, because I ain't right with me.

January 7, 1979

It's a new year, but nothing has changed. I guess I shouldn't have expected much change to happen in a week, but I was hoping.

I keep thinking about Ms. Prindle's words: "New year, new start." I just don't see how a new start is ever going to happen living here.

Mama told me that she expects me to do better in school this year. I told her I would, but I know I won't. Why should I try? It ain't going to get me off this mountain. All Ms. Prindle's pretty stories and clever poems ain't going to change what can't be changed no matter how hard I wish they could.

February 14, 1979

Valentine's Day

I saw Dallas Cutler today. I see him most days, but today was the first time since we broke up that he looked at me. I mean really looked at me.

I think I loved him. I'm not sure, but I think he may have loved me.

This was before he hated me. At least that's how it has seemed for a long time.

But today when he finally looked at me, I didn't see hate or love. I saw nothing.

I have no more to say about that.

March 28, 1979

Frank got into another fight today. In the past few years, Frank has gotten into a couple of scuffles, but lately all he seems to do is fight. Being the oldest boy and having no daddy, Frank feels like he has to be the man of the house. He thinks that fighting is what makes a man.

What Frank doesn't know is that a man is measured by much more than the speed of his hits and the number of his fights, but Frank don't know it because he ain't a man, he's just an angry little boy.

I miss the boy who was quick to love. This boy who is quick to hit and to hurt scares me. I worry about him, but that don't matter much to Frank—not anymore.

May 2, 1979

I'm bleeding. It started this morning. I want to tell Mama, but I don't want to upset her because I think I may be dying.

I don't know what's causing the dying. I didn't fall. There ain't no cut. I didn't even know a person could bleed from there. It's hurt there sometimes, especially after it happens, but it ain't ever bled.

I've been praying so hard to God to get me off this mountain that I'm thinking maybe he finally decided to do something about it. I guess dying make sense since that seems to be the only way I will ever make it out of here.

When I think about it some more, I wonder if God is punishing me for not stopping it—stopping him.

Truth is that I don't want to die. I just wish living didn't hurt so much.

June 5, 1979

I'm not dying.

Mama found my underwear. I had stuffed them under my bed when I couldn't get the blood out. She showed them to me and asked when. I told her that there was no way of knowing how long I had left.

She just shook her head and told me I wasn't dying. She said I'd become a woman. She thought for a minute before saying that she guessed in a way the little girl

*part of me did die. I didn't tell Mama how that part of
me died long before the bleeding started.*

*I bled again this month. Mama said that this is the
way it will be until it's not. My stomach hurts so bad
that I've spent most of the day doubled over in my bed.
I can't eat and my head hurts.*

*I used to pray to God to get me off this mountain,
now I pray to God to make this stop.*

August 21, 1979

*I am fifteen today. I was hoping for some small change
in me, but everything is still the same.*

*I don't expect Mama to do much for my birthday,
and this year I don't care. I'm too tired to care. Baby
Curtis has been crawling into my bed for over a
year now. I wouldn't mind except for his kicking and
screaming wears me out.*

*He has nightmares. Well, he has one nightmare.
It's about a monster with too many legs and arms. He
hadn't had it for a while, but last night it came back.
Even after he's awake, he cries and hugs me so tight I
can barely breathe.*

*I never push him away because I've been that
scared, and all I want is for someone to hold me until
the monster goes away. Since I ain't got no one to do
that, I hold Baby Curtis until his monster goes away.
But just like all monsters, it always comes back.*

September 8, 1979

It's been a week since school started, and I still don't see why Mama sent me back for another year. There ain't nothing they're going to teach me that's going to get me off this mountain. And there ain't nothing I'm going to learn that's going to make me want to stay.

So, I go to school because Ms. Prindle says I should and because Mama says I have to and because I have nowhere else to go.

January 15, 1980

Four months. I haven't opened this diary in four whole months.

I wish it was because my life has been too busy. Fun. Wonderful. But the truth is that my life has been too hard. Fighting. Hurting. Who wants to write about that? I'm only writing now because a new year, new start. I know it won't make no difference, but I just can't seem to stop hoping. I guess hope is what you got when you don't got nothing else.

February 22, 1980

Today gave me another reason to hate school.

I saw Dallas with Cathy McQuinn. They were together, hugging and kissing each other. When I saw

*them I wasn't sure if I was going to cry or be sick. I
looked away and tried to pretend I didn't see them. But
somehow they made their way in front of me, and I had
to watch as she slipped her hand into his pocket, and he
leaned close and whispered in her ear.*

*I didn't want to see them like that, but I couldn't
look away. I just stood frozen as Cathy walked over to
me and hissed that Dallas is her boyfriend now.*

*Then she grinned, thinking she took something from
me, but what she don't know is that it was taken from
me long before she tried.*

March 9, 1980

*Today, Mama came home early from her Sunday trip. I
still don't know where she goes. I just know it won't do
any good to ask.*

*She wore her cornflower blue dress today. I love
how the blue makes Mama look soft and pretty, but
I hate how the baggy folds make her look small and
weak.*

I still ain't sure if it's the dress or if it's Mama.

April 13, 1980

*Today, I followed Mama on her Sunday trip. I waited
until I heard the screen door shut, then I got out of
bed and watched as Mama crossed the yard. She was*

wearing her yellow skirt. Her cheeks were rouged and her hair hung loose on her neck. She looked pretty until she turned, and then she just looked sad.

As she started up the hill, I snuck out and quietly followed her. She paced around Ms. Keefer's cabin for a bit before doubling back to his. I hid in the bushes across the way and watched as Mama stood in front of Piney Boyer's cabin.

She didn't go in. She didn't even cross the yard. She just stood there. After a long time, she sat down and stared. Ants were crawling on me, making my skin itch, but I didn't move because Mama didn't move.

After forever, Mama stood then walked in a few small circles before heading down the road toward our house. I cut behind the Royer's backyard and ran the whole way. I stood inside, trying to catch my breath as I waited for her.

She walked in only minutes later. Her skirt was unwrinkled. Her lipstick wasn't smudged, and her hair didn't need combed.

I thought this would make her happy, but when she looked at me I saw she wasn't happy. She was afraid. She didn't say so. She didn't have to. I saw the worry lines stretched tight across her face.

Now I wonder…does she know?

May 19, 1980

*Today was the last day of school. I'd be happy if
Ms. Pringle hadn't told me that she was leaving our
school for a position in Oakridge. I like Ms. Pringle.
I like her so much that I was hoping someday I could
tell her. I guess I could have told her today, but it didn't
make any sense to hand her a burden that wasn't hers to
carry and one she couldn't set down. So I said nothing.*

*She gave me another diary. It's a pretty blue. Before
I could thank her, she pulled me into her arms and held
me tighter than Mama ever has. Then she pulled back
and told me that she picked a blue diary so I would
remember that even after the darkest storms, blue skies
return.*

*It ain't Ms. Pringle's fault, but she just ain't lived in
these mountains long enough to know that some storms
don't ever end.*

August 6, 1980

It happened again.

*I've prayed and prayed for it to stop. I've prayed
hard every morning and every night. I've prayed on my
knees.*

*Aren't you listening, God? Don't you hear me!
Six times. It's happened six times! And You stay silent
while I suffer. What god does that?*

He takes my body like it's his. I don't fight anymore.
He can have my body. It's my soul I am now fighting
for. It's breaking and he's taking pieces faster than I can
gather them.

I haven't told anyone, but how do they not know?
How does Mama not know? How does she not hear how
loud I'm screaming on the inside?

Is she even listening? Is anyone?

August 20, 1980

Tomorrow is my birthday. I'm going to be sixteen.

Mama says now I'm more woman than girl. This
scares me because I've seen what this mountain does to
women.

I gave God one last chance to help me. I prayed that
he keep me a girl, and I think that this time he listened.
It's been almost a week and I still haven't started my
monthly bleed.

I'm not sure, but I think God has finally answered
one of my prayers.

Lottie laid her mother's diary, still open to the last
page, next to her pillow. Yawning, she stretched her body as
long as the tight covers would allow, then she pulled back the
corner of her quilt. Lottie was amazed to see that the room
was as dark as when she crawled beneath her covers. An entire
day—Christmas day—had passed.

Lottie had spent it alone, reading, pacing, praying, and waiting. She wasn't exactly sure what it was she was waiting for, but she knew it was something she needed, and she felt certain it would come if only she was patient.

Pulling her mother's third and final diary close to her, Lottie burrowed back beneath her blankets. She softly ran her thumb down the length of the cover before opening the diary to the first page. Lottie hadn't read more than the first sentence before her eyes gently closed.

Chapter Twenty-Four

The food Effie had left for Lottie outside her room sat cold and untouched. Effie carefully slid back the tray before slowly turning the doorknob. The room was dark except for the sliver of light that slipped through the crack in the slightly opened door. Effie quietly followed this stream of light to her granddaughter's bed.

Drawing an imaginary line from her softly closed eyes to her delicate cheek, Effie could still see the baby she rocked and the little girl who begged for barrettes, but now she also saw something else. She stared a bit longer, trying to sort out the difference. Perhaps, Effie thought, it was the deep lines newly set in her furrowed brow or the way her muscles tensed even in sleep. Effie wasn't sure, but she knew something in her girl had changed.

As Effie turned to go, her hip brushed one of the diaries off of the bed. Effie quickly caught the book before it landed loudly on the floor. It was Effie's intention to place the book beside Lottie's bed, which she would have done if she hadn't noticed the handwriting. The script that looped and flowed across the page was as familiar to Effie as the lines that crossed her hand. Effie stifled a gasp, nearly dropping the diary. She then placed the book beside her granddaughter before carefully stepping back from it as if it were a ghost she'd rather not disturb.

Effie quietly crept backward out of the room and softly closed the door. Leaning against the frame, she covered her mouth to muffle her breathing, which now came hard as her heartbeat quickened. It was Sarah's writing. She knew it just like she knew the feel of her girl's silken hair or the touch of her hands.

Effie slowly made her way into the living room, where she sunk heavily into the couch cushion and leaned her head back. Roughly running her fingers across her forehead, Effie wondered how Sarah had managed to slip into her house without her knowing. Muddled memories tangled with a thousand thoughts and wound tightly around Effie's brain. It wasn't long before Effie's eyes were as heavy as her heart and she was fast asleep.

Effie woke early the day after Christmas to the sound of staccato taps like rain hitting a tin roof. Bleary-eyed she looked into the kitchen, where she saw her granddaughter sitting alone at the table. Lottie's nervous habit of rocking her foot against the chair rung was the source of the sound.

Most days, Effie would have paid no mind to the rapid little flicks of Lottie's small foot, but to Effie these tiny taps now seemed to shake the ground beneath them. Careful not to startle the girl, who now seemed quick to flee, Effie soundlessly watched her granddaughter as Lottie stared into the space above her untouched glass of milk.

Unnoticed, Effie studied Lottie. She noted the sharp lines of her jaw, the soft curve of her shoulder, and the sweet shape of her mouth. A silhouette of perfection in Effie's mind, Lottie looked like a mythical creature. One who Effie watched transform, changing the very skin and bone of her being like casting off one coat for another. It was both beautiful and frightening, and Effie shuddered to see it.

After picking up a spoon that clattered to the floor, Lottie turned to meet Effie's gaze, and the trance was broken. Feeling like a caught thief, Effie scrambled to her feet and awkwardly began making breakfast. She could feel Lottie watching her, and she wondered what *she* saw—a cold and distant grandmother, a worn woman, or worse?

The clank of pans against the cookstove and the rattle of spoons sang loudly next to Effie's words, which came quickly and nervously. "You want some biscuits? I can have 'em mixed up in a few minutes. I'll make 'em extra sweet and fluffy."

Without looking at her grandmother, Lottie slowly shook her head no.

Determined, Effie continued, "I know you didn't eat nothing yesterday." Effie turned and muttered under her breath, "Even though I left you a whole tray of food." Turning back to Lottie, she said more cheerfully, "I'm a going to mix these up and you're going to love 'em."

At an even quicker pace than she was moving, Effie rambled on about the weather, the cost of flour, and the stickiness of the floor. Lottie responded to none of it, and even Effie couldn't be sure what she was saying or why. She just knew that she had to fill the empty spaces that now felt much too loud.

Effie carefully slid three freshly made biscuits onto Lottie's plate. Buzzing around the girl with syrup and silverware, Effie said, "Eat 'em while they're hot."

Without a thank-you or a nod in Effie's direction, Lottie stared straight ahead.

Although feeling jumpy, Effie lightly asked, "Cat got your tongue, girl?"

Lottie said nothing.

With her own limits pushed, Effie decided to push Lottie's a bit. "It ain't polite not to answer, girl. You been taught better than that. Now I know—"

Interrupting Effie with a steely look, Lottie abruptly asked, "Do you miss her?"

Stunned, Effie stepped back as though slapped, and in a way, in her heart, she had been. Without answering, she turned and put the pan back onto the stove, regretting that she'd chased the quiet away.

Effie avoided answering by pretending to be busy. She wiped clean counters and washed unused plates. Lottie, however, was just as stubborn and not so easily ignored. "Well, Granmom, do you? Do you miss my mom?"

Effie stopped wiping and scrubbing but never turned to face Lottie. Instead she stared out the small, grease-splattered window, wondering why Lottie chose now to break their silent pact. The one that Effie believed they'd both forged the day Sarah left. Effie had spent all these years thinking that it was at that moment a heartbroken mother and an abandoned little girl made an unspoken agreement to carry the wound and never ask about the one who made it. Effie now realized she'd made that deal alone.

Frustrated with Effie's silence, Lottie demanded, "Well? It's a simple question."

Without turning, Effie answered, "But it ain't a simple answer, girl. Not simple at all."

Lottie heaved a sigh and said, "I don't see how it's not."

Effie also exhaled before saying, "You don't see it because you're too young to understand that life ain't black and white. It would be real neat and tidy if it was, but the truth is most of us live in the grays."

Unsatisfied with her grandmother's answer, Lottie argued, "There ain't nothing gray about it. You miss her or you don't."

Finally turning to face Lottie, and in many ways her own heartache, Effie softly said, "She made the choice, girl. I know it hurts, but she was the one who left you." Choking up a bit, Effie added, "And me."

Feeling bold, Lottie said, "If you live in the grays, Granmom, then you should know it ain't that simple. Haven't you ever thought that maybe she ran because something chased her away?"

Effie dropped her eyes and said nothing. The truth was she had thought about it, but Effie had made another pact with herself long ago to never ask the questions that she feared the answers to.

Lottie's chair screeched as she pushed it back from the table. The sound sent a chill down Effie's back. Lottie stood with her fingers wrapped tightly around the rungs of the chair. Effie could see her knuckles whiten. It was as if Lottie was grasping on to anything to keep her tied to this place, and Effie could sense that, like her mother, she was ready to run. Effie cautiously stared at her granddaughter's small, clenched hands for what seemed like forever before Lottie suddenly released the chair and walked out of the room.

Feeling drained from the empty space she left, Effie sank into the nearest chair. If Effie wasn't certain before, she was now—Sarah had definitely found a way back into her home, and she wasn't sure she liked it.

Safely hidden behind the kitchen curtain, Effie watched as Curtis and Lottie slowly trudged across the thick drifts of snow. Soon the distance that made them small swallowed them completely, leaving only their footprints sunk deep across the yard. Curtis said they were going for a walk, but he didn't say where or when they'd be back. Seeing Lottie's scowl, Effie didn't ask.

Since Effie wasn't sure how long they'd be gone, she wasted no time. She didn't even bother slipping on her coat. It wasn't until her stiff fingers fumbled with the cold steel box that she regretted not grabbing her gloves. Because Effie didn't know when Curtis and Lottie would be home, she decided not to waste precious time on going back in to bundle up. Blowing a few puffs of hot breath onto her hands, she rubbed them together quickly to warm them before she tentatively reached around her neck and released the clasp.

Still warm from resting against her chest, the skeleton key slipped easily into the frosted lock. The quiet click seemed to echo loudly against the hush of the snowy landscape, causing Effie to instinctively look around. Fearful she would be caught, she quickly pulled the folded paper from beneath the gun. Closing the lid and pushing the steel box back into place, a shadow of grim smile cast across her face. It wasn't lost on Effie that her treasure chest held only torment.

Effie again vigorously rubbed her hands, trying to get the blood to flow back into her numb fingers. It was several minutes before the stinging subsided and she was able to reach into her pocket to pull out the piece of wrinkled paper. She held it in her hands, gently turning it front to back. It was yellowed and torn at the edges, and Effie knew what was held within—her gift. Her curse. Effie didn't want to open it, but she knew she had to face her fear. So, with trembling hands, Effie unfolded the crinkled paper, and as she did, a part of her life unfolded with it.

"I ain't going to bury him myself. It's enough I'm doing the diggin'," Piney grumbled. Still stunned, Effie sat watching Piney as he heaved shovelfuls of dirt over his shoulder. Watching him easily scoop out mounds of dirt, Effie wondered how such a small man could be so strong. She also wondered where he got the shovel. Maybe he left? Maybe he had it with him? She couldn't remember. What Effie couldn't forget was Charles Derrick. Averting her eyes from his dead body, Effie looked up. She watched as soft pink hues scattered across the sky slowly fading into a deep orange.

Angrily throwing his shovel to the side, Piney whisper-shouted, "What you lookin' at, girl?"

Without looking away, Effie answered, in barely above a whisper, "The colors. They're so pretty."

Angry, Piney snapped, "What the fuck you talkin' about, girl?" Kicking dirt with his boot, he grumbled, "Dumbass girl mooning over colors when we got a dead body to bury." Seeing Effie still standing dumbstruck, Piney snarled, "Are you stupid, girl? Do you know what the hell those colors mean? It's about to get dark and ain't no way we're burying him in the pitch black."

At the mention of Derrick's body, Effie forced herself to look at him. Seeing his empty eyes and his tongue lolled to the side of his mouth caused her to turn quickly as her stomach lurched. She heaved and choked, but nothing came up but bile, which burned her throat as the tears stung her eyes.

Having picked up his shovel, Piney sighed in disgust as he muttered, "Damn, useless women."

Hearing him and refusing to be seen as weak, Effie pushed herself up. Dizzy, she staggered over to Piney and took the shovel. As she hefted a shovelful of dirt over her shoulder,

Piney sniggered and said, "Well, looks like we both all in now, huh?"

Darkness swallowed the remaining light of the day just as Piney and Effie finished covering the fresh mound of dirt with rocks and branches. Piney stepped back, taking measure of their work, he said, "That should hide it."

Effie, choking on the word, sputtered, "*Should*?"

Piney sniffed, "Well, ain't much more we can do now, is there? We just cover him up and hope no one finds out."

Effie hoarsely squeaked out, "What if someone does find out? What will we do?"

Piney shook his head. "Just git yourself cleaned up and keep your mouth shut."

Watching Effie stare at her dirt-smeared hands, Piney said, "It ain't nothing a little soap and water can't fix."

Effie looked at him helplessly, knowing that no amount of scrubbing would wipe clean the memory of this horror.

Picking up his shovel, Piney stepped close to Effie, and in an uncommon moment of sympathy, he said softly, "It always gonna hurt, but time has a way of taking out the sting."

Effie looked at him, her eyes glistening with tears. In vain, she searched his face, trying to see compassion and kindness. She saw neither. Uneasy in her stare, Piney turned and mumbled, "You git on home now." As Effie turned to go, Piney reached back for her hand and said, "You remember, girl, we're in this together."

Piney wrapped his boney hand around Effie's, and she nodded as they shook on his words. In that moment, Effie knew deep in her soul that she'd just made a deal with the devil.

A week and half passed and still the police hadn't come to Effie's door. Terrified of being caught and tortured by the image of Charles Derrick's cold, dead body, Effie rarely left the house. As the days passed, the soreness between her legs subsided, and her bruises gradually faded to a pale yellow. Effie's body was healing. Her spirit, however, was still shattered.

With her father rarely home, Effie stumbled through her days alone. Because she'd become used to quiet, empty rooms, Effie was startled when she saw her father sitting at the kitchen table. A cup of cold coffee and a half-smoked cigarette burned in the ashtray as Eugene held his head in his hands.

Without a word, Effie sat down at the table. Eugene slowly looked up. Passing his hand through the morning light that streaked across the table, he said softly, "I don't see much of the sun no more."

Quietly, Effie asked, "Do you miss it?"

Eugene tilted his head and considered her question before answering, "Your mama was my light, and when that went out, well, I guess I didn't much care no more."

Numb, Effie said nothing.

They were both quiet a bit longer before Eugene offhandedly said, "One of the mining bosses has gone missing."

Feeling as though her heart stopped beating in her chest, Effie gasped.

Eugene raised his eyebrows and said, "It happens, girl. He could have gotten lost in one of the tunnels or he could be lying shit-faced in a ditch." Eugene sniffed, lit another cigarette, and said, "All anybody does know is that no one gives a shit."

Seeing his daughter's eyes widen, Eugene said, "Charles Derrick was a son of a bitch who had coming whatever he got." Eugene blew out a puff of smoke as he stamped out his cigarette.

Interlaced, Effie's fingers whitened as she squeezed them tightly together, trying not to scream. Looking up at her father, Effie saw his eyes glistening with the threat of tears. Abruptly standing up, Eugene took a quick swig of coffee and stuffed the pack of cigarettes into his shirt pocket. He grabbed his helmet and headed quickly toward the door.

With his back to his daughter and his hand on the doorknob, Eugene said quietly, "You look like your mama." Opening the door, he whispered, "It hurts." Eugene closed the door, leaving Effie alone again.

Three more weeks passed before Effie could finally relax enough to take a full breath. It was then that the wind was knocked out of her. After a day spent scrubbing floors and washing dishes, Effie had sunk heavily into the couch. Startled awake by three loud raps on the door, Effie stumbled across the room and pulled back the yellowed lace curtain from the window. Soaked to the skin and staring back at her was Piney Boyer. Effie's heart raced.

"I see you, girl. Open the damn door! I ain't gettin' no drier standing out here."

Effie opened the door a crack. Piney pushed his face close and hissed, "Ain't you gonna let me in?" Effie shook her head. Forcing the door open wider, he threatened, "I think you forgot who saved your ass. Maybe you need reminding."

Effie quickly stepped back as Piney stepped inside.

Piney took off his hat, and the water that pooled in the brim spilled onto the floor.

Taking an uneasy breath, Effie asked, "Is it about *him*?"

Shaking his head, Piney grinned and said, "Nope. That boy ain't goin' nowhere." Then, scratching the stubble on his chin, he reconsidered and added, "Unless, of course, this here rain floods him up."

Pacing nervously, Effie said, "No. I mean does someone know?"

Piney sniffed and said, "Well, if someone did know then it wouldn't be me making puddles on your floor."

Without hesitation and without compassion, Piney said, "Your daddy's dead."

Piney watched, waiting for Effie to scream or cry or fall into a heap on the floor, but she didn't. Explaining, Piney said, "They ain't too sure about what happened. It's likely something fell on his head. It could have been—" Stopping him short, Effie pushed Piney toward the door as he protested, "Whoa. Hey! There ain't no need to shove. I was nice enough to come tell you. I don't see no one else coming out in the rain to—"

Effie pushed harder and yelled, "Just go!"

Stumbling onto the porch, Piney grabbed on to the rail. Regaining his balance, he wheeled around and forced open the door as Effie struggled to shut it. Jutting his head in the crack, he looked around the cramped shack and said snidely, "This place looks awful big now that you're by your lonesome. Might be nice to have someone here to protect—"

Before Piney could get out his last word, Effie slammed the door shut and locked it. Piney stepped off the porch, slapped his hat back on his head, and grumbled, "Ungrateful bitch."

Effie sat alone with her grief for several weeks. She was still afraid to go into town, so Mr. Goodwin delivered her father's final paycheck and a few groceries. Since her father's death, time had liquefied. Every minute dripped into the next until the hours were no more distinguishable from each other than two drops of rain. Effie soon lost track of the days. It wasn't until she passed the worn calendar she'd tacked up next to the icebox that she saw it was July 15—her eighteenth birthday.

Effie walked over to the mirror and studied her reflection. Only a year older but she could have been a hundred years older, Effie thought as she looked at her pale skin pulled tight around her sunken cheeks. Turning, she quickly headed out of the room. Effie didn't know if it was because she was restless from being cooped up or if it was because it was her birthday, but suddenly, she was drawn to her father's room.

Keeping her footsteps light as if her presence might still disturb him, Effie went in and carefully sat on his bed. Looking around the small room, which smelled of coal dust and whiskey, Effie saw only the bed, a nightstand, and a few crates stuffed with worn clothes.

Effie reached over her father's rumpled pillow and slowly opened the nightstand drawer. Lying in the center was a Bible that had belonged to her mother. Effie took out the book and laid it beside her. Then she opened the drawer wider to find a gun tucked in the back corner. Cautiously, she touched the grip for only a moment before pulling back her hand and shutting the drawer.

Effie picked up the book and walked out of her father's room. Mindlessly carrying it by the spine, she'd taken only two steps before she heard the soft swish of paper falling to the floor. Effie picked it up, opened it, and read the first few sentences, which, although she didn't know it, would determine the course of her life.

Clutching the paper in her hand, she ran at full speed until she reached Mr. Goodwin's porch. Effie rapped her knuckles against the door until she heard Mr. Goodwin's heavy footsteps. "Hold on. Now, hold on," Mr. Goodwin said as he slowly opened the door to a winded Effie, who stood panting to catch her breath.

"Effie? What's going on? Are you okay?" Mr. Goodwin asked, concerned.

Without a word, Effie shoved the paper into his hands. As her only explanation, she said, "I found it in Daddy's drawer."

Mr. Goodwin nodded as he read it. Folding the paper in half, he looked at Effie and said, "He didn't tell you about this?"

Effie shook her head.

"No, of course he didn't," Mr. Goodwin said before adding, "This is good, Effie. It's real good for you."

Grabbing the paper from him, Effie said, "No! I won't take it. He got this doing wrong."

Mr. Goodwin considered it a moment before he said, "Maybe, but his sins ain't your sins."

Effie argued, "His wins ain't my wins neither."

Smiling, Mr. Goodwin said, "Maybe, but the truth is you ain't done no wrong to no one, but you sure had wrong done to you." Patting her shoulder, he added, "You deserve this, Effie."

Effie shrugged.

Mr. Goodwin wrapped his arms around her and whispered, "Take it."

Taking Mr. Goodwin's advice, Effie packed her few belongings and moved out the next day.

Enraged, Piney yelled, "You can't do this! You have no right."

Effie calmly held the deed under his nose before saying, "This here says I have every right."

Backed into a corner, Piney hissed, "I did you a favor, girl. Seems to me you be owing me one back."

Remembering how he'd callously kicked Derrick's cold body into the grave he'd dug, Effie shuddered and said, "You did, but it weren't out of the goodness of your heart, was it, Piney Boyer?"

Piney smirked and said, "It don't change the fact that I helped you bury a man you killed in cold blood."

Effie's eyes widened and her cheeks blanched. "Cold blood?" she shrieked. "He...he..." she stammered. Holding on to her stomach as it seized, Effie turned and vomited. Retching until she only heaved, Effie, sweating, slumped down on the step. Doing nothing to help her, Piney carefully studied Effie as she wiped the saliva from the corners of her mouth.

Grinning, Piney said, "You ain't just no regular sick, is ya, girl?" Effie looked at Piney, who was confident he had the upper hand, and said, "I seen that look before. I'm guessin' the rabbit died."

Effie stared, unblinking. She hadn't been completely positive until that moment.

Piney snickered and said, "Yep. You's pregnant."

Feeling his new power, Piney grabbed his bargaining chip and gleefully tossed it on the table. "A young girl like you is gonna need a daddy for that baby."

Effie forcefully shook her head and shouted, "I don't need nobody!"

Piney pulled a cigarette from his pocket, lit it, and took a long drag. Exhaling slowly, he said, "Maybe not. But my mama knew the sting of squawking women's gossip. It nearly killed her and she was a lot stronger than you."

Although Effie stared coldly into Piney's eyes, he could still see the fear, and he used it to strike his final deal. "Look here, girl. The way I see it we could both use each other's help." Piney paused before adding, "You let me live on my land, and I will make claim to this baby so's you ain't no whore."

Giving it no more than a minute's thought, Effie defiantly said, "I ain't taking your deal, Piney Boyer. I claim this baby, and I don't give no shit what anyone has to say about it."

Piney snorted, "You ain't got what it takes."

Standing, Effie shrugged and said, "Maybe not, but I guess we both about to find out."

With nothing left to bargain, Piney threatened, "I helped you out, girl, and I kept my mouth shut." Pushing his face close to her, he hissed, "Maybe now I feel like talking."

Effie stepped back. Knowing he had the upper hand but refusing him the win, she countered, "You can live here, but I live in the big house." Pointing to the field behind them, she said, "You can pick one of them shacks."

Piney scoffed, "Big house? This ain't no plantation, and you sure as shit ain't no lady."

Now Effie pushed her face close to Piney and said, "Maybe I ain't a lady, but what I am is the owner. So, Piney Boyer, I will live where I want, and you will live where I say."

Piney sneered, "And if I tell?"

Through clenched teeth, Effie said, "Whether I like it or not, we are in this together. If I go down, you go down."

Piney said, "Maybe we is and maybe we ain't. The way I see it, little girl, it's your word against mine."

Pressing his nose almost to Effie's, he added, "And who's gonna believe a knocked-up girl with no man?"

Piney's laugh, hollow and hard, scared Effie, but she didn't back down. Instead, she said, "Who is gonna believe a bastard?"

Piney's cheeks reddened, and his fists clenched. "You bitch! Those are lies."

Stiffening her back and straightening her shoulders, Effie said, "All I know, Piney Boyer, is you were born in the dirt and you live in the dirt. Maybe in a weak moment I crawled down in there with you, but it don't mean I have to stay."

Piney slumped against the steps, and stubbing out his cigarette with his boot, he said, "You sure is uppity for a knocked-up murdering bitch." Reaching toward Effie, he traced her jawbone with his boney finger and whispered, "But you'll crawl back down here with me every now and again, you'll see."

Effie shuddered with the thought, then taking a deep breath, she picked up her suitcase and headed to the house that was to become not just her home but also her destiny.

It wasn't long before Effie realized that Piney had been right. A piece of paper and a promise loosely kept wasn't enough for her to feel safe, and so Effie did crawl back in the dirt with Piney—too many times to count. The price of Piney's silence was steep; the costliest payment was the birth of Effie's sons.

Each time a newly born screaming baby was put into her arms, Effie was reminded of her crime, her sin, her curse. She loved her boys, but there was always a moment when she caught a shadow of him in one of them, causing her to feel her greatest fear. The terror tore at her and the filth of this fear sunk so deeply into her skin that Effie never again felt clean no matter how much she scrubbed or sacrificed.

Effie's memories receded. Trembling, she stared at the paper without seeing the words. She didn't need to read them. She'd memorized them a long time ago. With her index finger, she traced the familiar looping curves of her father's signature.

She no longer needed to know why her father hadn't shown her the deed. What she did know was that he was a good card player, and probably an even better cheat, and that Cletus Boyer was desperate. Effie also knew that while her father had nothing to lose, Cletus had everything to lose. So because the deck was stacked, Effie now held this paper, which she placed back into her pocket. Smiling, she thought how in the end, fate had found a way to even out the odds.

Chapter Twenty-Five

The sky's crimson curtain of early morning lifted, and bright blue sky swept across the snow in a horizontal blur. Lottie and Curtis trundled and nearly toppled as they wove between the mounds of snow. The drifts quieted the world around them, so their voices echoed off of the trees and bounced softly back to their ice-tipped ears.

"She did not!" Lottie cried, pushing gently on her uncle's arm.

Grinning, Curtis said, "I ain't lying. She did too. Your mom was a great shot."

Lottie stopped and, looking up at her uncle, asked, "Really, Uncle Curtis? You're telling me the truth?"

Curtis forced a serious face and said, "Really. Your mom shot a squirrel between the eyes at twenty feet."

Disbelieving, Lottie shook her head.

"Okay, maybe it was more like ten feet."

Lottie raised her eyebrows and cocked her head.

Laughing, Curtis said, "Okay, okay. Maybe it was five

feet, but she did shoot it. And…" Curtis pulled Lottie along as he added, "It was delicious."

Lottie stopped again. "Eww, you ate it? That's really gross."

Rubbing his belly, Curtis said, "Nope. It was delicious."

Disgusted, Lottie asked, "How could you eat *squirrel*?"

Curtis chuckled. "Same way you do."

Lottie argued, "No! I have never eaten squirrel." Feeling less confident, she asked, "Have I?"

Laughing harder, Curtis asked, "Do you really think it's always chicken?" Seeing Lottie turn suddenly pale, Curtis quickly said, "It's chicken. It's always chicken."

Looking at each other, they both laughed.

Trampling forward through the snow, Lottie shivered as she pulled her coat more tightly around her. Noticing, Curtis asked, "Are you cold, Lottie-Pops?"

Lottie answered, "A bit." Dusting the snow from her hair, she added, "I mean, it is winter, Uncle Curtis." Lottie took a few more labored steps then asked, "Why did you want to take a walk *now*?"

Slowly clumping beside his niece, Curtis said, "Well, I guess I thought since you were holed up in your room all day yesterday, it might be nice to spend some time together."

"It was just one day."

Curtis shrugged and said, "It was Christmas Day."

Lottie softly said, "I needed it."

Curtis nodded. "I understand. I guess I'm just wondering what you did all day."

Looking into the distance, Lottie said, "I just wanted some time to myself."

With a doleful smile, Curtis said, "I know I've been sticking real close to you for a while, Lottie, and I know that lately you can't really seem to shake me." Curtis's warm breath caught in the cold air, turning to little white plumes as he sighed then said, "I've just been so worried about you especially after..." Dropping his head, Curtis mumbled, "You know."

Lottie said nothing.

Lottie pulled up her heavily booted foot and sunk it back into the deep snow as she trudged forward at a faster pace. Unsure by her sudden change in mood, Curtis plodded after her.

"Lottie?" The only answer returned was the soft padding of her footfalls. Winded, Curtis finally caught up. "Lottie, What's wrong?"

Lottie didn't answer and she didn't stop.

Frustrated, Curtis shouted, "Lottie. Stop!"

Sunk deep in snow, she stood still and stared straight ahead as Curtis came to her side. "Lottie, what is wrong?"

Acting every ounce of the fifteen-year-old she was, Lottie huffed, "Nothing. I'm fine."

Putting his hands on her shoulders, Curtis gently turned her to face him. "I know you've been through a lot, Lottie."

Shaking off his hands, Lottie said, "I don't want to talk about it."

Curtis shoved his hands deep into his pockets and said, "Okay. Okay, Lottie. Let's just go back home."

Lottie shook her head. "No."

Confused, Curtis asked, "No. You don't want to go back home?"

Suddenly angry, Lottie snapped, "No. It's not *my* home."

Curtis argued, "Yes it is."

Lottie said sharply, "No, *my* home is the one with my mom. Remember my mom?"

Stunned, Curtis answered, "Of course I remember. We were just talking about her."

Lottie quickly shot back, "No! *You* were talking about her. I don't know those stories. I don't know any stories." Lottie added, "I don't remember her voice or the way she smelled or the way she held me." Crumpling into an ice-tipped snowdrift, Lottie, teary-eyed, said, "I don't remember if she loved me."

Sinking down next to his niece, Curtis looked at her and said, "She loved you very much, Lottie." Pulling his hand from his pocket, he wiped a tear from her cheek. "I don't know why she left. God knows livin' on this mountain ain't easy and maybe—"

Cutting Curtis off, Lottie said bitterly, "I know why she left."

Shocked, Curtis asked, "You know?" Stammering a bit, Curtis asked, "How do you know?"

Avoiding his eyes, Lottie said, "I found more diaries."

Looking away, Curtis asked, "Why, Lottie? Why didn't you tell me?"

Guilty, Lottie answered, "You all have so many parts of Mama. I just wanted one part of her that was all my own." Finally looking at her uncle, Lottie said, "I'm sorry, Uncle Curtis."

Meeting his niece's eyes with his own, Curtis said, "No. Don't be sorry, Lottie. You deserve to have a part of your mama." Hesitating for a moment, Curtis took a deep breath and asked, "Did someone hurt her?"

Lottie dropped her head and said, "I think you know."

Curtis said, "Who was it, Lottie?"

Lottie didn't answer.

Curtis pressed, "Who?"

Lottie softly said, "I don't want to tell you."

Frustrated, Curtis demanded, "You have to tell me, Lottie!"

Boldly, Lottie snapped, "No, I don't!"

Taking a deep breath, Curtis slowly exhaled and gently said, "No, you're right. You don't have to tell me." Heaving another deep sigh, Curtis added, "I loved her too, Lottie. She's my sister." Rubbing his chin with the back of his hand, Curtis said softly, "And she left me too."

Wrapped up in her own pain, Lottie had never noticed that same pain in her uncle's eyes until today. Ashamed she'd missed it for so long, she relented and said, "Okay, I'll tell you, but you have to promise not to tell Granmom."

Although uneasy about this deal, Curtis said, "I promise."

Lottie fidgeted with the buttons of her coat as she said, "He tried to hurt me too."

The flash of Piney's sick and twisted face swiftly brought Curtis to his feet. Enraged, he shouted, "I'll kill the son of a bitch!"

Terrified, Lottie stood, and grabbing her uncle's coat sleeve, she pleaded, "No, Uncle Curtis! Please! Piney Boyer ain't worth it." Pushing her face into her uncle's, she sobbed, "Please. Please. I don't want you to go to prison. You can't leave me here."

Pulling Lottie to him, Curtis promised, "It's okay. It's okay, Lottie. I won't leave you. Not ever." Feeling that her clothes were soaked from sitting in the snow, Curtis said, "Come on. Let's go home so we can get you warm and dry."

They said nothing more until they reached the porch, and Curtis said, "I should have protected her."

Lottie abruptly stopped. "No, Uncle Curtis. It ain't your fault."

Curtis stomped his foot on the first step and said, "It is my fault."

Lottie grabbed her uncle's arm. "No, it's *her* fault."

"Who?"

Pointing sharply at the house, Lottie hissed, "Hers."

Confused, Curtis asked, "You're saying Ma is the reason Sarah left?"

Lottie jutted her chin forward and nodded her head hard.

Curtis evenly asked, "How is any of this Ma's fault?"

Saying nothing, Lottie walked up the steps and stood waiting on the porch.

"Are you sure you just don't need someone to blame?"

Lottie said simply, "I have someone to blame."

Curtis stepped onto the porch next to Lottie. "Come on, Lottie. Ma didn't do nothing."

Looking sharply at her uncle, Lottie said, "That's right. She didn't do nothing."

Pulling off her glove, Lottie put her hand on the cold doorknob and asked her uncle, "Why doesn't Piney pay rent? Why does he live here?" Turning the knob, Lottie said quietly over her shoulder, "Why don't we know the answers, Uncle Curtis?" Without waiting for his reply, Lottie opened the door and went inside.

Curtis stood alone on the porch with only the cold and his dark thoughts. He mindlessly stamped his boot on the snow-crusted slats as he cursed himself for not knowing, for not protecting her, for not saving her. Clenching his hands into tight fists, Curtis relaxed for a moment in the rush of rage that flushed his cheeks and warmed the bitterness in his bones. Silently he promised his sister, he promised himself, that he would protect Lottie—no matter what. Opening the door, Curtis went inside with a new determination and a new plan.

Chapter Twenty-Six

Curtis had mulled the plan over in his mind for weeks. He'd spent every day since the day he found out about Sarah working out the details and gathering his courage. Pacing now on the porch, he waited for Jimmy Dobson. Curtis and Dobson, a lazy drunk who Curtis said talked more shit than he shoveled, both worked for Ernest Weddell. Although shifty, Jimmy could be relied on when the price was right. Curtis met that price with half his paycheck and a case of beer. In exchange, Jimmy loaned Curtis his truck for the day.

Anxious, Curtis stomped down the steps just as Jimmy drove up in his rusted-out 1986 Ford. Not sure of how long he had before his mother and Lottie got home, Curtis ran up and stuck his head in the driver's-side window.

Startled, Jimmy said, "Whoa, partner. Wait 'til I put her in park."

Curtis didn't wait, and swinging open the door, he said, "Get out, Jimmy."

Confused, Jimmy asked, "I thought you were driving me home first."

Curtis pulled him from the seat before he slid in and said, "That was before you were an hour late."

Irritated, Jimmy asked, "What am I supposed to do?"

Curtis revved the engine. "Walk." Then, with a sharp cut of the wheel, Curtis pulled around and headed toward Calver County.

Calver County was only about a two-hour drive north, but Curtis knew with the snow and back roads it was going to take a lot longer. He cursed Jimmy's name for costing him another hour as he sped up and wove around cars, trying to make up the time. Trying to distract himself, Curtis turned on the radio, but only static snapped back from the cheap speakers. He switched it off and nervously tapped his thumb against the steering wheel in time to his thoughts.

In his mind, he replayed the words—the ones he'd worked and reworked—that he was going to say. He nodded as he practiced. Then, turning down Chapel Street, Curtis muttered, "This is crazy." Curtis wanted to go home, but gripping the wheel until his knuckles whitened, he kept straight. As he headed down the long drive, the brown building, institutional and cold, was now directly in front of him. Holding his breath and keeping his foot steady on the gas pedal, Curtis whispered over and over, "I can do this. I can do this."

Curtis didn't have much to hand over, but the guards made certain to take anything that wasn't buttoned or zipped onto him. Everything else, which wasn't much, was placed in the basket. Then an overweight guard whose gut hung heavily

over his low-slung pants patted him down before gruffly bark-
ing at him to move forward.

Given instructions and a few warnings, Curtis was
told to take a seat. Sitting on a yellow hard-plastic chair bolted
to the floor, he looked around. The only other people waiting
were an elderly couple who sat hunched together and a skinny,
young girl whose collarbone seemed to protrude farther than
her pregnant belly. Catching Curtis staring, she shot him a
nasty look before walking over to the vending machine filled
with KitKats and SunChips. Sitting in the corner, the machine
glowed a soft yellow that Curtis found oddly comforting if
only for a bit.

Nervously bouncing his knee up and down, Curtis
watched as the sweep hand clicked off another second on the
clock. It was already fifteen minutes into the visiting hour and
still no one had called his name. With each panicked thought,
Curtis's knee bounced harder. He'd just reached the worst con-
clusion in his mind when a guard called out, "Bilfrey. Curtis
Bilfrey."

It wasn't until Curtis stood up and hoarsely said,
"Here," that he realized he really was *here*.

Directed to a small room with a short row of black
chairs, Curtis chose one and obediently sat. Straight-backed
and perfectly still, he waited. After only a few minutes, Curtis
watched him walk into the room and slowly slide into the
chair across from him. Although the glass between them was
thick and smudged, Curtis could still see the hollows beneath
Frank's eyes. His face was gaunt with cheeks that dipped below

his bones like fallen valleys. His steel-gray eyes had darkened, and his tightly set jaw belied a determined calm.

Dropping his gaze for a moment, Curtis reconsidered asking Frank, but with no other choice, he picked up the phone and waited for his brother's snide remarks and cruel words. Frank, however, put the phone to his ear and simply said, "Hello, Curtis. It's good to see you."

Taken aback by his brother's civility as well as his sincerity, Curtis took a few seconds before he said, "You too, Frank."

Frank asked, "How is everyone?"

Small talk seemed even more insignificant here, but Curtis didn't know how to start, so he answered, "Okay, I guess."

Questioning, Frank raised an eyebrow.

Curtis added, "Well, not everyone is okay."

Leaning forward, Frank asked, "Is it Ma?"

Surprised to hear the concern in his voice, Curtis answered, "No, it's not Ma. It's Lottie."

Frank grunted, "Oh."

Trying to plead to any feeling Frank might have for the girl, Curtis said, "She is *your* niece, Frank. Don't you care even a little bit?"

Frank huffed and snapped, "What do you want, Curtis?"

Curtis had intended on explaining everything to Frank. He was going to tell him about Sarah's diaries and Piney, but facing Frank's hard stare, Curtis decided to cut to the point. Seeing two broad-shouldered guards standing at the door, Curtis thought through his words carefully before he asked, "Do you remember when you and Gene played cops and robbers?"

With his brow furrowed and his jaw tightly set, Frank hissed, "What the fuck are you talking about?"

Curtis smiled and said, "You guys never let me play. I always wanted to, but you said that I was too little and too weak."

Frank pushed his face close to the glass, trying to control his anger. Spittle dotted the phone as he spat out, "My ass is in prison, and you come up here to bitch that I didn't play with you?"

Seeing that he was only enraging his brother, Curtis was worried he wouldn't be able to make Frank understand.

Trying again, Curtis took a deep breath and said, "You and Gene had those plastic pop guns. I loved those pop guns. I always wished I could have one of my own. I still do." Curtis added, "I always wanted to know where you got them." Leaning close to the glass, Curtis lowered his voice and asked, "Where did you get them, Frank?"

His anger receding, Frank leaned back. Only a suggestion of a smile slipped across his face as he realized what Curtis wanted.

Leaning forward again, Frank said, "It's probably best you didn't play with us, considering where Gene and me is sitting now." Shaking his head, he said, "Besides, I ain't so sure you could have handled those pop guns."

Dropping his voice low, Curtis said, "I can handle it, Frank, and considering where you and Gene are sitting, I have to handle it."

Frank nodded and said, "We got them from the Cutlers."

Curtis asked, "The boy Sarah dated?"

"Yep."

Still disbelieving, Curtis asked, "Doesn't he work at Sawyer's Mill?" Before Frank could answer, Curtis asked, "Isn't he married? With kids?"

Frank said, "Who gives a shit?"

Before Curtis could answer, a thick-necked guard called, "Time!"

Leaning close to the glass, Frank pressed the phone to his mouth and said quietly, "Watch what you play with, little brother."

Curtis slid back his chair. "I ain't playing, big brother."

Frank's sudden flash of pride was so subtle that only Curtis could see it, and only for a moment, but it was enough.

Before hanging up, Frank said, "Tell Ma that I love her. And Curtis, I—"

Without waiting, Curtis said, "Thanks, Frank."

Making good time, Curtis arrived in Devil's Fork—a dirt road that split sharply into two directions—by three o'clock. He took the road that veered south and turned onto Potter's Lane. He'd gone only a few feet before he saw Dallas Cutler staggering down the center of the road. After pulling over to the side, Curtis jumped out of the truck. Slowly jogging, he easily caught up to help Dallas to his feet after what was obviously not his first fall.

Slurring, Dallas said, "Thanks, man. I must have trupped. Tripped."

Curtis turned his head, trying not to gag from the smell of cheap corn whiskey and vomit as he let Dallas lean on him. Together, they walked unevenly to a small run-down shack. Curtis took his arm from Dallas, who fell into a small heap on the steps. It was too cold to let him sit outside, so Curtis pulled Dallas up and led him inside.

Narrowing his eyes as he tried to adjust them to the dark room, Curtis walked Dallas to an old brown couch with busted springs. After helping him lie down, Curtis looked around the cramped space. Empty beer bottles littered every surface thick with dust and cigarette ash. Hearing Dallas softly snore, Curtis stepped over a pile of dirty clothes and walked into the only other room.

Dank with a rancid smell that forced Curtis to pull his T-shirt over his mouth and nose, Dallas's bedroom had nothing other than a sunken bed and cheap dresser in it. Curtis opened the top drawer. Empty. He then opened the rest of the drawers to find only a few T-shirts, a pair of torn jeans, and some socks. Unsatisfied, Curtis went back into the other room.

On the other side of the room from the couch was a broken table with a stack of papers, which Curtis rifled through, finding nothing important. Curtis then opened the cupboards, but all he found was two cans and a half-smoked pack of cigarettes. Curtis wasn't sure what or why, but he knew he was searching for something.

Turning in a slow circle, Curtis took in the entire room. There were no pictures, no curtains, no comfort, and in between the smell of trash and neglect was the distinct and familiar smell of sadness floating on unseen motes.

Hearing Dallas wake, Curtis grabbed the cleanest cup he could find, filled it with cold coffee, and handed it to Dallas, who was now sitting up. After a few gulps, Dallas's eyes, now clearer, focused on Curtis. He said, "I think I know you."

Sitting down next to him, Curtis nodded and said, "You did once."

Dallas titled his head as if to jar the memory. "How?"

"You dated my sister, Sarah."

With a slip of a smile, Dallas said, "You're Sarah Bilfrey's kid brother."

Curtis nodded again. "The brother part is right. I ain't sure the kid part fits anymore."

Uneasy, Dallas rubbed his hands up and down his legs before quietly saying, "I was real sorry to hear about Sarah." He quickly added, "She was a great girl." Then he awkwardly asked,

"She just up and run off, huh?"

Curtis said quietly, "Yeah."

Dallas pursed his lips. "Well, it was probably for the best. There ain't nothing here worth staying for." Sobered up enough to see the wounded look in Curtis's eyes, he clumsily added, "I don't mean you all. I just mean there ain't nothing…" Slowly looking around, he said, "Here."

Curtis looked at Dallas. "She didn't just leave us. She left her daughter."

Curtis wasn't sure, but he thought he saw Dallas wince at the mention of Lottie. If he had, he shook it off quickly before he said, "Yeah, that shit's hard." In that moment Curtis wanted to ask Dallas if he was Lottie's father. Sitting next to him, Curtis knew that this was most likely the last time he would ever get the chance. So Curtis swallowed hard and asked, "Dallas, are you…" Losing his courage, he finished, "Okay?"

Dallas snorted and said, "You see where I live."

Finding no argument, Curtis sighed and said, "I came here for something, Dallas. My brother Frank told me you're the person who could help me."

Picking up a half-empty bottle of whiskey, Dallas took a swig and said, "Sure. Anything for Sarah's kid brother."

Once he had what he needed, Curtis thanked Dallas and opened the door, but before he walked out he took one last look around Dallas's dark, dirty shack. Curtis didn't need to see it because he felt it. He'd felt it since the day his sister had left them without reasons or answers or apologies. It now struck him that what he'd been searching for was Sarah—a piece of her, a sense of her. Feeling the thick misery of this room in his throat, he knew he'd found her or at least the loss of her.

After returning Dobson's truck to him, Curtis walked the remaining two miles home. Cold, Curtis slipped his hands into his pocket. Feeling the cold touch of the metal, he wrapped his fingers around his new talisman. It felt heavy and dangerous in his hand. With his arm at his side, he held it tightly and pressed the weight of it into his leg. A buzzing like an electric current seemed to flow from it into Curtis's blood, making him feel powerful. Curtis knew that he now had what he needed to protect Lottie.

It was dark by the time Curtis got home, making it easier for him to sneak into the shed unseen. Quietly stealing to the back, he picked up a pile of greasy rags carelessly thrown on the floor. He wrapped the rags around it and carefully tucked the bundle into the corner of the back wall. Satisfied it was well hidden, he stepped outside. Closing the door, he jumped at the sound of Lottie's voice.

Turning and seeing her only a few feet away, Curtis grabbed his chest and said, "You almost gave me a heart attack."

Although Lottie looked curious, she didn't ask. Instead she said, "Granmom is looking for you."

Curtis grinned and asked, "Do I need a shovel or a backhoe for this trouble?"

Lottie shrugged and said, "Bring both."

Curtis laughed and slung his arm around her shoulders.

Reaching the steps, Lottie shook loose his arm and said, "I'm not going to ask where you've been today, Uncle Curtis, but I missed you."

Curtis gently bumped her shoulder and said, "I missed you too." Together they walked into the house to see Effie standing, arms crossed, waiting. Curtis wasn't sure what he was about to face, but looking at Lottie, he knew it was worth it.

Chapter Twenty-Seven

Effie stood in her garden, the sun stretched across her back, warming her bones, which had felt cold for too long. It was finally April, and with it came the start of spring and the end of Effie's long wait, which had lasted for four months. During that time there wasn't a day or a moment when Effie didn't think about Sarah's diaries—the ones she'd seen next to a sleeping Lottie on Christmas night.

Effie didn't know what her daughter had written, but she did know that Sarah's words had woven their way into her granddaughter's heart, had taken root, and now threatened to bloom. Effie feared that those blooms would cast upon a wind she couldn't control, and she would forever lose Lottie. Although she knew she couldn't harness her granddaughter's spirit, she knew she had to try her best to hold Lottie a bit longer to this place, to her own heart.

Effie believed the only chance she had of pulling Lottie back to her was by reading Sarah's diaries, so every day that Lottie left for school, Effie raced to her room to search for them. She looked under the bed, behind the dresser, and under drawers, but she found nothing. It was an entire week before Effie realized that Lottie was taking them with her. Disappointed but not discouraged, Effie waited.

Effie pulled a soft new leaf from an otherwise withered plant and turned it over in her hands, examining the small thin veins. Only God, she thought, would allow such perfection to exist where few noticed and even fewer cared. Effie opened her hand and let the leaf flutter softly to the ground. Hearing Lottie and Curtis, Effie stepped over the abandoned leaf and headed toward the porch.

"I don't see why we have to go all the way to Cutcher's Hollow," Lottie whined.

Effie said, "I told you, girl, it's the best place to get jam."

Lottie shook her head. "You make your own jam, Granmom."

Effie gently placed her hand on Lottie's shoulder. "Not like this."

Lottie shook off her grandmother's hand and stomped down the steps.

Curtis smiled sympathetically before saying, "Teenage girls."

Effie nodded and again repeated the instructions she'd already given him earlier. "You need to go all the way to the south end of Cutcher's Hollow to a small stand called Eddy's Fruit and Wares. Buy what you see fit, just don't be back before five o'clock."

Raising an eyebrow, Curtis asked, "What are you up to, Ma?"

Effie gently pushed Curtis forward before saying, "Never you mind. Just do like I ask, okay?"

Curtis didn't answer.

Effie grabbed hold of his shoulders and turned him to face her. She asked again, "Okay, Curtis?"

Curtis nodded, stepped off the porch, and ran to catch up to Lottie.

"You two be safe and have fun," Effie said cheerfully.

Lottie turned only long enough to glare before turning back around and stamping toward the road. Effie's smile faded but not her hope.

Quickly she went inside, locked the door, and headed to Lottie's room. Thanks to a bit of spying, Effie knew exactly where to look. Pulling the hidden screwdriver from her pocket, Effie pushed back the bed, dropped to her knees, and began to pry loose the floorboard. The strip of wood finally released, allowing Effie to stick her hand into the narrow cavern beneath it. Months of watching and waiting were finally rewarded as Effie pulled Sarah's diary from beneath the floor. She exhaled slowly as she ran her thumb down the spine of the book before laying it beside her. Effie reached in again to search for more; she was almost certain there was more than one.

Effie stood and swiftly searched the room. She circled the small space several times, breathing rapidly as she raced to uncover what her granddaughter had so cleverly hidden. Effie stopped pacing long enough to go over in her mind the plan she'd worked on for weeks. She'd made sure that Lottie took nothing with her today, she'd made sure she had the house to herself, and she'd made sure she knew where to find the diaries.

Frustrated, Effie smiled in spite of herself. It was in the Bilfrey blood to keep secrets, and she couldn't fault Lottie for being a Bilfrey even if she did pity her for being one. Seeing the time, Effie quickly picked up the diary and pressed it to her chest. Looking around the room once more, Effie knew that she had to sacrifice some secrets in order to discover others. She just hoped what she had was enough.

Effie sat on the couch and held her daughter's diary close to her. She didn't open it. Instead, she savored the safety held in the brief moment when she blissfully knew nothing but possessed the possibility of knowing everything. It was both powerful and humbling, and it both excited and scared Effie. Sourcing her strength from her love for Lottie, Effie took a deep breath and turned to the first page.

January 3, 1981

I can no longer deny it. I've tried for months, but as my belly swells it pushes out the space in my head where I pretend it isn't happening. It seems unreal even as I write it. I'm pregnant.

January 24, 1981

I don't want Mama to find out—not yet—so I try not to be around her much. When I am around her, she stares at me like she's trying to sort out my secret without coming out and asking. I worry she will figure it out before I have the courage to tell her.

February 2, 1981

Today Mama did more than look. Without a word, she stepped close to me and pulled up the sweatshirt I've been wearing to hide my belly. I didn't say nothing and neither did she. Her face, both angry and sad, said more than I could bear to hear. I tried to explain what I couldn't explain, but she just turned away. She wouldn't listen. I guess it was too much for her to hear too.

February 17, 1981

Mama hasn't talked to me in two weeks. She doesn't even really look at me. I feel less than the nothing I know she now thinks that I am.

February 21, 1981

Mama made biscuits today. She hummed, but with Mama humming don't mean happy. She was thinking. I just don't know about what. I watched her for a bit before she turned and looked at me for the first time in weeks.

*I could still see the sadness, but the anger seemed
gone. I was grateful until she asked about the father.
I wanted to answer, but the words stuck in my throat,
choking me silent. Her anger came back quick and
doubled. She told me I should feel shame for letting this
happen. I stopped short of telling her the same.*

March 8, 1981

*My pregnancy is a secret to no one now. Stares and
hateful looks have been slung at me, but none have
stung so much as Frank's words today. Looking at me
with cold, dark eyes, he called me trash and said I
wasn't worth the effort it would take to pick me up and
throw me away. I know he's been angry with me for a
long time. I just didn't know he hated me.*

March 15, 1981

*Mama moved all of my things into one of the shacks.
She said it was best for the baby and me, but I know she
means it's best for her. It's a little easier not to feel shame
when you don't have to look at what's causing it.*

March 17, 1981

*Even with another soul inside me, I'm lonely. I wonder...
has God cursed me?*

March 22, 1981

Mama and I fought today, longer and louder than we ever have. It was about paint, but I am pretty sure by the end it wasn't about the paint no more. She called me uppity and ungrateful.

What Mama don't understand is that I don't think I'm better, I just want better. I want it for me, and now I want it for my baby.

March 29, 1981

I stepped on my porch this morning and saw three cans of stain tucked beside the door. I don't why she did it, but maybe there's a chance that Mama wants more too.

April 10, 1981

I was rubbing my belly today and the strangest feeling came over me. I don't know how, but suddenly I just knew it was a girl. For me, I'm happy. For her, I worry.

April 22, 1981

The baby almost never stops kicking. I don't think she'd fight so hard to get out if she knew what was waiting for her. God, I hope I'm enough.

May 17, 1981

*Today my baby—a small cherry-lipped and dark-eyed
girl—was born. When the pain started, I was scared, but
Mama never let go of my hand until my baby was tucked
in my arms. I stared into her eyes for the longest time.*

*When I did look up, Mama was gone, but I'm
okay—I have my girl.*

May 20, 1981

*I've named my baby girl Lotus Bilfrey. Mama flat out
told me she thought it was an ugly name, then she tried
to talk me into calling her Rose or Daisy.*

*I found the name in Mama's special book that she
thinks she hid so well. It's called, "A Lady's Companion
to Wildflowers," and if Mama actually knew about all
the flowers in it then she would know why I picked this
name. She would also know that it is far more fitting
than Rose or Daisy.*

August 21, 1981

*Today is my birthday. I am seventeen years old. Lotus is
three months old. I didn't think I would make it to see
either.*

December 26, 1981

*Yesterday was Christmas. I knitted Lotus a pink
blanket. I wrapped her in it and went to Mama's house.
I knocked on the door, and I waited a long time, but
she never answered. I told myself she's out, but I know
Mama wouldn't go nowhere on Christmas.*

 *I took Lotus home and rocked her for hours. We
cried ourselves to sleep.*

February 13, 1982

*Lotus is crawling, babbling, growing. She is changing
so fast, and I'm afraid to turn around for a minute and
miss even one moment.*

February 23, 1982

*Lotus is always smiling. She makes me smile. She is my
only happy, and I am grateful for her—every day.*

April 17, 1982

*Lotus will be a year old in one month. Every day of this
year has been hard, sad, scary, and wonderful in more
ways that I can count, and when I look at her I can't
believe that I ever thought even for a moment that she
was anything other than a gift.*

May 17, 1982

Lotus is a year old today. She has been trying to walk for weeks. She falls a lot, but she never gives up. Just like a Bilfrey. She's strong, and I'm thankful for it.

July 3, 1982

Mama comes around more now. Lotus lights up when she sees her. I do a bit too, I guess.

August 8, 1982

I saw him today. I was playing in the yard with Lotus when I felt him watching me. He was standing behind a tree just staring. It made my whole body go cold. I grabbed up Lotus and ran inside, locked the door, and held her until my fingers went white.

September 14, 1982

It's happening again. I want to tell Mama.

September 20, 1982

Yesterday, he grabbed me by the arm, pulled me off my porch, and dragged me around to the backyard. Then, while my baby was napping inside, he shoved me

*against the side of the house and ripped another piece
from me.*

October 1, 1982

How does she not know?

November 19, 1982

*I don't struggle. I don't twist or turn or fight. Am I
giving up?*

December 25, 1982

*Christmas. Today was good. Me and Lotus sat at
Mama's table. I ate her biscuits and listened to my
brothers' stories. I laughed.*

*It's been so long that it sounded odd, but it felt good.
I wish I could live in today forever—safe, warm, and
wanted.*

February 9, 1983

*I don't want this for Lotus. I don't want this for me.
I don't know what to do other than give in, give up. I
think about it until I look at her and then I feel the fight
come back.*

March 24, 1983

I can't have another baby. I just can't.

April 21, 1983

I visited Mama today. I sat across from her at the table and looked into her eyes. I thought that maybe if she looked at me, really looked at me, she would see it.

She would see how every time he steals what he wants from me, another piece of me breaks, falls, and silently slips away. She saw nothing. How can she see nothing?

April 24, 1983

I worry that soon there won't be enough of me left for my Lotus.

April 26, 1983

I need a plan. I need it now.

As the last words of the last sentence soundlessly slipped from Effie's mouth, she looked up, trying to focus her vision. Strained and teary, her eyes blurred with the fatigue of reading each and every word without once looking away from the page.

Shock, sadness, and shame coursed through her veins with a speed that seemed to thicken her blood with the emotion. Her heart raced and her muscles tightened even though she didn't make the slightest motion. The combination of fearing the unknown and knowing what to fear turned into a simple and pure terror, which drove Effie to run into Lottie's room.

Dropping to her knees, she practically threw the diary back into its hiding space before quickly replacing the board. As Effie backed out, she scanned the room for any traces she might have left of her intrusion before hurrying to her bedroom.

Once safely behind her closed door, she dropped onto her bed. Restless, she lay there only a minute before sliding off and sinking onto the floor. Stretching her arm beneath her bed, she pulled out Sarah's sweater. The one she'd saved and kept safe, only pulling it from its secreted space when its smell, its feel, its warmth was all that could comfort her.

Holding the sweater close to her cheek, Effie crumpled into it like a child and cried. She never heard the turn of the lock as she whispered repeatedly, "Please God. Please Sarah. Forgive me."

Chapter Twenty-Eight

Lottie set three jars of jam onto the table. Curtis kicked the mud from his boots and put two more jars next to them. Irritated, Lottie blew air through her tightened lips and said, "Five jars! We spent all day walking, tiring ourselves out, to buy five jars of jam."

Curtis shrugged one shoulder. "I guess she wanted jam."

Lottie raised an eyebrow and asked, "She wanted jam even though she makes her own?"

Curtis gently bumped Lottie's arm and said, "I don't know, Lottie-Pops. I find it best not to question Ma too much." Curtis smiled and headed back down the hall.

Lottie twisted open one of the jars. With her finger, she swiped the inside rim, scooping out a big lump of gooey jam, which she stuck into her mouth. The sugar rush caused a euphoria that temporarily calmed her. Lottie took one last lick then screwed on the lid. Setting the jar down, she smiled. *A fool's errand*, she thought. Pushing the jar next to the others, she whispered, "Only I'm not the fool."

Inside her bedroom, Lottie shut the door then leaned against it and listened. She could hear the faint sound of the shower, so she knew she didn't need to worry about Curtis. What she couldn't hear was her grandmother, and that meant she couldn't be sure she wouldn't barge in at any moment. Lottie considered calling out to her. Worried she might answer, Lottie decided against it. Instead, she took her chance at being caught and moved quickly.

Lottie pulled her mother's first two diaries from the waistband of her shorts. Wincing, she examined her sides to see angry red welts where the books had chafed her skin. She gently touched the tender skin and whispered, "Worth it."

Lottie then pushed back her bed and pried up the floorboard. Lying where she'd left it as if untouched was the diary. Lottie had decided to leave only the third one. Because she was never sure what her grandmother might do, she couldn't risk losing all of them, and besides, the third diary said all she wanted her grandmother to know. All she should have known.

Lottie delicately placed her fingertips on either side of the book then carefully lifted it from its hiding place. Turning the diary over in her hands, she looked but saw nothing. Peering into the shallow hole, she saw it—a tiny white string crumpled and stuck to a large splinter of wood. Lottie smiled. It worked.

Earlier that morning, Lottie had painstakingly placed the thin thread in a tight straight line before putting the book on top of it. She knew that if the string moved so had the diary. Lottie grinned, thinking about how she'd set the trap and how her grandmother had so easily taken the bait.

As Lottie sat flipping through the pages, it soon sunk in that her grandmother hadn't just moved the diary. She'd read it. Rereading the entries, Lottie wondered what her grandmother thought and felt as *she* read them. Did she cry? Did she feel ashamed? Lottie picked up the diaries, cradled them close to her, and thought about the most important question. *Now that she knows, what will she do?*

For weeks, Lottie carefully studied her grandmother. She watched her as she made breakfast, washed dishes, and folded laundry. Lottie patiently waited as she tried to take notice of some subtle shift or change. She looked for a darkening under her eyes, a sadness within them, anything that belied her grandmother's steadfast hold to the routine. Yet each moment of every day Lottie saw nothing more than her grandmother's resistance or—as Lottie feared—her inability to feel. As the days wore on so did Lottie's patience.

Although still May, the bright morning sunlight glared against the glass, making Lottie's tiny room hot. Restless, Lottie tossed and turned until her blankets, heaped high, tangled around her legs. Kicking them off of her, she pushed them onto the floor. Lying on the cool sheet, she stared out the window. Spring had beautifully dressed the backyard in emerald greens with buttons of flowering white buds. Bleary-eyed and anxious, Lottie didn't notice this beauty. Instead she lay there listless for a long time as her mind raced.

Dropping her arm over the side of the bed, Lottie touched the board where the diaries lay secreted beneath. As she mindlessly traced her fingers back and forth over the small wooden space, she thought about how she once believed that these diaries would answer all her questions, connect her to her mother, and somehow make it all a bit better.

Bitterly, Lottie admitted to herself that instead of feeling closer to her mother, she only felt more profoundly the distance between them, and it hurt. She also now had more questions than answers, but she was also more determined to figure them out. Swinging her legs over the side of the bed, Lottie sat up without fully knowing that she'd made a decision deep within her heart.

Lottie walked into the kitchen and stood silently watching her grandmother as she sifted flour and cracked eggs.

Effie asked, "Are you hungry?"

Lottie shook her head.

"Well, you better get hungry because I made two batches of biscuits."

Lottie sidled closer and asked, "Why so many?"

Without turning, Effie answered, "I do my best thinking when I'm baking biscuits."

Baiting her, Lottie asked, "What are you thinking about?"

Dropping another blob of biscuit dough onto the pan, Effie answered, "Life, I guess."

No longer in the mood to play her grandmother's cat and mouse game, Lottie abruptly asked, "Why didn't you look for her?"

Effie's body stiffened. The sticky dough slowly dripped from the spoon as Effie held it midair, frozen. She didn't move. She didn't answer. Lottie's precision aim hit the nerve she'd targeted, but not yet satisfied she said, "You know she would have never left me unless she had a reason—a good reason. So, why didn't you go after her?" Stepping even closer, Lottie lowered her voice and asked plaintively, "Why didn't you look for my mom?"

Effie set the baking sheet on the counter and wiped her hands on her apron. Trying to sound indifferent, she said, "I don't know her reasons."

Angered by her grandmother's coldness, Lottie hissed, "Maybe you didn't know then, but you know now, and I don't see you making no move to bring her home. To make it right."

Feeling her own ire well up, Effie snapped, "Girl, don't you—"

Lottie quickly cut her short. "I know you read it, Granmom."

Effie sank back against the cupboards. Knowing it wasn't an empty accusation, she didn't deny it.

Effie dropped her head. Barely above a whisper, she asked, "You knew I would read it?"

A shadow of a smile slipped across Lottie's lips. "You couldn't even come up with a better story than jam."

Guilty, Effie said, "I just needed the time, Lottie, to figure out what's been going on with you."

Lottie shot back, "With me? Why didn't you ever take that time to figure out what was going on with my mother?"

Defensive, Effie said, "It's not as simple as those words on the page."

Lottie snapped, "Simple? You think what Mama wrote was simple?"

Effie cut in, "No, not simple, just not the whole story."

Like a caged dog, Lottie paced. Effie's eyes tracked the dizzying back-and-forth shifts as she waited for the next blow, which Lottie landed swiftly when she said, "She was in pain. *Your* daughter was in pain. How did you not see it? How did you not *feel* it?"

Grasping for an explanation that she knew would never be good enough, Effie weakly said, "Lottie, you have to understand."

Turning on her heel, Lottie wheeled around and said coolly, "*I* have to understand. No! *You* have to understand. I lived most of my life without my mother, believing she dumped me, believing she didn't love me." Lottie's voice trembled. "You let me believe it. You wouldn't answer my questions. You wouldn't let me talk about her." Lottie sunk onto the floor in defeat and whispered, "You tried to erase her."

Her granddaughter's pain was palpable, and Effie felt it keenly. She wanted to help her, heal her, but she knew the wounds were far too deep. Effie knew that a lifetime of bad choices and wrongs committed in the name of right couldn't be explained to a sad and angry motherless child whose own pain drowned out the sound of everything else. So, Effie didn't try to comfort her granddaughter, instead she sat distant, quiet, and still.

Lottie, though angry, desperately wanted comfort, and only seeing what she believed was her grandmother's refusal to give it caused Lottie's love for her to twist into an unharnessed hatred. Slowly Lottie stood, and glaring at her grandmother, said, "If you won't save her, I will."

Whether a threat or a promise, Effie said no more than "I hope you do."

Chapter Twenty-Nine

Lottie woke early on her birthday. It had been ten days since she vowed to her grandmother, and more importantly to herself, to find her mother. She could think of no better day to begin than today. Lottie lay still for a few moments listening to the familiar creaks of the house keep time with the singing of the morning birds. She then waited for the sound of the shower, pans being banged against the stovetop, and finally the slam of the screen door. Knowing her uncle and grandmother wouldn't be gone for long, Lottie got out of bed and hurried to her closet, where she retrieved the diaries from her new hiding place.

Taking the third one in hand, she mindlessly flipped the pages. Whether by luck or fate, the sheet that fluttered to a stop in her palm had on it the last entry that read, "I need a plan. I need it now." Like a divining rod from the page to her being, the message found its meaning in her heart, and in that moment, Lottie had her own plan.

Stacked and set on her bed, the diaries lay next to piles of clothes that Lottie pulled from her dresser and closet. Jeans were heaped next to shirts, a comb, and a few barrettes. With her drawers emptied, Lottie studied the room. It took only seconds to realize that all that mattered was what lay on the bed and in her heart.

Lottie took measure of the mounds of clothes before heading to the kitchen for a garbage bag. Halfway down the hall, she stopped midstride and said out loud, "The suitcase." Headed back toward her grandmother's room, she sang out, "*My* suitcase." It had been well over a decade since she'd seen it last, but she knew it had to still be here. She *felt* it.

Once in her grandmother's room, Lottie looked in the closet, behind the dresser, and finally under the bed. As Lottie pulled out three dusty shoeboxes and one abandoned slipper, she brushed her hand against something soft. With another tug, she pulled out a yellow-and-blue-striped sweater, which easily slipped from its hiding spot. Turning it over in her hands, she knew it wasn't her grandmother's. She pressed it against her cheek for a moment then quickly took it to her room where she gently laid it between her clothes and the diaries. Then she hurried to the shed to keep searching.

The acrid smell of gasoline and grease caused a pinch of pain in her head as Lottie stepped inside. Carefully walking around tools and old newspapers that littered the floor, Lottie headed to the back of the shed. Tipping back warped and pitted boards she found only rusted mousetraps and forgotten marbles.

Discouraged but determined, she slowly looked around the small space until her eyes focused on the dust motes that

danced on the light streaming through a cracked window
pane. Caught in this stare, the world stilled for a moment,
until a bright glint sliced across Lottie's sightline. Seeking the
source of reflected light, Lottie moved broken rakes and old
boxes to find it resting in the back corner near her uncle's
worktable. As she picked it up, its rag covering dropped softly
to the floor, revealing one more Bilfrey secret and Lottie's
new plan.

With her new find in hand, Lottie had forgotten
the suitcase until she nearly stumbled over it. Leaned up
against the wall next to the door was the tattered pink case
that Lottie's mother had packed with her tiny clothes sixteen
years ago. Grabbing the handle tightly, Lottie ran straight to
the house without stopping until she reached her room. After
shutting the door, she put the suitcase on the bed and popped
open the metal latches. Looking inside, Lottie marveled at its
small size.

Shrugging her shoulders, she sighed and grabbed the
first stack of clothes. Shoving them into the shallow hollows of
the case, she struggled to make them all fit. Lottie closed the
lid and sat on top of the suitcase as she pulled and tugged at
the zipper, which only made it around the first corner before
snagging and stopping. Lottie groaned and jumped off.

Lottie yanked on the stuck zipper, and when she heard
a sharp tearing, she flipped open the top to see the light pink
satin lining ripped and hanging loose. Grabbing tightly to the
tattered edges, she tried to pull it back to its stitching, but it
refused to budge. Trying to stretch the material, Lottie stuck

her hand behind the lining, and that's when she felt it. A thin, stiff, and folded piece of paper hidden and waiting for her.

Lottie's fingers shook as she opened the letter that began simply:

Lotus,

Please forgive me. The only way I know how to save you is by saving myself. This mountain is swallowing me up, and I don't want it to take you with me.

I'm leaving you with Mama because I know she will keep you safe. She will do better by you because she couldn't do better by me.

There are two things I need you to know and never forget. The first is that I love you now and forever. The second is why I chose your name.

Mama wanted me to call you Rose or Daisy, but you, my baby girl, are not a delicate flower growing in gentle soil. These mountains are hard, and you have to be strong and determined to survive them.

Like the lotus flower, you have been forced to grow under dirty water surrounded by bugs and weeds. It is my greatest hope that you will rise up through it all.

Push through the mud, Lotus, push through and bloom.

Love,
Your mother

Lottie refolded the paper and placed it back behind the lining of the suitcase. She didn't cry; she no longer felt the need. Instead these words, not found and read secretly but words written just for her, moved Lottie to push forward no matter the risks, the cost, or the losses. Deciding to take only what would fit, Lottie easily closed the suitcase. Then, without even a final glance, she left her room, closed the door, and headed for his house.

Setting the suitcase on the porch, Lottie banged on the door. She waited only seconds before turning the knob and stepping inside the dark room. Stumbling a bit from the dizzying stench of cheap whiskey and stale smoke, Lottie leaned against the wall to steady herself. She wanted nothing more than to slide to the floor and rest, but her thoughts of a still moment were sharply broken by his thick wheezing, snapping her back to this life, this room, this moment.

Turning slowly toward the sound of strained breathing, Lottie saw a gaunt figure sunk deep in an old chair. Staying buried in the shadows, he said, "Does your granmom know where you are, little girl?" Struggling to stand, Piney took a few uneven steps closer to Lottie before saying in a snake-slick voice, "I don't think she'd like it." Staggering to the kitchen, he slurred, "I'd offer you a drink but"—he shook an empty bottle at her—"I'm all out." With quivering arms, Piney lowered his wasted frame onto a wooden chair with an audible groan.

Lottie didn't move. Standing soundless and still, she stared at him, yet no matter how closely she looked, all she could see was bones bagged up in dirty coveralls. With a wrinkled face that twitched and gnarled hands that shook, Piney was no more than a funhouse reflection, a warped and strangulated version of the monster she'd remembered.

The man—who tortured and ripped apart her family until they were nothing more than hanging filaments floating loosely on any breeze that blew across this godforsaken land—was broken. Weak and sick of body now as well as soul, Piney was nothing more than a frail old man, but Lottie felt no pity, only rage.

Small droplets of sweat beaded on Lottie's forehead as her fury beat red and hot against her skin. Wrapping her hand tightly around her steel confidence, she stepped forward and said, "I know what you did."

Piney snickered and taunted, "I did lots of things, little girl."

Taking a step closer, Lottie hissed, "I know what you did to my mother."

Piney leaned back and nodded. "Do tell."

The acidic words stung Lottie's tongue even before she said them. Taking a breath, she slowly spit each one out, "You. Raped. Her."

Piney laughed in choked bursts until it eased into a coughing fit that lasted several minutes. He thumped his chest a few times before spitting phlegm into a dirty coffee mug, then wiping spittle from his dry, cracked lips, he smirked and said, "You can't take what someone is giving away."

Sickened, Lottie shrieked, "You liar!" She pulled the gun from behind her back, steadying her trembling hand with her other one as she leveled the sight line at Piney's head.

Unfazed, Piney leaned forward, and in a guttural voice growled, "You gonna shoot me, girl?"

Lottie nodded and calmly answered, "Yes."

Pushing back his greasy hair, Piney tapped the center of his forehead and said, "Go ahead."

Lottie didn't loosen her grip, but she also didn't pull the trigger.

Suddenly on his feet, Piney jutted his jaw out and snarled, "You're just like your granmom. She didn't have the guts to shoot neither. I'm the one that had to put the bullet through that boy's chest. I saved her worthless life and all she gave me was three useless, gutless boys and this here shit shack."

Rage took hold of any reason Piney had left. Shoving back his chair, he pounded the table with his fists as shouted, "I would've killed her along with her daddy if I'd known that bastard would give her my land." Flat palmed, he banged his chest as he howled, "You hear me, girl? *My* land!"

Hearing his hateful confession, Lottie dropped her arm—and the gun—to her side as she shuddered to think she shared his blood. Piney steadied himself against the table, then taking a step closer, he coolly hissed, "Maybe I don't make the same mistake with you."

A humorless smile spread across Lottie's lips as she said, "You are nothing but a sick, rotten old man."

Stiffening with the insult, Piney barked, "Who do you think you are?"

As if to undo her ties to him, Lottie bound herself tighter to the Bilfrey line by saying, "I am Effie Bilfrey's granddaughter, I am Sarah Bilfrey's daughter, and I am the girl who is going to put you in your grave."

When Piney saw the familiar flash of retribution and hate in her eyes, his anger dissolved into fear. Bartering once more for his life, he said quickly, "I know what happened to your mama."

Lottie's resolve crumbled a bit beneath these words. Holding on to the last shards of hope, which cut far more than they soothed, she said cautiously, "You're lying."

Picking up his trump card, Piney arrogantly said, "Then shoot me, but when I'm a gone so is your chances of ever finding your mama."

Lottie took the gamble and listened. Every sound, every syllable uttered from his vile mouth sent ripples of shock and horror across her skin. His story caused Lottie an agony that seared her flesh and ripped through her bones, leaving her broken in ways unimagined.

After his last hateful word hissed against her ear, Lottie slowly and with intent lifted her arm and aimed the gun once more at Piney's head. Smirking, he said, "Ah, there you go, girl. I knew you had my fire."

Wrapping her finger tightly around the trigger, Lottie spit back, "I don't got nothing of yours, not even your soul on my conscience." Lottie closed her eyes, squeezed the trigger, and listened gratefully to the dull thud of Piney's body as it fell to the floor.

Chapter Thirty

Effie peeked into the empty kitchen before walking in and setting the diary on the table. Worried about being caught, she called out Lottie's name. Hearing nothing, she waited a few seconds and called out again. Effie decided it was just like the girl lately not to answer.

She thumbed through the blank pages and then closed the ebony-colored cover. She pulled out pink paper and wrapped the new diary she bought for Lottie's birthday. Sticking on a crushed green bow, she sized up her gift and frowned. Effie worried she would never find her way back to Lottie, especially since Lottie blocked every path Effie tried to take.

After smoothing the wrinkled sides and taping a new pen to the top, Effie stood back and admired her work. She hid the book in the cupboard behind the flour, which she then pulled out to bake Lottie's cake. After piling her ingredients onto the cramped counter, Effie reached for her mixing bowl beside the stove.

Her fingers had barely grazed the edge of the bowl when she instinctively pulled back and gasped. A feeling more than a sound sliced the air, causing a shiver to course down her spine and surge back through her nerves, which suddenly felt awake and raw. Without thought or reasoning, Effie began to yell out Lottie's name, demanding the girl answer.

Led by her gut, Effie raced from room to room, shouting Lottie's name. It wasn't until she again stood in the kitchen that a singular thought, overwhelming and netted deep in her bones, caused her to stop. Wild-eyed, she looked around the room. Forcing herself to swallow her panic, she grabbed a steak knife and ran out the door.

Panting hard and with her heart beating fast inside her chest, Effie charged open Piney's front door. Wielding the knife wildly in front of her, she shouted, "Where are you, you son of a bitch?" Effie tipped over chairs and kicked blankets from under her feet as she cursed and threatened Piney, who lay, unseen, close to her feet.

Believing the house was empty, terror took a stronger hold of Effie's senses. Pacing back and forth, she pleadingly prayed, "Please God, not Lottie. Not Lottie, not Lottie, not Lottie." Her legs, weakened from fear and the run, buckled under her, causing her to stumble. Trying to gain her footing, Effie slipped in a warm and thick liquid that streamed across the floor in tiny red rivulets.

A flourish of arms and legs sent Effie careening to the floor. Landing on her side, Effie moaned as she rubbed her hip, which took the force of the fall. Placing her hands behind her, Effie carefully pushed herself up. It was then that she saw Piney Boyer, slack-jawed, still, and with a bullet hole torn through his forehead. Effie didn't scream or swear or pray. She simply stood up and swiftly kicked Piney's leg. Satisfied he was dead, she walked out, closed the door, and headed home.

Effie had barely trampled the grass in her front yard when another thought, darker and heavier, rested on her heart. Her steps quickened as her mind raced. Soon Effie was in a dead run with every footfall chased by dread. Scrambling to the porch, Effie dropped to her knees and reached her arm under the wooden slats. Ducking her shoulder under the railing, Effie contorted her body as she tried to grab the lock box. She stretched her fingertips, straining, but they only danced across the cold, steel top. She pulled hard, groaning in frustration and pain, as she shouted, "Come on! Come on!" Finally, the rock that caught and held it rolled loose. Effie wrenched it free and dragged it out.

Effie reached around her neck and snapped the chain she'd worn for over twenty years. As the links softly slipped across her shoulders, an imperceptible weight and a thin skeleton key fell with it. Effie quickly snatched it up and stuck it into the lock, which she turned until she heard a quiet click. As unease crawled across her skin, Effie slowly reached her quivering hand into the box.

Never considering the absurdity of someone opening the box without the key, Effie was relieved when her hand wrapped around the gun. Setting it on her lap, she steadily exhaled and closed her eyes as she leaned her head against the porch. Her reprieve was swiftly shattered when she heard his voice. "What are you doing, Ma?" Effie looked up to see her son standing over her. Startled, she dropped the gun into the lock box and quickly shut the lid.

Effie didn't answer. She was suddenly running her own questions through her mind. Each one pierced and poked until she, without a second's hesitation, leaped from seated to standing. Wrapping her hands tightly around Curtis's shoulders, she demanded, "Did you shoot him?"

Curtis's eyes widened as he shook his head, confused. "Who, Ma?"

She was now shaking him, her voice reaching a shrill pitch as she shouted, "Piney!" Lowering her voice, she forced out a raspy, "Piney Boyer is dead."

Curtis stepped back from his mother's tight grasp. Shocked, he stammered, "How? Why? Who, Ma? Who?"

Ashamed, Effie dropped her arms to her sides and whispered, "I thought that Lottie…" Stopping short of saying it, she nodded toward the lock box and said, "The gun is still there. It wasn't her. She couldn't have because…" Effie exhaled deeply and said, "The gun is still there."

Curtis's face drained of color. Without a word, he sprinted to the shed with Effie on his heels. Throwing open the door, Curtis knew immediately. Boxes lay strewn on the floor next to toppled rakes. Curtis closed his eyes and whispered a quick prayer before looking down to see the discarded rags he'd used to wrap the gun. Picking them up, he turned to look at his mother standing in the doorway. Her eyes, crazed and wild, darted from the rags to Curtis's face. In a brittle voice, Effie asked, "What, Curtis? What?"

Shaking his head rapidly, he sputtered, "A gun. I had a gun, and it's gone."

Taking two quick steps closer, Effie demanded, "What do you mean you had a gun? Why?"

Curtis weakly explained, "I got it to protect us."

Effie snorted, "Protect us from what?"

Angry, Curtis shot back, "Protect us from Piney. God, Ma. He tried to rape Lottie, and I am sure he raped Sarah." Shaking his head, he said, "How do you not know?"

Defensive, Effie artfully turned the blame. "How did you get a gun?"

Curtis sighed. "Frank."

Incredulous, Effie said, "Frank is in jail."

Curtis slumped against the worktable and said simply, "He knows people, Ma."

Effie was quiet a for minute as she worked out the questions and the answers. Disgusted, she asked, "You just left it lying here for anyone, for her—"

Cutting her short, Curtis said, "No! I hid it."

Effie snatched the greasy rags from Curtis's hands and shook them in his face as she screeched, "You hid a gun under rags?" Before Curtis could answer, Effie asked, "Did she take it?"

Curtis shrugged a shoulder. "I think so."

Decided, Effie said, "Come on, we have to find her. Piney's body was still warm, so she couldn't have gone far."

In one stride, Curtis had his mother in his arms. Holding her tightly, he promised, "We'll find her."

Effie stiffened, then pulling herself free from his grasp, she stormed out the door.

They walked in silence for more than twenty minutes. Effie struggled to keep pace with Curtis, whose steps seemed to double with each stride. Quickening her own steps, Effie took little notice of the roads they walked down or the paths they cut across. Instead she focused on trying to quiet her mind, which was loud and relentless in its worry. She pushed down the thoughts of *what if* and *what now* that threatened to cleave her heart completely by forcing herself to believe they would find Lottie.

As turns taken led only to barren paths and stones stepped over uncovered nothing, Effie's faith flagged. Although Effie regarded trust as an emotion felt only by fools, she's proffered it to her son. This act of kindness, however, was not without limits, and seeing Curtis's failure, she withdrew it sharply. "Where the hell are we going, Curtis?"

Without turning, Curtis answered, "Heaven's Clutch."

Heaven's Clutch was a ledge formed from gray stones silvered in the sun and dappled with blue. It is the highest point of Talon Ridge, cresting the mountain and stretching out from its edge as though reaching for the other side. Across it lay land lush with pines that bellow when the wind swiftly rises up from the drop that falls steeply for over two hundred feet. Crescent shaped—drawn long and round—the ledge appears like a hand longing to clasp and hold the world, which, just out of reach, waits.

Effie lagged behind, weighing Curtis's decision. Then,

questioning it, she asked, "Why the hell are we going to Heaven's Clutch?"

Without stopping, Curtis answered, "We're going because I think she'll be there."

Effie scrambled to catch up. Reaching Curtis, she twisted him toward her and demanded, "Why? Why there?"

Patiently, Curtis said, "I took her there once. I wanted to show her that the world is bigger than this mountain. I wanted her to know she didn't have to stay penned up here. I wanted her to know she had choices."

Insulted, Effie snapped, "Well if this here mountain is so bad then how come you ain't never tried leaving?"

Curtis dropped his head. "I never left 'cause I ain't got what it takes, but Lottie does. She deserves more than here, and in your heart you know it's true."

Effie said nothing. Curtis turned back around and kept walking.

Curtis guided Effie down a narrow path with turns that cut sharply and climbed ever upwardly. Rounding a razor-edged ridge, Effie slipped on scattered stones, nearly falling before Curtis caught her arm and pulled her to her feet. Hearing the echo of loosened pebbles ricochet against the rock and fall into the cavernous abyss, Effie swallowed hard and sputtered, "I...I almost fell."

Pulling her closer to the safer side of the path, Curtis said, "But you didn't."

Breathless from clambering over rocks, Effie panted, "This is going to kill me."

Curtis looked back, smiled, and said, "Not likely." Grabbing her hand, he pulled her up to the next rise before saying, "We're almost there." Digging her heels more firmly into the ground, Effie cautiously again started after Curtis. Bracing herself against him, she stooped and bent, trying to avoid brambles that fell like piercing veils, pricking and tearing at her bare skin.

Busy wiping the blood that dotted her arms, Effie was unaware they'd reached the top until she smashed into Curtis, who'd stopped abruptly. Annoyed, Effie hissed, "Curtis!"

Before she could say anything else, Curtis whispered, "Shh."

Hearing his voice pulse with fear, Effie looked up and felt her own blood run cold.

When Effie saw her standing a hair's breadth from the edge, her senses ignited with terror. Sweat beaded her forehead as her nerves danced on fire. Effie's vision blurred and narrowed so that only what she saw in front of her mattered. Helpless, Effie watched the bone of her bone and the blood of her blood bide precariously close to the precipice, knowing that the sudden drop meant certain destruction for them all.

Gone was reasoning as her sanity slipped, leaving only the primal need to protect, to rescue, to save her own. Knowing the only way to silence the screams inside her mind was to run to her, Effie lurched forward, only to be stopped and caught by Curtis's outstretched arm.

Evenly, Curtis whispered, "No, Ma. Don't."

Pushing against Curtis's shoulder, Effie begged, "Curtis, please."

Curtis refused. Keeping his mother behind him, he warned, "We have to be careful. We have to do this right."

Looking only at Lottie, Curtis said nervously, "Lottie-Pops."

Staring into the expanse outstretched before her, Lottie said nothing.

Curtis tried again, "Lottie. Everything is going to be okay. I just need you to step back a bit." Curtis forced the calm into his voice, but Effie could hear where fear cracked the edges and it terrified her more. "Please, Lottie. Please," Curtis pleaded.

Lottie slowly turned her head in Curtis's direction. Looking through him rather than at him, she took three steps backward from the edge.

Exhaling deeply, Curtis said, "That's good, Lottie-Pops, but just a few more steps, okay?" It wasn't until Lottie had reached a safe distance that Effie and Curtis could finally breathe.

Impatiently, Effie pushed against Curtis's back. "I have to go to her."

Curtis grabbed Effie's wrist as she started forward. "Slow. Just go slow."

Fighting every urge in her body to run, Effie took measured steps toward Lottie, who had again turned to face the outstretched sky that dipped and dropped not far from her feet. Panic warped time so that Effie felt as though she'd walked years until she'd reached Lottie. Gently grabbing her granddaughter's shoulders, she turned Lottie toward her then swiftly pulled her into her arms.

Rigid and without returning Effie's affection, Lottie stood still. Feeling the sting of her refusal, Effie only held tighter until Lottie broke from her embrace.

Steely-eyed, Lottie held her grandmother's stare and said, "I'm leaving." With these words, the wind again got knocked out of Effie, who, frenzied, nearly screamed, "No!"

As Lottie edged back, Effie could see she no longer held that power.

Settling herself, Effie tried again, "Please, Lottie. You don't have to go. It's okay."

Lottie exhaled sharply. "It's not okay. It's never going to be okay as long as I stay here."

Shaking her head firmly, Effie said, "We can fix this. We'll burn down his shack."

Staring hard into her grandmother's eyes, Lottie said, "Maybe burning down his shack will hide that I killed that sick son of a bitch, but will it hide that I share his blood or that he wears my mother's on his hands?"

Numb and confused, Effie asked, "What do you mean?"

Lottie answered bluntly, "Mama never left."

Shaking her head as if to erase the possibility, Effie insisted, "Yes, she did. I saw her leave."

Lottie argued, "No. You saw her leave your house. You didn't see where she went, and you didn't bother to find out." Lottie told her grandmother what she'd discovered as

Effie murmured "no" like a fervent prayer. "Before I put the bullet into his head, that bastard told me what happened to my mother. Scared and alone, she came here. He followed her then he stood behind a tree and watched her walk to the edge. He didn't stop her. He just watched as she jumped to her death."

Effie gasped, "No! Lottie, no!"

Ignoring her grandmother's outburst, Lottie continued, "She couldn't take it anymore. The raping. The abuse. The loneliness. No one tried to save her so she tried to save herself the only way she knew how." Lottie's words then turned cruel as she angrily spit out, "My mother is dead because you built a life on bad deals and lies."

Never one to bend under the weight of heavy blame, Effie said, "There's a lot you don't know. That man tangled me up in his web when I was just a girl."

Without hearing more, Lottie cut in and said, "You didn't shoot him, Granmom. He did, and you bartered our souls for a piece of land."

Determined to make her listen, Effie grabbed Lottie's shoulders, and pressing her face close to her granddaughter's, she said, "No, Lottie, not land. I sold *my* soul for the price of this family's freedom."

Effie let go of her grasp and said, "Living on this mountain ain't easy. It's mostly scraping and scratching to survive. I had no mama, and my daddy was a drunk, and one day I was forced to make a deal with a man no better than the devil. I know I've done wrong, Lottie, but I swear to God that any bad I did was for the good of my family." Like a stone, Effie sank to her knees. "Please, Lottie. Please forgive me. Please don't leave me."

Lottie looked down at her grandmother. Having never seen tears streak her face, Lottie said with compassion, "My mother named me Lotus because she knew that just like the flower, I would have to grow up through all this mud and meanness." Putting her palm gently on her grandmother's face, Lottie said, "What Mama didn't know is that the lotus flower's beauty depends on its ugliness. Maybe, Granmom, I didn't bloom in spite of you but because of you." Lottie leaned down and softly kissed her grandmother's cheek before picking up the small suitcase.

Crumpling smaller into herself, Effie put her head in her hands and sobbed a lifetime of tears. Curtis, who stood silent and strong, watched it all unfold with sadness and pride. Unable to see her pain anymore, Lotus turned away from her grandmother and looked at Curtis, who smiled and nodded. Squaring her shoulders, Lotus took her first steps away from her grandmother and Talon Ridge, and as she did her heavy heart lightened knowing she was the first Bilfrey to finally be free.

Made in United States
North Haven, CT
12 January 2025

64269901R00186